TOO CLOSE FOR COMFORT

"Now, stop arguing with me or I'll kick you out of the car and leave you in the middle of nowhere."

It was an empty threat.

But instead of being cowed she stuck her chin out. "Fine. Dump me here if you want. I've no problem with that."

Damn, she was actually serious.

What kind of guys had she been dealing with? Then he thought of the seedy motel and had a pretty good idea.

"Yeah? Well, unfortunately I do."

"Then take me back to the motel. I'll get my stuff and stay somewhere else."

Maybe it was the flinty determination in her voice, or the way her gaze never wavered, but he wanted to believe her.

Which only made him sure he shouldn't. Ten years on the force had taught him that trust was a dangerous thing—and following your gut instead of having proof could get you killed.

He slid the car into Reverse. "Forget it. You're staying where I can keep an eye on you."

DEAR READER,

This is my first book for Harlequin's fabulous new KISS line, and because of that I knew I was gonna need a scorching-hot hero and a smart, sassy, super-great heroine to make my story shine in such illustrious company. Pressure!

But as it happens I had Mr. Scorching waiting in the wings. Zane Montoya was one of those heroes who set light to the keyboard as soon as he first appeared as Nate Graystone's secret half brother in my last book (my fourteenth!) for Harlequin. Relaxed, charming, witty, sexier than sin and so gorgeous he makes women drool, Zane appeared to be the perfect KISS hero—almost a little too perfect, frankly.

But then along came Iona MacCabe, a feisty, determined Scottish lass who is Zane's worst nightmare—a damsel in distress who doesn't want to be rescued. And before you can say "the trouble with love," Iona is discovering there's a dark side to Zane's white-knight routine—and Zane is discovering that Iona's not the only one who needs rescuing.

I love to hear from readers, so if you want to have a chat about Zane or Iona or why Mr. So-Not-Perfect is a lot more irresistible than Mr. Perfect, you can contact me on my website at www.heidi-rice.com.

Heidi

TOO CLOSE
FOR COMFORT

———

HEIDI RICE

Recycling programs
for this product may
not exist in your area.

ISBN-13: 978-0-373-20717-6

TOO CLOSE FOR COMFORT
Copyright © 2013 by Heidi Rice

THE WEDDING DRESS DIARIES
(Prequel to The Wedding Season continuity)
Copyright © 2013 by Aimee Carson

ABOUT HEIDI RICE

———

Heidi Rice was born and bred and still lives in London, England. She has two boys who love to bicker, a wonderful husband who, luckily for everyone, has loads of patience, and a supportive and ever-growing British/French/Irish/American family. As much as Heidi adores "the Big Smoke," she also loves America, and every two years or so she and her best friend leave hubby and kids behind and *Thelma and Louise* it across the States for a couple of weeks (although they always leave out the driving off a cliff bit). She's been a film buff since her early teens, and a romance junkie for almost as long. She indulged her first love by being a film reviewer for ten years. Then a few years ago she decided to spice up her life by writing romance. Discovering the fantastic sisterhood of romance writers (both published and unpublished) in Britain and America made it a wild and wonderful journey to her first Harlequin novel.

Heidi loves to hear from readers—you can email her at heidi@heidi-rice.com, or visit her website, www.heidi-rice.com.

This and other titles by Heidi Rice are available in ebook format—check out **Harlequin.com.**

Special thanks go to fellow authors Scarlet Wilson and Libby Mercer for their help in making my Scottish heroine and my Californian hero sound real (I hope).

And to the lovely Roberto, who gave me invaluable insight into the culture and traditions of California's Mexican-American community—any mistakes in the portrayal are entirely mine.

CONTENTS

TOO CLOSE
FOR COMFORT

ONE

'Hey, Mitch, was there anything on a kid in Demarest's file? About five-two or-three, hundred and ten pounds?'

Zane Montoya squinted into the shadows of the motel parking lot, trying to make out any other usable details. But whoever the kid was, he was being real careful not to stray into the pools of light cast by the streetlamps, making the fine hairs on Zane's neck prickle. He'd been staking out Brad Demarest's motel room for five hours—taking over right after Mitch had called in with the flu—and Montoya Investigations had been on the guy's tail for six months now. Getting the tip that this by-the-hour motel on the outskirts of Morro Bay was Demarest's latest bolt hole had been their first break in weeks. And his gut was telling him the kid was casing the joint. And he didn't like it, because if Demarest showed up the last thing Zane needed was some little troublemaker alerting the guy to their presence—or, worse, spooking him before they could do a citizen's arrest.

'Is this kid a girl or a boy?' Mitch's voice croaked.

'Don't you think I would have...?' Zane's frustrated

whisper cut off as the kid stepped back and the yellow glow of the streetlamp illuminated a sprinkle of freckles, vivid red-and-gold curls springing out from under a low-riding ball cap and the curve of a full breast beneath the skintight black tank she wore over camo trousers and boots. 'It's a girl.'

A girl who had to be up to no good. Why else would she be dressed up like GI Jane?

'Make that a young woman—eighteen to twenty-five—Caucasian with red shoulder-length hair.'

The girl melted into the shadows as he tried to picture the intriguing features he'd glimpsed on a mugshot.

'She doesn't look familiar,' he murmured, more to himself than Mitch.

He'd reread Demarest's file while gorging himself on the endless supply of junk food Mitch had stashed in the glove compartment, but he couldn't remember any of Demarest's known associates fitting her description.

Mitch gave a weighty sigh. 'If she's hanging round his motel room, she's probably another mark.'

'I don't think so—she's too young,' Zane replied. *And way too cute.* He cut off the thought. If she was mixed up with Demarest, she couldn't be that cute. A one-time B-movie producer who'd taken a brief detour into porn before finding a more lucrative income duping rich women by promising to make them movie stars, Demarest was a typical LA parasite. But this kid with her pale skin, her freckles, her silicone-free breasts and her furtive activities looked anything but his typical mark.

'Don't be too sure,' Mitch replied. 'The guy cast a wide net and he wasn't choosy.'

'Oh, hell,' Zane muttered as the girl approached the

door to Demarest's room. 'Call Jim for back-up,' he added sharply. 'And get him over here now.'

'Has Demarest showed up?' Mitch's croak rippled with excitement.

'No.' *Thank God.* 'But Jim'll have to take over the surveillance. We've got trouble.' He glared across the lot, his irritation levels rising as his stomach sank. 'Because whoever the heck she is, she's just broken into his motel room.'

He shoved the cell into his back pocket as he lurched out of the car and headed across the parking lot.

Just what he needed after five hours sitting in a damn car—A GI Jane lookalike with freckles on her nose screwing up a six-month-operation.

Iona MacCabe eased the door open, and clutched a sweaty palm around the skeleton key she'd spent a week doing the job from hell to get hold of. The tiny strip of light coming through the curtains was alive with dust motes, but didn't give her much of an idea of the room's contents bar the two queen-size beds.

Her heart pounded into her throat at the footstep behind her, but as she whipped round to slam the door a tall figure blocked the doorway.

Brad!

Her stomach hit her tonsils as the apparition shot out a hand and wedged the door open.

'I don't think so,' came the gruff voice—tight with anger.

Not Brad.

The knee-watering shaft of relief was quickly quashed as an arm banded round her waist. Her back hit a chest like a brick wall, knocking the wind out of her, as he lifted her off her feet.

'Let go,' she squeaked, her reflexes engaging as the shadow man hefted her backwards.

'What the hell do you think you're doing?' she yelped as he kicked the motel door shut and carted her across the parking lot to who knew where.

The muscular arm tightened under her breasts and her lungs seized as she figured out that getting abducted might actually be worse than being caught by Brad—the thieving love rat.

'I'm stopping a felony in progress,' the disembodied voice growled. 'Now shut up, because this'll go a lot worse for you if someone spots us.'

She grabbed his arm and tried to prise it loose, but he was holding her too tightly for her to get any leverage. The tensile strength under her fingertips made the panic kick up a notch. She heard the heavy clunk of a car door opening and began to struggle in earnest. He was kidnapping her.

No way!

She'd come five thousand miles, lived on her wits for a fortnight, been cleaning toilets for a week in the grottiest motel in the world and hadn't had a decent meal since the day before yesterday, only to get murdered by a nutjob in a motel car park a few feet from her goal.

Fury overtook the panic. 'If you don't put me down this instant I'll yell my head off,' she whispered, then wondered why she was whispering—and why she was giving him a warning.

She drew in a breath and a callused palm slapped over her mouth. The ear-splitting scream choked off into an ineffectual grunt.

She kicked furiously, but only connected with air, as the scent of something clean and intensely male cut through the aroma of rotting garbage that hung in the night air.

He doesn't smell like a low life.

The thought disconcerted her long enough for him to twist round and dump her into the passenger seat of the car.

With his hand no longer cutting off her air supply, she hitched in a shaky breath—only to have the palm cover her mouth again. His forearm held her immobile.

She tried to bite him, but her jaws were wedged shut. His dark head loomed over her, the features still disguised by the shadows—and her heart battered her ribs with the force of a sledgehammer.

The enticing scent enveloped her as he hissed next to her ear. 'You let out a single sound and I'm going to arrest you on the spot.'

Arrest.

Her mind grabbed hold of the word.

He's a cop. He won't kill me.

But while her heart stopped pummelling, the panic still crawled across her skin and made sweat trickle between her breasts.

Not being murdered thousands of miles from home was good. But getting caught by a cop breaking into Brad's room was definitely bad. The temporary work visa she'd spent two months getting a hold of would be revoked. She could get deported and then she'd have no chance of getting even a fraction of the twenty-five thousand pounds of her dad's money Brad had absconded with.

'Nod if you understand me?' he said again, low and apparently seriously pissed off.

She nodded, her fingers curling around the key she'd used to get into Brad's room. She slid the key under her bottom.

He lifted his hand and she sucked in a deep breath.

'Why didn't you identify yourself as a cop sooner?' she demanded in a furious whisper, deciding attack was the best form of defence—and a good way to distract him until she could get away from him. 'You scared ten years off my life.'

'I'm not a cop, I'm a private investigator.' He tugged something out of his back pocket and flipped it open. She guessed the card he was showing her was some form of ID, not that she could see it any better than she could see him in the darkness.

'Now put your seatbelt on, we're leaving.'

Outrage welled up her throat as he shut the car door, skirted the bonnet, climbed into the driver's seat and turned on the ignition.

He's not even a proper cop?

She grasped the dash as the car reversed out of its slot. 'Hang on a minute—where are you taking me?' Maybe she'd been a bit hasty assuming he wasn't a kidnapper.

'Put the seatbelt on now or I'll put it on for you.'

'No, I will not,' she announced as he drove down the block of doorways and braked in front of the motel office. 'I have a room and a job here. I'm not going anywhere. And if you're only a fake cop you can't make me.'

She reached for the door handle, intending to dive out. But he leaned across her, the roped muscle of his arm skimming her breast, and clamped his hand over hers on the door handle.

'You're not staying here any more.' The menacing growl

was so full of suppressed anger she flinched. 'And I *can* make you. Just try me.'

She tried to flex her fingers, the iron-hard grip merely tightened.

'Let go now,' he murmured, his minty breath feathering her earlobe and making her nape tingle. 'Or so help me, I'm calling this in and to hell with the investigation.'

'I can't,' she snapped back, her anger not quite as controlled as his. 'You're holding on too tightly.'

He released her hand and she let go of the handle, shaking her numb fingers in a bid to restore the blood supply before she got gangrene. 'That hurt. I think you may have crushed a finger.'

The huff of breath suggested he didn't care if he had.

A large, square open palm appeared under her nose. 'Now hand over the key.'

'What key?' she squeaked, struggling to sound innocent while the key burned into her left bum cheek.

'The key that's under your butt.' He snapped his fingers, making her jump despite her best efforts to remain aloof. 'You've got ten seconds or I'm going to get it myself.'

And then he started to count. Her nipples tingled at the memory of his forearm wedged under her breasts.

She retrieved the key and slapped it into his palm, conceding defeat at the unpleasant thought of those long, strong fingers delving under her bottom.

'There, fine, are you satisfied now?' she asked, disgusted with herself as well as him. 'I had to scrub fifty toilets to get that. And believe me, the toilets in this dump need more than their fair share of elbow grease.'

The scoffing sound sent another inappropriate prickle of reaction shooting up her spine.

What the heck was wrong with her? This guy was the

opposite of sexy. Clearly a fortnight spent living on a shoestring budget doing dead-end jobs in an alien, unfriendly country had melted her brain cells.

'Don't go anywhere,' he said, getting out of the car. 'You won't like me if I have to come get you.'

She folded her arms across her chest, tense with indignation. 'I don't like you now.'

He gave a humourless chuckle.

Iona glared at his back as he walked into the motel office and indulged in a brief fantasy of running off into the night. But as his tall frame stepped into the office—and the lean athletic build rippling under a tan polo shirt and dark trousers became apparent under the harsh strip lighting—she let the fantasy go.

After a ten-minute conversation with Greg, the night clerk, he strolled back towards her, silhouetted by moonlight again. As he approached she became painfully aware of the mile-wide shoulders, narrow hips, long legs and the predatory stride.

Flipping heck.

Whoever this guy was, he was a lot stronger and bigger than she was—and she already knew he didn't mind using his physical advantage. Which meant she was going to have to wait to make a clean getaway.

He paused next to the car and pulled out a smartphone. As he talked into the device, the blue light from the neon Vacancy sign hit his face.

Iona gasped. Her abductor could make a living as a male supermodel.

A bubble of hysteria built under her breastbone as she stared at the firm sensual lips, the aquiline nose with a slight bump at the bridge, the sculpted angular cheekbones, the olive-toned skin and the shadow of stubble on his jaw. He glanced towards her and her lungs stopped as she absorbed the deep sapphire-blue of his eyes and the unusual dark blue rim around the irises. Was that a trick of the light? Even Daniel Craig's eyes weren't that blue. Surely?

He finished the call—not a word of which she'd managed to catch due to the loud buzzing in her ears from a lack of oxygen—and slipped the smartphone back into his pocket.

He settled into the driver's seat, thankfully casting his stunning face into darkness again.

She looked away and concentrated on breathing. So what if he was better looking than Adonis? He was still a bullying jerk.

She repeated the mantra in her head as he drove off without acknowledging her.

'If it's not too much to ask,' she said as they left the motel's lot, 'where exactly are you taking me? Because my purse, my passport and all my worldly goods happen to be in room 108. And I don't want someone to nick them.'

Not that she had a great deal of money in her purse, or many worldly goods, but her credit card was kind of important, and her passport if she was ever going to get out of this Godforsaken country.

'That's cute, coming from you,' he said as he flipped the indicator and turned onto Morro Bay's main street.

She bristled. 'I'm not a thief, if that's what you're implying.'

'Uh-huh. So what were you doing in Demarest's room? Planning to scrub his john after hours?'

The mention of Brad's name had her bristling even more. So he knew Demarest? Or knew of him? She tried to decide whether this was good or bad.

'This is the way it's gonna work,' he said, his voice domineering—and deadly calm. 'Either I report you to the Morro Bay PD and they put you in a cell to keep you out of my way or you do what I say and tell me everything you know about Demarest.'

His thumb tapped rhythmically against the steering wheel as the car drifted out of the small town—taking her farther away from her goal, and her passport.

'It's not stealing if someone's already stolen from you,' she offered, after considering her options. She didn't plan to tell this arrogant stranger anything but she didn't want to end up in a cell either.

His thumb tapped three more times. 'No, actually, technically it's still stealing.'

Great, the man wasn't just a bullying jerk, he was a self-righteous bullying jerk—with eyes bluer than Daniel Craig. Her pulse spiked.

Get over the eyes. Looks can be deceiving—you know that.

'How much?'

'How much what?' she asked, confused by the question.

'How much did Demarest take you for?'

The toneless enquiry had all the pain and humiliation charging up her throat and threatening to gag her. She swallowed down the bitter taste. So she'd made a mistake. A stupid, selfish mistake by believing in a guy who had never been what he seemed. But she'd spent the last two weeks trying to put that mistake right—that had to count for something.

'Not me, my father.' She stared out of the window into the darkness. The car had reached the bluff over Morro Bay and even though she couldn't see the ocean, she could sense it.

She hit the button to slide down the window, suddenly desperate for the scent of fresh air. The dry ache in her throat caught her unawares as the musty scent of earth, and sea and tree sap brought with it a vivid picture of Kelross Glen. The little Highland town in the foothills of the Cairngorms she'd spent the first twenty-four years of her life trying to escape. And every second of the last two weeks wishing she could return to.

She hit the up switch, sealing out the painful memories. She couldn't go back, not until she made amends for Brad and the childish wanderlust that had drawn her to him in the first place. She had to get at least some of her father's money back. And if that meant tracking Brad the Cad through every dive on California's coastline—and putting up with the arrogant guy seated beside her—she'd do it.

'How much did he take your father for?' The sharp question jolted her out of her thoughts.

'Twenty-five grand,' she said. Her dad's life savings. Peter MacCabe had believed he was giving Iona a shot at her dream—but Brad's promises of setting her up as a wildlife artist in Los Angeles had been as false and shallow as he was.

She pushed out a shaky breath.

Stop being a drama queen.

Once she'd given Detective Sexy the slip and worked out a way to get back into Brad's room, she'd finally be able to look for her dad's money.

'You don't seriously think he's got twenty-five grand in Irish bills stashed in his motel room do you?'

The incredulous statement had her head whipping round. And her eyes narrowing.

'I'm not Irish, I'm Scottish,' she said, indignation ringing in her voice—how come no one in California knew the difference between a Scottish and an Irish accent—hadn't any of them ever watched *Braveheart*? 'And I don't see where else he would put the money. He's not likely to be using a bank account, is he?'

'When did he hit your old man?'

'December.'

December the twenty-third, to be precise. What a merry Christmas that had turned out to be. To think she'd actually believed the story he'd told her about popping over to Inverness to get her and her father a Christmas present. Until her father had dropped the bombshell about cashing in all the bonds he owned to 'give you a chance at happiness with your new young man.' She hadn't even had the heart to tell him she and Brad were hardly a love match.

'That's three months ago.' She heard the note of pity in the detective's voice, and hated him for it. 'The money's long gone by now.'

It couldn't *all* be gone. Not all twenty-five grand. 'How? He's not exactly spending it on his accommodation.'

'He's got a cocaine habit. He could lose that much up his nose in a weekend.'

'But...' A cocaine habit? Was that why he'd seemed so fragile and vulnerable when he'd walked into the Kelross giftshop?

'I'm taking it he kept that quiet while he was in...' The detective paused. 'Where are you from?'

'The Scottish Highlands,' she said absently.

'So that's why he disappeared from our radar for a couple of months,' he murmured more to himself than her. 'I figured he might have skipped town to avoid his marks, but I didn't think he had the imagination to skip all the way to Europe.'

'He has other marks?' she said dully.

'*Querida,* he's a high-end hustler with a class-A habit—where do you think I come in?'

'I don't know, where *do* you come in?' she snapped. Did the guy really have to be quite so patronising?

'My name's Zane Montoya. I own and operate a private investigations firm based in Carmel. We've been investigating Demarest for six months. Gathering evidence, witness statements, establishing a money trail, all on behalf of an insurance company who made the mistake of insuring some of his victims.' He waited a beat as she struggled to absorb the information.

So her father hadn't been the only one who'd fallen for Brad's clever lies? This hadn't been some arbitrary, opportunistic con? Her stomach pitched at the thought.

Had she really believed this couldn't get any worse?

She'd got over her ludicrous fantasy that Brad Demarest cared about her and admired her artwork—enough to help her get out of Kelross Glen—months ago. But Montoya's revelations felt like the final rusty nail in the rotting coffin of her pride and self-respect.

'A complex, high-level investigation,' Montoya continued. 'That your dumb stunt came close to screwing up tonight.'

She ignored Montoya's irritation. If he expected an apology for her 'dumb stunt,' he'd be waiting until they were serving snow cones in hell. She couldn't care less about him or his anonymous insurance company or his complex, high-level, 'almost screwed up' investigation.

All she cared about was her father.

Peter MacCabe was a good man, who'd wanted to give

her a dream. A dream she'd destroyed by letting a professional conman into their lives.

They rode in silence for the next few miles. Iona stared into the darkness and tried to get her head around what she was going to do next. It had taken her over two weeks to track Brad this far, in the hope she could get some of the money back. But if all the money was gone, was there even any point in confronting him? The hopelessness of the situation felt debilitating.

The lights of a strip mall shone in the distance as they approached another seaside town, but her mind had gone numb and she simply could not get it to engage.

Even her bones felt tired. She'd been running on adrenaline since she'd got to California, trying to live on as little as possible while she waited for Brad to return to the motel she'd had staked out. Tears of frustration and weariness pricked her eyes. She sucked them up. Crying never solved anything.

The yellow sign of a fast-food franchise flickered on the side of the road. Her stomach protested audibly and the hot flush of shame fired up her neck. Seemed the coffin of her self-respect hadn't completely rotted away because she'd be mortified if Montoya had heard her hunger pains.

No such luck.

The car bounced across the cracked pavement in the fast-food restaurant's forecourt, then stopped at the drive-through window.

He slanted a look at her belly. 'What do you want?'

'Nothing, I'm good,' she said, even though she hadn't eaten since the coffee and doughnut she'd splurged on at breakfast. She'd rather die of starvation than accept charity from this jerk.

'What'll it be, sir?' The teenage girl in the drive-through window blushed profusely before letting out a choked sigh—clearly suffering from the same asphyxiation problem Iona herself had had after her first good look at Detective Sexy.

He glanced at her over his shoulder and she got another unwelcome eyeful of that staggering face. An alarming series of pinpricks shimmered across her nerve endings.

'You sure?' he asked.

'Positive.' She lifted her chin.

The flat line of Montoya's lips curved up at one end, sending a dimple into his cheek. The pinpricks gathered and concentrated in all sorts of inappropriate places.

A dimple? Seriously? Give me a break.

The hint of a smile was more rueful than amused, but there was no denying the spectacular blip in Iona's heart rate—or the loud answering growl of the lion in her stomach still hoping to get fed.

'Suit yourself.' He turned back to the blushing teen. 'I'll have two double cheeseburgers with a couple of large fries and a chocolate malt, Serena,' he purred, reading her name off the badge pinned to her heaving bosom.

'Yes, sir, coming right up.' The girl jumped to attention. 'That'll be six dollars fifty, sir.'

Iona rolled her eyes. What was with the sir? Couldn't Serena see Detective Sexy already had an ego the size of Mars? Stroking it would turn it into a supernova.

He paid for the food, thanked Serena with what Iona guessed must have been the full dimple effect—because the girl's face went radioactive—then drove to the pick-up window.

'Here, hold these.' He passed her the two grease-spotted paper bags.

The delicious aroma of grilled meat and freshly fried potatoes swirled around Iona as he steered the car to a parking space one-handed while taking a loud slurp of his malt.

A giant chasm opened in her stomach and began to weep as she thrust the bags back as soon as the car was stationary. 'Why did you get two?' she snapped, drool pooling under her tongue. 'I told you I'm not hungry.'

Was he trying to torture her?

'They're both for me.' He patted what appeared to be a washboard-lean stomach, the rueful twist of his lips mocking her. 'Stake-outs are hungry work and all I've had since lunch is ten Twinkies and a gallon of Dr Pepper.'

She glared across the console. 'My heart bleeds for you.'

The mention of the sugary treats was torturous enough, but then he produced an enormous cheeseburger from one of the takeout bags.

The lurid orange substance that passed for cheese dripped from the sesame-seed bun as the savoury scent filled the car. The chasm in Iona's stomach yawned as his Adam's apple bobbed up and down while he demolished the cheeseburger, then made equally fast work of the fries. The crunch of crisp golden potato and the heady fragrance sent her taste buds into overdrive.

He balled up the empty bag and flipped it into a bin outside the car window. She licked her lips as her stomach rolled into her throat.

One down, one to go.

He peered into the second bag, lifted out the last

cheeseburger. Wrapping the serviette round one half, he brought it to his lips in slow motion.

'Wait.' Her hand shot out to grab hold of one thick wrist as the lion howled.

'Something you want?' His tone sounded strangely alluring in the darkness. Her tortured gaze met his mocking one.

'Yes...I...' Her tongue swelled, the drool choking her. 'Please.'

One dark eyebrow lifted. 'Please, what?'

The bastard was going to make her beg.

'Could I have a wee bite?' She begged, ready to sacrifice her pride, her self-respect and anything else he might want for one little nibble.

The intensely blue gaze dipped as her teeth dug into her bottom lip—and the pinpricks radiated up and out from all those inappropriate places. She dismissed her response. It had to be some weird physical reaction brought on by starvation.

She waited, ready for him to torture her some more, but to her relief his lips quirked—making the damn dimple wink at her—and he handed over the precious burger. 'Knock yourself out.'

She paused for a second as her fingers sank into the spongy bun, then ripped off a huge chunk with her teeth.

Her taste buds sang a hallelujah chorus as the meat juices and the creamy, salty cheese caressed her tongue. A low moan of gratification eased out round the mouthful of burger and his gaze locked on her mouth, the mocking smile gone.

She swallowed quickly and took another massive bite. She could feel the disturbingly intense gaze as she stuffed the rest of burger in—but she didn't care.

Let him be as appalled as he liked by her terrible table manners. She hadn't had a decent meal in days. And it hadn't been her idea to get kidnapped.

Why did that look so damn hot?

Heat shot into Zane's crotch as the wide full lips shone from the coating of grease.

'Slow down, you'll make yourself sick,' he murmured.

She peered at him, her expression wary as she continued to devour the burger like a ravenous wolf. He shifted in his seat, suppressing the urge to lick off the trickle of juice dribbling down her chin. She swiped the back of her hand across her mouth, wiping off the trickle, but the tug of arousal made it impossible to drag his gaze away.

I must seriously need to get laid.

Had it been six months since he'd had that weekend fling in Sonora with Elena, the public defender? Six months wasn't that unusual for him—he'd always been choosy about his sexual partners—but this time the abstinence had to be messing with his radar.

The girl was cute, no question. The slanting chocolate eyes, thick red-gold curls, her wide kissable mouth and pale freckled skin made a unique package—but cute was hardly his type. And then there was the biggest turn-off of all. He was involved with her in a professional capacity. She was definitely a witness, possibly even a perp. And he never crossed that line. Ever.

The heat subsided as he watched her gulp down the last of the burger as if her life depended on it. Exactly how old was she? With that petal-soft skin it was hard to tell, but she could be a teenager.

He forced his gaze from her lips as he lifted the bag of

fries off the dash, and passed them to her. 'How long's it been since you had a decent meal?'

She stiffened. 'Not long,' she said grudgingly but took the bag.

Yeah, right.

She popped the fries into her mouth, but continued to watch him, as if she expected him to snatch them back at any moment.

He suppressed the dart of compassion.

Grab a dose of reality, Montoya.

She's no damsel in distress—she's a resourceful little operator with her own agenda. Getting a job at Demarest's motel had been a neat trick. And how the hell had she tracked the guy from Scotland, when they'd had trouble tracking him across California? Until he had the full story of how she fitted into the picture with Demarest, he didn't plan to trust her an inch.

But that didn't solve his immediate problem. What to do with her tonight? He hadn't planned much past getting her away from Demarest's motel.

He couldn't take her back to Morro, and booking her into another motel wasn't an option either, because she'd skip.

Of course he could dump her on the cops. But while handing her over would 'contain' the problem, he couldn't quite bring himself to do it.

'So how did you find out Demarest had a room at the Morro, Iona?' he asked, deciding it was about time he started interrogating her properly—and stopped fixating on those damn lips.

She stopped shovelling fries into her mouth. 'How do you know my name?' she said in that lilting Celtic brogue.

'The motel clerk was real talkative when I told him about your crime spree with his key.'

Her rich chocolate eyes went squinty with temper. 'You told him? How could you? I'll lose my job.'

'You're not going back there anyway,' he said, dismissing the prickle of guilt. He wasn't the one who'd decided to indulge in some after hours B and E. 'I don't want you alerting Demarest to our presence.'

'I'm not going to alert him. Why would I?' She sounded aggrieved. 'How am I going to pay my bill now? They probably won't even give me the wages they owe me.'

'I settled your bill.' He'd also paid the clerk to keep her valuables in the motel safe. If Demarest showed up tonight, he might not need the bargaining chip Iona's ID documents represented, but he had a feeling it wasn't gonna be that simple. Because nothing about this damn case had been simple so far.

And the biggest complication of all was sitting right in front of him.

A complication made a whole lot worse by his perverse reaction to her.

He'd never before got a kick out of manhandling a woman—even on the force he'd earned the nickname Lancelot, because of his preference for using persuasion and persistence when interrogating female suspects, instead of threats and intimidation.

But there was no getting away from the fact that when he'd caught her in Demarest's room tonight—he'd noticed the generous breasts propped on his forearm and the fresh, subtle fragrance of her hair. And while he might have been able to ignore that momentary loss of control—because it had been six months since he'd had a woman, any woman in his arms—that excuse was nowhere near good enough to explain why he'd come close to getting a hard-on just watching her eat.

'But you can kiss your paycheck goodbye,' he said, making sure the chill stayed in his voice.

Her big brown eyes widened, making him feel as if he'd just kicked Bambi.

'Now stop arguing with me or I'll kick you out of the car and leave you in the middle of nowhere.'

It was an empty threat, he wouldn't do that to any woman, especially not one who had no money, no ID, who'd just devoured a burger as if she hadn't eaten in days and who had eyes like Bambi.

But instead of being cowed, she stuck her chin out. 'Fine, dump me here if you want. I've no got a problem with that.'

Damn, she was actually serious.

What kind of guys had she been dealing with? Then he thought of the seedy motel, and her connection to Demarest and had a pretty good idea.

'Yeah, well, unfortunately I do.'

'Then take me back to the motel. I'll get my stuff and stay somewhere else. I won't interfere with your case, I swear. I want Brad caught as much as you do.'

Maybe it was the flinty determination in her voice or the way her gaze never wavered. But he wanted to believe her.

Which only made him sure he shouldn't. Ten years on the force had taught him that trust was a dangerous thing—and following your gut instead of having proof could get you killed.

He slid the car into reverse. 'Forget it. You're staying where I can keep an eye on you.'

'Why?' she said, the hitch in her voice telegraphing

her shock. 'This is ridiculous. You dislike me as much as I dislike you.'

Unfortunately he didn't dislike her nearly as much as he should, but he let the observation pass.

Her brow creased. 'All you have to do is trust me a little bit and we never have to lay eyes on each other again.'

'Trust you?' He sent her a long look. 'You think?'

'Oh, for Pete's sake,' she hissed. 'I already told you Brad stole money from my father.'

So it was Brad now.

'I was trying to get it back,' she finished, crossing her arms, and making her breasts plump up under the scoop neck of the tank.

'Yeah, but I don't have a heck of a lot of proof.' He dragged his eyes away from her cleavage. Annoyed with himself. And her. Was she doing that on purpose? 'And until I do, we're stuck with each other.'

He reversed out of the lot, deciding the argument was over.

'Now hang on,' she piped up. 'If you don't trust me, why the heck should I trust you? You say you're a private investigator, but for all I know you could be an axemurderer.'

'I showed you my licence,' he said, humouring her.

'Which you could have had forged for you by axemurderers.com.'

His lips quirked at her tenacity, but he bit back the chuckle. The accusation wasn't funny, it was insulting.

He braked and pulled out his smartphone, then keyed in the number for the LAPD. He passed the phone to her as it started ringing. 'Ask for Detective Stone, or Detective Ramirez in Vice, whichever one is on shift. They can vouch for me.'

He waited while she spoke to the dispatcher, and spent some time verifying that she was talking to a genuine LAPD officer—and not one of his axe-murdering pals.

Smart girl.

'Excuse me, Detective Ramirez,' came her smoky voice when she got his former partner on the line. 'My name is Iona MacCabe and I'm here with a man called Zane Montoya. He says he's a private detective and that you know him. Is that true?' She listened for a moment, her teeth releasing her bottom lip as she nodded. 'Can you tell me what he looks like?' Her gaze roamed over his face as she listened to Ram's reply. Her scrutiny was sharp and dispassionate, and so unlike the glassy-eyed stares he had come to expect from women that something perverse happened. His nape heated, triggering a flash back to high school, when those glassy-eyed stares had allowed him to charm any girl he wanted into his bed—or more often the back seat of his uncle Raoul's Chevy.

He rubbed a hand over the back of his neck.

Damn it, Montoya. Get real. You're not in high school any more and you don't want Iona MacCabe in your bed, or anywhere else.

'All right, I guess this is the same guy,' she murmured, that smoky accent only making him more uncomfortable. 'And you're sure he's no an axe-murderer?'

Her eyebrows inched up her forehead and then she laughed, the sound low and amused and so unexpected it arrowed right through him.

He didn't even want to think what Ram had said. His ex-partner had a sense of humour coarsened by twenty-five years spent in a squad car and a locker room. It wasn't exactly subtle.

At last she passed him back his phone. 'Okay, you

check out,' she said a little grudgingly. 'The detective wants to speak to you.'

Terrific.

'Hey, Ram,' he said without a lot of enthusiasm. He usually enjoyed shooting the breeze with the guy, but not now, not with this woman in the car—who was becoming way more of a complication than he needed.

Ramirez's amused voice boomed down the phone. 'Lancelot, man, who's the *chiquita*? She sounds cute.'

Zane kept his eyes on Iona, and hoped she hadn't heard the dumb remark. 'I'm on a case, man,' he said sternly, relieved when Iona broke eye contact and stared out of the window, ignoring him.

'I'll bet.' The rusty laugh caused by two packs a day wheezed out as Ram replied. 'What happened, man? You finally find one you can't charm out of her panties with that pretty face of yours?'

'I appreciate you vouching for me, Ram,' he said, wishing to hell it had been Stone on the late shift tonight—whose sense of humour was about as animated as his name. And ended the call.

He dumped the smartphone on the dash, tunnelled his fingers through his hair. This night had started badly and gone downhill from there.

'Satisfied?' he asked Iona.

'I guess so,' she said, sounding snotty again.

She wasn't the only one in a snit now, though.

He started the car and pulled out.

'You still haven't told me where we're going.'

'Monterey,' he said, being as vague as possible. 'It's about two hours' drive so you might as well get comfortable.'

'And why are we going there?'

'I have a friend who owns some vacation rentals in Pacific Grove,' he said, remembering the key he still had in his glove compartment to Nate's property, which he'd stayed at a month ago while his kitchen was being remodelled. He could stash her in the picturesque little cottage for tonight, then review his options.

Without a car, or any cash or ID, she wouldn't be able to get far. And it was close enough to his place on Seventeen Mile to be convenient.

'You can stay there tonight—and I'll bring over your stuff tomorrow.'

When he planned to interrogate her—and find out exactly what she knew about Demarest.

It had been on the tip of his tongue to tell her he was taking her back to his place for the night. He had five bedrooms in the timber-and-glass beach house he'd bought a year ago, and it was a little more remote than Pacific Grove. But he'd kicked the idea into touch almost as soon as it had occurred to him.

He rarely did sleepovers, even with women he was dating. And he'd sure as hell never had one he was planning to interrogate stay over. Plus, given his unpredictable reaction to Iona already, having her under his roof had the potential to turn a complication into a catastrophe.

'And what if I don't want to stay at your friend's vacation rental in Pacific Grove?' she demanded.

'I turn you over to the cops,' he said, not sure why he wasn't doing that already. 'Your choice.'

The weighty silence told him what his passenger thought about the proposed sleeping arrangements.

'Why are you even giving me the option?' she said at last, the note of caution making it clear she'd accepted the lesser of two evils. 'I could wreck the place to spite you.'

Good question, and not one he wanted to answer.

'True enough, but you'd be facing a lot more than a B and E charge when I caught you.' He slanted her a long look, frustrated that he trusted her even though he didn't want to—and letting every ounce of that frustration show. 'And I would catch you.'

Her musical voice didn't pipe up again until they hit the coastal highway.

'Fine, I'll stay where you put me—until tomorrow. But only because I don't have a choice.' The Celtic mist of her accent did nothing to disguise the annoyance. 'But I'm not your *chiquita*. So don't get any funny ideas, Lancelot.'

Zane's fingers tensed on the wheel until he could feel the stitching on the leather biting into his palms.

Gee, thanks, Ramirez.

TWO

—

The vicarious pleasure at getting the final word didn't last long when Montoya's only response was the creak of leather—as he held the steering wheel in a death grip.

Way to go, Iona. Why not draw attention to his reputation for charming women out of their knickers? Because that's just what you want, to make this encounter personal.

'Did Ram say something dumb about me?' he asked after twenty seconds that had stretched over several lifetimes.

Iona risked a glance at him. His eyes remained fixed on the road as if he were trying to burn off a layer of tarmac.

'Maybe,' she said carefully, feeling increasingly awkward. Why hadn't she kept her smart mouth shut?

With a face like that, the guy probably got hit on by supermodels—despite his less-than-charming personality—which meant snide remarks about being indifferent to his charms probably made her sound delusional.

He sighed. 'Ram's got a big mouth and he gets a kick out of busting my balls. Don't pay any attention to him.'

The knot of tension in Iona's stomach released. He didn't sound angry; he sounded embarrassed.

'So you don't have a reputation for charming the *chiquitas* out of their panties?' she said, intrigued by his reaction.

Instead of taking the bait, he laughed. The low rumble of amusement shivered down her spine and re-ignited the stupid pinpricks she'd been trying to forget.

'I do,' he conceded. 'But I didn't do a whole lot to earn it.'

She didn't believe him. Either he was being falsely modest, or he was lying. From the lazy, casually seductive tone he'd slipped into so effortlessly, she'd bet he could charm the average *chiquita* out of her panties from five hundred paces.

'Ramirez tends to exaggerate my exploits.' He protested a bit too much. 'Because he's been happily married for twenty-five years.' He sent her a dimpled smile and the pinpricks were toast. 'Don't worry, Iona, you're safe with me.'

The pulse of awareness that warmed the air at his softly spoken guarantee had her nipples hardening under the thin black camisole. She folded her arms over the tell-tale buds and cursed the knee-jerk thought that she wouldn't completely object to a little danger.

'Good to know,' she replied, trying to convince herself she was grateful he had no designs on her panties.

Given her disastrous relationship history, the last thing she needed right now was to develop some ridiculous crush on Detective Sexy. She was already at enough of a disadvantage with the man.

'So how did Demarest manage to relieve your old man

of twenty-five grand?' he asked, sliding effortlessly from charm offensive back to cop mode.

'Why do you ask?' she said, attempting to deflect the question. While she'd much rather be dealing with Montoya the cop, than Montoya the pantie charmer, she had no intention of revealing the grim details of her affair with Brad.

'It's not Demarest's usual MO.'

'What is his usual MO?'

He paused, and she had the uneasy feeling he had seen right through the stalling tactic. 'All the victims we questioned were women, mostly over fifty, recently divorced or widowed. He poses as a producer, gives them a line about casting them in his latest movie, sweetens the deal with a little recreational sex and then asks for an investment.'

The flush spread up Iona's throat at Montoya's matter-of-fact statement. But she managed to choke back the urge to correct him.

Sex with Brad had been the opposite of recreational, at least in her experience. He'd been rough and demanding, but because he'd been her ticket out of Kelross Glen, she'd wanted to please him. Her stomach sank to her toes, her scalp burning at the memory of how hard she'd tried. Hard enough to persuade herself she actually liked Brad.

When Brad had dangled the carrot of knowing a wealthy benefactor in LA who might be keen to commission her artwork, she'd had no qualms about mentioning the opportunity to her Dad. But while her gullibility made her sick with shame, it was the way she'd let Brad use her in bed that made her feel sordid.

'Demarest's a sick bastard,' Montoya continued. 'The money's not the main kick for him, it's sleeping with the women he's exploiting,' Montoya hesitated. 'Which is why I'm wondering how your old man fits into that? Where was the kick?'

She flinched at the perceptive comment. Montoya wasn't buying it. Had he guessed her father hadn't been the real mark? And why did the thought that he might find out the truth only make her feel a thousand times more unclean?

It really shouldn't matter what this man knew or didn't know. He was a stranger. And she didn't even like him. In anything other than a hormonal sense, she added grudgingly.

But somehow it did matter.

'Demarest was going to make a tourist film for my dad,' she said, remembering one of Brad's earlier carrots—that her father hadn't taken. 'We have a gift shop in Kelross. Demarest suggested making a movie about the history of the place for US investors,' she added. It had *almost* been true.

'How long was this movie going to be?'

'I'm not sure...' She scrabbled around trying to remember if Brad had even got that far with the con. 'An hour, maybe.'

'An hour? For twenty-five grand?' He gave an incredulous laugh. 'Your old man sounds like an easy mark.'

Iona bristled, knowing she'd been the easiest mark of all. 'He just doesn't know much about movie making.' And unfortunately neither did she.

'Although it still seems kind of weird,' Montoya murmured, the continued scepticism making her tense. 'For there not to be a woman in there somewhere.' He bumped his thumb against the steering wheel, the insistent tapping making Iona feel like Captain Hook listening to the tick-tock of the approaching crocodile. 'What about your mother? Where does she fit into the picture?'

The question was so unexpected, she answered without thinking. 'Nowhere. She ran off when I was small. We haven't seen her since.'

The recently eaten burger turned over as the ugly truth made her feel suddenly vulnerable, scraping at an old wound. A scabbed over, forgotten wound that she thought had healed years ago.

'That's tough.' Montoya's gruff condolence only made her feel more exposed.

'Not that tough. I can barely remember her,' she lied, ashamed of having revealed too much, too easily.

She curled away from him, gazed at the stars sprinkled over the dark line of the cliffs, and closed her eyes, trying to shut out the memory of her mother—so beautiful, so careless and so indifferent.

Don't think about her. You've got quite enough to deal with already.

Fatigue made her eyelids gritty. She blinked furiously, determined to stay awake. She couldn't afford to give into sleep yet, because that would mean trusting Montoya and she'd known ever since she was a child she shouldn't trust anyone.

And her experience with Brad had only confirmed that.

Montoya didn't offer any more useless platitudes or ask any more probing questions. Something she was pathetically grateful for as she pressed her cheek into the soft leather, listened to the soothing hum of the car's engine—and plummeted into a dreamless sleep.

* * *

Zane braked gently in the driveway of the small cottage—and studied his sleeping passenger.

She'd dropped off like a stone an hour ago, and hadn't made a sound since. The engine stilled and the only sound was the chirp of crickets and night crawlers and the distant hum of a passing car. He unclicked her seatbelt, eased it over her bare shoulder and got a lungful of her scent.

The fresh fragrance of baby talc and some flowery soap mixed with the sultry scent of her invaded his senses, and the inevitable pulse of arousal hit.

He tensed, annoyed with his inability to control the response. The cottage's nightlight illuminated her pale face and the varying shades of red in her unruly hair. The thick lashes resting on her cheeks and the even breathing made her look impossibly young. The heat subsided as he imagined her as a kid, losing her mother. The dart of sympathy was sharp and undeniable.

What would he have done if Maria had abandoned him? And she'd had more cause than any mother.

He shook his head, to dispel the thought.

Don't make this personal, Montoya. You're having enough trouble keeping a professional distance.

He didn't even know how old she was. Or how much of her story was true.

And exactly how mixed up with Demarest was she? She'd lied to him about the con. He'd spotted it straight away, the hitch in her breathing, the hesitation as she stumbled over the explanation. Had she been the mark all along? Was that why she'd been so determined to get her father's money back? Because she felt responsible for the loss? Exactly how much danger had she put herself in, while tracking Demarest?

And why did the thought of that bother him so much?

She wasn't his problem, not in the long-term.

He retrieved the key buried in the glove compartment. Then thrust a hand through his hair as it occurred to him he was glad she was here tonight, and under his protection, instead of back at that seedy motel.

He got out of the car, walked around to the passenger door and stared at her cuddled into the seat. He should shake her awake, get her to go into the cottage under her own steam, but she looked so peaceful, he couldn't do it.

Without giving himself too much time to think, he scooped her into his arms.

The sultry scent enveloped him as he carried her onto the cottage's porch. She let out a puff of breath and her soft hair brushed against his chin as she burrowed into his chest like a thrusting child.

He fumbled with the key, pushed the door open with his foot and stepped into the dark interior, an emotion he didn't like banding across his chest.

She didn't stir as he placed her on the small queen-size in the cottage's only bedroom, untied the laces on her combat boots and slipped them off, then covered her with the throw before he got fixated on the slow rise and fall of her breasts beneath the tank.

He found a note pad in the kitchen, scribbled a note and pinned it to the corkboard above the fridge. Unplugging the phone and tucking it under his arm, he walked out of the door, closing and locking it behind him. Then dropped the key through the letter slot.

As he drove back to his place he sent a voicemail to Nate's business line, to inform him of his new house guest, and left one with his PA.

If they didn't pick up Demarest tonight, he was diverting every free man he had to the case tomorrow. He needed to get this damn case closed, before it got any more complicated.

THREE

Stay put, I'll be back tomorrow to tell you what's going to happen next.
Montoya

Iona ran her fingers through her damp curls, tucked the towel between her breasts and glared at the thick black writing—particularly the shouty capitals.

Where did Detective Sexy get off giving her orders like a pet dog?

No one told her what to do. She'd been taking care of herself since she was ten years old. And taking care of her dad too. And okay, maybe she hadn't exactly been doing a stellar job of it of late, but that hardly gave him the right to treat her as if she were his to command.

And what exactly did he mean by *'to tell you what's going to happen next'*?

She struggled to hold on to her indignation and ignore the little blip of disappointment at the fact that so far the only person she'd seen was one of his detectives. A rotund guy called Jim with a gruff but friendly manner, who'd woken her up an hour ago to deliver a bag of groceries, her rucksack—conspicuously minus her purse and passport—and the news that Mr Montoya was busy with the case but would be in touch later in the day.

Pulling the note off the corkboard, she scrunched it up and dumped it in the kitchen bin. Well, hooray for Mr Montoya—it must be nice to get to order everyone around like a demigod.

Goosebumps rose on her arms. She marched back into the cottage's tiny living area and grabbed fresh under-wear, jeans and a T-shirt from her rucksack. He'd better bring her passport when he showed up or there would be trouble. Returning to the compact bedroom, she hunted around for her boots, then stopped dead when she spotted them—placed neatly together on the rug by the bed-side table, the laces undone.

Her heartbeat bumped her throat as a picture formed in her mind's eye. The picture she'd been holding at bay ever since she'd been woken up by the sound of knock-ing at the front door, snuggled cosy and content and well rested under a clean quilt that smelled pleasantly of fab-ric conditioner.

The picture of Montoya carrying her into the cot-tage, taking off her boots and then covering her with said quilt.

The pulse of reaction skittered up her spine, making the pinpricks shimmer back to life and party with the goosebumps.

She swallowed heavily, trying to ease the ache in her throat.

The thought of being fast asleep in his arms was dis-turbing enough, but much worse was the thought of him putting her to bed so carefully.

When was the last time anyone had bothered to treat

her with that much care and attention? Her father had been unable to care for himself after her mother left, let alone her. So at ten years old, she'd become the parent—caring for both of them while he struggled to pull himself back from the brink of depression. She'd had a few boyfriends before Brad, but they'd been young and reckless—providing nothing more than the easy thrill of youthful companionship. And as for her brief liaison with Brad, well Brad had been a user, always quick to take, never willing to give.

Big deal. He just took your boots off for you.

Perching on the edge of the bed, she grabbed one of the boots and shoved it on, staunching the ridiculous tide of her thoughts.

Zane Montoya didn't care about her; he just cared about his case. And she didn't care about him either. So why was she turning one moment of consideration into a primetime drama?

She returned to the kitchenette and began taking the groceries out of the brown paper bag Jim had delivered, determined to put the moment of vulnerability behind her and concentrate on finding a solution to her situation.

She almost wept with joy when she found a tin of coffee. She filled the kettle, looking out of the window to find a sweet little patio garden carpeted with climbing vines. As the rich smell of brewing coffee filled the kitchen, a strange contentment settled over her.

The cottage was tiny, but so clean and pretty—and completely adorable compared to the dives she'd been forced to stay in of late. Pouring herself a steaming cup, she smiled as a hummingbird fluttered into view and settled over the bright yellow pegonias in the window box, and began gathering nectar in its long beak. Putting down the mug, she rushed back into the living room and dug out her art supplies, her palms itching to detail the blurred lines of the bird's movement in the static medium of paper and graphite. Settling in front of the kitchen window, she sketched furiously, trying to capture as much as she could before the bird disappeared. As the hummingbird flitted from flower to flower and the clear lines began to form on the heavy paper the leaden feeling of failure that had bowed her shoulders for so long began to lift.

She relaxed as the bird flew off, and gazed at her drawings. More than enough to create a detailed watercolour later. Refilling her now lukewarm coffee, she took a muffin out of the deli-bag on the counter and realised that for the first time in a long time she felt the bright sheen of possibility peeking out from under the dead weight of failure.

And she had Detective Sexy to thank for that.

When he appeared, she would be conciliatory instead of combative. The truth was, she'd been aggressive and unnecessarily snotty with him last night. Because she'd been exhausted, hungry and terrified—she might as well admit it. But she'd had her first full night's sleep in weeks. Which meant she owed Montoya—however highhanded he'd been with his little note.

But once she'd thanked Montoya and was on her own again, the bigger picture was more complicated. Still, now she was well rested her prospects didn't seem nearly as bleak as they had seemed last night.

She had some money left and a work visa that lasted another five months. There was no reason why she couldn't look for a better place to live now, away from

the seedy motels Brad frequented. And perhaps sell a few more sketches. She'd managed to sell all the hand-painted postcards she'd produced in the cafés along Morro Bay's Main Street, but keeping an eye on Brad's motel room had meant she hadn't had time to replenish her work. But now she was free of Brad-surveillance she could actually devote herself to finding a decent job and spend her evenings sketching. Monterey was supposed to be arty and bohemian—as well as being a tourist mecca. Surely there were bound to be places she could sell her stuff and look for a job. The summer season was only weeks away, so casual work shouldn't be too hard to find.

The most important thing of all, and the main reason she'd come to America to track Brad, was to stop her dad from ever finding out that he'd been conned again by someone he trusted. And while she most likely wouldn't be able to get him his money back, she could still achieve that much.

She'd told her father she was travelling to LA at Brad's invitation, that her 'new man' had come through with his promises of a showcase for her work. Even though the lie had nearly choked her at the time, it had kept her father happy. And while getting a gallery showing had always been a foolish pipe dream, in five months if she worked hard and applied herself she might be able to return home with at least some money to replace what her father had lost—and a small degree of success to show for his bogus investment.

She frowned as she grabbed another muffin. But first she had to convince Montoya she was of no significance to his case. To do that, she needed to be polite and cooperative—and keep things impersonal.

Wiping the crumbs off the surface and rinsing out her

coffee mug, she picked up her sketch pad again, feeling almost euphoric. Until Montoya arrived, she planned to indulge herself and do what she loved for a change.

Zane tucked the cottage's phone under his arm and rapped on the front door. The early evening light beamed off polished wood but as he peered inside it was obvious there was no one in the front room.

He rolled his shoulders as the muscles cramped. He hoped she'd done as she was told and stayed put. After the day he'd put in already, the last thing he needed now was to have to scour Pacific Grove for her.

The original plan had been to swing by first thing that morning. But after having his night's sleep disturbed by way too many sweaty dreams involving firm breasts, wide caramel-coloured eyes, worn tank tops and full kissable lips glossy with burger grease, he'd held off, and sent Jim to deliver the groceries instead.

Iona MacCabe had an unpredictable effect on him, and until he figured out what—if anything—he was going to do about it, keeping his distance was the smart choice.

Then the case had exploded at ten when Demarest had shown up at the Morro Motel—and all hell had broken loose. Zane had been tied up with the Morro Bay PD for the rest of the day, handing over the case files and contacting the LAPD to make sure Demarest got transferred there before the day was out. As a courtesy, Stone and Ramirez had let him observe their interrogations. He massaged the back of his neck to ease the tension headache that had been building ever since.

Just as he'd guessed after their original profiling, in the interview Demarest had been slick and supremely arrogant. But he soon lost control under pressure, and proved how volatile and dangerous he was.

Zane shuddered. What the hell had Iona been thinking breaking into the guy's room? What would have happened to her, if it had been Demarest who'd caught her last night and not him? At some point he planned to give her a damn good talking to about personal safety.

The thought of any woman being at the guy's mercy had sickened him—but worse had been the moment when they'd questioned Demarest about his trip to Scotland. Demarest had laughed and boasted about the Scottish girl who'd been 'begging for it' and Zane had been forced to walk out—the urge to leap through the mirrored partition and strangle the guy triggering the sickening memory that had haunted him most of his adult life.

He eased the kinks out of his shoulders and rapped again.

He should be feeling great now. Six months' work had finally paid off and Montoya Investigations was in line for a nice fat bonus payment. Plus his firm had been instrumental in catching one of the nastiest and most parasitic low lives in California and bringing him to book. But somehow it didn't feel like enough—because it could never undo the damage the bastard had done.

He squinted through the clouded glass again, and a little of the tension dissolved as he spotted the petite silhouette coming to the door from the back of the house. Then the door swung open and the punch of lust hit full force.

The setting sun glinted on her hair, highlighting the different shades of red, and making her skin almost transparent. Her rich caramel eyes glowed with energy, and, while the wary caution of the night before was still there, the bruised shadows underneath were gone. In a pair of old jeans and a T-shirt that hugged the generous breasts he recalled a little too well pressing against his forearm, her feet encased in the boots he'd taken off her the night before, she should have looked like a tomboy. She didn't.

'Hello, Mr Montoya. Sorry I didn't hear you knocking—I was in the back garden.' The Celtic lilt and the hitch in her breathing called to his inner caveman.

Down, Montoya. You're here on business. Not pleasure. However tempted you might be to stray over that line.

He noticed the pad under her arm, which was covered in a series of intricate drawings of a small bird.

'You're an artist?' he asked, although the answer was obvious from the quality of the work.

'Yes, I...' She shrugged. 'I specialise in drawing flora and fauna. It's a passion of mine.'

She stumbled over the word *passion* and two pink flags appeared on her cheekbones, making the sprinkle of freckles on her nose more vivid.

'A passion, huh?' he said, not quite able to hold back the grin when she squirmed. So he wasn't the only one struggling to remain professional.

Good to know.

'Come in, Mr Montoya,' she said, the cool, polite tone disconcerting as she stepped back and held the door open. He wondered what had happened to the firebrand he'd met last night.

'The name's Zane.' He dumped the phone on the coffee table. 'I brought this in case you want to call your father. You got the groceries okay this morning?'

'Yes, you should tell me what I owe you for them,' she

said, the cool tone turning chilly. 'Although it's going to be hard to pay you without my purse.'

He tugged her purse and passport out of his back pocket. But when she reached for them, he lifted them above her head. 'Not so fast. I'll need your word you're not going to run off.'

The beguiling almond-shaped eyes narrowed. And the firebrand came out of hiding.

'And what would you be needing my word for?' she asked, propping her hands on her hips and making her breasts flatten against the tight T-shirt. 'If you don't believe a single thing I say?'

'It'll go some way to putting my suspicious mind at rest,' he said, enjoying the view probably a bit too much.

The fire in her eyes flared. 'Is it just me you don't trust?' she asked her tone dripping with sarcasm. 'Or do you have this low an opinion of all women, Mr Montoya?'

He choked out a laugh. No one had ever accused him of that before. Especially not a woman. But then Iona MacCabe was turning out to be an original in more ways than one.

His gaze wandered over her face and he watched with satisfaction as her cheeks pinkened. 'On the contrary, I have a very high opinion of women.'

The pulse of awareness warmed the air as her cheeks heated to a dull red. And pert nipples protruded against the T-shirt.

It was a crisp spring evening outside, but the sun shining through the cottage's front window meant the atmosphere was warm and close.

She crossed her arms to cover the stiff buds.

Too late, your secret's out, querida. You're no more immune to me than I am to you.

'In fact,' he added, 'I can't think of a single thing about women I don't enjoy.'

Professionalism be damned. Iona McCabe was too cute to resist flirting with.

'So perhaps we should start over—and forget about last night.' He held out his hand. 'Zane Montoya, at your service.'

Suspicion clouded her eyes, but then she thrust her slim hand into his much larger, much darker one. He clasped her fingers for barely a second, the handshake quick and impersonal, but the cool, soft touch of her skin contrasted sharply with the arrow of heat that darted straight to his groin.

She stuffed her hand into the back pocket of the jeans. But her pupils dilated with something he recognised only too well, before her gaze flickered away.

You felt it too.

Endorphins flowed freely through his system. He'd always been a connoisseur of women, in all their myriad and wonderful varieties. Which was why he didn't have a type. But for some reason, this girl hit all his happy buttons, without even trying.

And he was through fighting it.

As of today, Demarest was in a cell and would be for a very long time. The case was closed as far as Montoya Investigations was concerned. So there was no professional reason why he shouldn't push a few of her happy buttons right back.

'I've got some news on the case, Iona,' he said, planning to ask her if she wanted to discuss it over dinner, but before he could say any more her head shot up.

'News about Brad?'

He frowned, his happy buttons not feeling all that

happy any more. 'We picked him up at ten this morning. He's in a cell facing more charges than he can count.'

'I see.' Her voice sounded casual, but then she fixed him with that cautious gaze and he knew it wasn't. 'Did he have any of my dad's money on him?'

He shook his head and her face fell.

'Right.' She looked down, but not before he saw the shadow of distress.

He shoved his hand into his pocket, resisting the urge to run his finger down her cheek, and stroke the distress away.

For one tense moment he thought she might cry. But then she seemed to pull herself back from the brink.

'Well, I guess this is where we part company, then, Montoya,' she murmured.

Something tugged hard under his breastbone. And that surprised him.

The threat of female tears didn't usually faze him, but there was something about Iona McCabe's stoicism—and those sultry eyes, so large and wary in her small face—that *had* fazed him.

She let out a weighty sigh. 'Do you think it would be okay for me to stay here another night? I could pay any rent that's due.'

His sympathy dissolved. She looked scared but defiant, like a puppy who expected to be kicked but was determined not to yelp.

He didn't deserve that.

He trusted her. In fact, she sort of fascinated him. She was feisty and unpredictable and refreshingly transparent and he hadn't been able to get his mind off her, even though he'd tried. But it was real clear that however attracted she might be to him, she didn't trust him. And while he'd understood her animosity last night, he was finding it hard not to take it personally now.

'Damn it, Iona, you can stay here as long as you need.' In fact, he planned to insist on it. She might think she was safe, but he knew different. A woman alone was always vulnerable, but especially a woman as impulsive as her. 'And there's no charge—the place was empty anyway.'

'Why would you do that? I'm not your responsibility.' She sounded genuinely confused, making his annoyance increase.

'Because, weirdly enough, I'm not the kind of guy who kicks women when they're down.' *Unlike your pal Brad.*

'Okay, well, thank you, I appreciate not having to leave tonight,' she said. But then her chin stuck out in a stubborn show of strength. 'But I'll make sure I'm gone by tomorrow.'

I don't think so. Not until I'm sure you'll be safe.

He bit back the retort, seeing the mutinous expression on her face. In his experience, pushing her only made her push back. And anyhow, he didn't want to argue with her. Not tonight.

'How about we talk about it over dinner in Santa Cruz? I know a place that does the best enchiladas on the West Coast.'

Her face went completely blank for a second and she blinked, her eyes going round with astonishment.

That had sure shut her up.

'You're n-not serious?' she stammered, her accent thickening.

Damn, she's even cuter when she's flustered.

Had Detective Sexy just asked her on a date? Or was she hallucinating?

'I'm always serious about Manuel's enchiladas,' he replied, while the tempting glint in his eye implied the opposite. 'My treat,' he continued, apparently not the least bit bothered by her shock.

But then she suspected he was probably used to that reaction from women.

What with that devastating face—not to mention that subtle I-can-have-you-any-time-I-want-you smile—she already knew he was an expert at charming women out of their panties. She'd only got a glimpse of his charm the night before—but she was standing in the full glare of it now, and getting a little light-headed.

Then she made the mistake of drawing a breath into her lungs. The fresh scent of laundry soap, a zesty hint of aftershave and something musky and entirely masculine drifted up her nostrils.

Good Lord, he's got so many let's-get-naked hormones pumping off him, I can actually smell them.

She pressed her arms into her breasts as her traitorous nipples began to ache.

'But why...?' she began, struggling to come up with a coherent response.

He leaned forward and whispered, 'Because I'm starving, *querida*. Aren't you?'

His breath feathered her earlobe and sent the pinpricks careering down her neck and straight into her nether regions. She drew her head back, and got fixated on those penetrating blue eyes. She didn't answer the question, because she was fairly certain they weren't talking about enchiladas any more.

His smile widened—and the nuclear blush radiated up her neck.

'Well, I...?' she began again, fighting to stem the tide of brain cells leaking out of her head.

He chuckled. 'Say yes, Iona. They really are the best. I don't lie to women.' He winked, the playful gesture as dazzlingly sexy as that azure gaze. 'It's one of my many charms.'

He probably lied to women all the time, but the firm 'no' that should have been hovering on the tip of her tongue wasn't.

Taking Detective Sexy up on his offer of a dinner date was probably not a smart move. Especially as she might end up getting zapped to a crisp by his let's-get-naked hormones. She'd promised herself she'd be polite and sensible and keep her interaction with him impersonal. But as soon as she'd opened the door, and seen him standing on the porch, a sunbeam spotlighting that blue-black hair and breathtaking face, she'd had to concede that impersonal was always going to be a hard sell. And then he'd started talking, in that patronising but oh-so-sexy way and polite and sensible had taken a nosedive too.

Plus she finally had something to celebrate. The news that Brad Demarest was out of her life for ever. It had been a blow to discover her father's money really was gone, but she wasn't going to worry about that. If she could make a go of her artwork in Monterey, at least something good might come of the loss.

And then there was the fact that she hadn't been out on a date in—well, for ever. The boyfriends she'd had in Kelross had never been able to stretch to much more than a visit to the local chip shop. And Brad had only ever been interested in getting her naked and then getting the sex over with as soon as he was satisfied.

She blitzed the thought.

Do not go there. Concentrate on the enchiladas—the best on the West Coast no less—they sounded delicious. And being in the company of a guy who made her pulse vibrate, instead of one who made her feel as if she didn't have a pulse.

Plus there was no danger of her doing anything stupid, no matter how much her pulse vibrated. Because post-Brad she was pretty sure she was man-proof—or at the very least man-averse—with or without the pinpricks.

And Montoya was probably only asking her because he felt bad about threatening to have her arrested last night. So this had to be a pity date.

'Okay, you're on,' she said, reckless excitement thrumming through her veins.

Brad had destroyed her confidence in ways she hadn't even realised. And she'd let him. But she couldn't think of a better way to get some of it back. If ever there was a cure for a woman's shattered ego, it had to be spending an evening with someone as drop-dead gorgeous as Detective Sexy.

FOUR

———

Iona tied the silk scarf around her head as Zane's vintage convertible bulleted down the coast road. She gazed out across the dark blue expanse of the Pacific Ocean. The rolling breakers created a mighty backdrop to the soft tangerine glow of sunset hitting the low cliffs. The zing of exhilaration made her pulse throb, especially as the dramatic splendour of Monterey Bay wasn't the only spectacular view on offer.

'Exactly how many cars have you got?' she shouted, stealing a glance at the man beside her.

He'd rolled up his shirt sleeves, giving her a gratifying glimpse of tanned forearms dusted with dark hair while he negotiated the road's hairpin bends. His dark hair ruffled in the wind around his face and made him look relaxed and gorgeous. A bit too gorgeous, really. Nerves fluttered.

Relax. Pity date, remember. Absolutely no call to panic.

The quick grin gave her a flash of even white teeth in his darkly handsome face. Designer sunglasses hid those diamond-bright eyes from view, thankfully, but she could still sense the twinkle of amusement. 'Several.' He glanced at her. 'Automobiles are a passion of mine.'

She stroked the shiny red paintwork, and laughed at the way he'd emphasized the word *passion*. He was definitely flirting with her. Which felt ridiculously good.

'So how did you get into drawing flora and fauna?' he asked.

'There happens to be a lot of it about in Kelross Glen, so it was a no-brainer really,' she replied.

'Kelross Glen? That's the town you're from in Scotland, right? What's it like?'

'Small,' she said—but decided not to elaborate. That was more than enough about her.

During the half-hour drive along the coast road, Zane Montoya had used those killer looks and that killer smile to prise information out of her about everything from her childhood, to her education, to her father's depression, to her job in the gift shop her dad owned in Kelross Glen, while at the same time neatly sidestepping any personal questions about himself. She'd basically undergone a charm offensive that Lieutenant Columbo would be proud of. No wonder the man made a living as a private detective.

But she was wise to his tactics now. And she wasn't going to divulge another iota of information about herself, until she managed to get him to reciprocate—because all the things he wasn't saying were making her unbearably curious.

The car slowed as they entered the city limits of Santa Cruz. The engine noise dropped to a well-oiled hum as the open road gave way to neighbourhoods of brightly painted clapboard houses with their obligatory picket fences. Teenagers skateboarded on sidewalks whooping out the joys of spring while grey-rinse cyclists thronged the bike paths leading to the boardwalk. Everything was so safe and normal and non-seedy it was enchanting.

The scent of sea salt and fish was a pungent reminder of the beach community's nearby marina. But instead of heading towards Santa Cruz's famous funfair, or the historic Main Street she'd read about in the guidebooks, Zane took a small side road, which wound its way down to a sandy cove.

The restaurant came into view perched on a bluff. A large wooden terrace packed with Friday-night diners jutted out over the ocean. The fairy lights strung from its canopy twinkled festively in the gathering dusk. Cars lined the narrow access road. The joint was jumping and Iona wondered where they were going to park. Her question was answered when Zane drove round to the back lot and slotted his convertible into the only available space under a huge yellow sign that read in ominous black letters: 'Unauthorized Vehicles WILL BE Towed, 24 Hours A Day.' And then underneath scrawled in red graffiti: 'Don't even think about it, Amigo.'

'Shouldn't you think about this, Amigo?' she asked, pointing to the sign as Zane opened the passenger door. He sent her a rakish grin. 'You're worried about me.' He offered her his hand as she climbed out. 'I'm touched.'

'I'm more worried about your beautiful car, actually,' she said, her pulse skipping pleasantly as his palm settled on her hip. His fingers slid against the linen of the short shift dress she'd changed into as he directed her to the restaurant's entrance.

The slope of her back felt as if it were being stroked with a low-voltage cattle prod, the sensation a little shocking and a lot exhilarating.

'And how I'm going to get home if it gets towed,' she finished, trying not to make too much of the possessive touch. He wasn't deliberately trying to electrocute her erogenous zones, it was all in her head.

His low chuckle rumbled through her, upping the voltage.

'Don't worry, I have connections.' He caressed the words the same way he was caressing her back, his palm skimming under the denim jacket she'd worn to ward off the spring chill. 'One of my *primos* owns the place,' he added. 'The Mustang will be safe.'

She shivered and he rubbed gently, the absent caress instantly chasing away the chill. The electrical tingles morphed into tantalising zaps of energy and her nipples drew into tight buds, trapped against her bra.

And she wished this date weren't as safe as his Mustang.

'You're cold.' His gaze dipped to her cleavage as he led her past the queue of people waiting in line for a table. 'Let's grab a booth inside.'

She spotted the booths against the back wall in the darkest part of the restaurant. Their high leather backs and the tea lights flickering on the tables made them look intimate and inviting—and a bit too romantic.

'I'm not that cold. Let's sit outside, over the ocean.' Sharing a booth with him and his let's-get-naked hormones would be risky. She might well get high on them and start purring, especially if he touched her again. And that had the potential to be embarrassing.

His brow quirked, the sceptical smile calling her on her cowardice. 'You sure about that? It's chilly tonight.'

'Absolutely, positively,' she said, determined to avoid purring at all costs.

Montoya's questions in the car and the light flirtatious banter had made her feel important and special. Even if it was a routine he used with every woman he met, her battered ego appreciated the boost. Not only that, but the restaurant was fabulous, the smell of roasting meat and Mexican spices almost as delicious as the lively buzz of friendly people having friendly conversations—and not shouting out obscenities at the top of their voices in the middle of the night.

She felt safe here and really rather fabulous under Montoya's attentive gaze—but she didn't want to get carried away.

A young waiter with bright ginger hair and an eager smile greeted Zane like an old friend and showed them to a table tucked at the end of the terrace.

Iona absorbed the sound of the waves lapping on the beach below and the glittering lights of the funfair across the bay, her stomach grumbling.

As pity dates went, this was shaping up to be one of her best.

Get your eyes off her butt.
Zane lifted his gaze from Iona's perfect rear end as Benji pulled out their chairs.

He kept his gaze above her waistline as he held her chair. But then she smoothed her dress over that delicious tush and planted it on the seat. And his blood pressure shot up another notch.

So now you're a butt man—when did that happen?
Then again, Iona McCabe had a lot of exceptional parts he decided as a gust of sea air plastered her dress against her breasts. Benji handed them both menus and Zane took in a lungful of the salty breeze to calm him-

self down. This was supposed to be fun and flirtatious—
and a fact-finding mission. He wasn't planning on taking
things any further till he knew a lot more about her. She'd
relaxed on the drive up and he'd managed to get some details out of her, but she'd clammed up again before he'd
even got to talking about her association with Demarest.

So he needed to relax, turn up the charm and stop
fixating on her assets, or he was never going to find out
what he wanted to know.

Benji filled their water glasses. 'Welcome to Manuel's
Cantina.' He nodded at Zane. 'I'll tell Mani you're here,
Zane.'

'Don't bother, Benj—I'm sure he's busy,' he said, tens-
ing up at the thought of seeing his *primo*. He liked Mani
well enough, and the food here was terrific, but he never
felt comfortable pretending their family connection
meant something.

'No problem,' Benji remarked, before reeling off the
specials and then leaving them to decide.

'That all sounded delicious.' Iona picked up the menu,
and he was struck again by how young she looked. He
knew now she was twenty-four—he'd checked out the
birth date on her passport—but she looked younger. The
image of Demarest sitting behind the mirrored glass with
a cruel smile on his face made his stomach knot.

Forget it. Whatever the guy had done to her, she was
safe from him now. He put his menu down on the table.
'So, Iona, what do you want?' he asked, making an effort
to keep his tone G-rated.

'Quite a lot actually,' she murmured, the sparkle of
flirtation in rich caramel making the knot sink lower.
A lot lower.

'Uh-huh, well, why don't I help you to decide?' He

stretched out his legs, rested his forearms on the table—
and forced himself to ignore the insistent pulse of heat.

He never slept with a woman on a first date, no matter how much he desired her, because it meant making
demands that might be misconstrued later. He respected
women, he enjoyed their company, but if sex was going to
happen it would be on his terms and at his pace.

'My personal favourite is the blackened catfish enchiladas with green chilli salsa.'

Her lips quirked. 'Are they now? And why's that?'

'Because they've got heat and spice—which is the way
I like my enchiladas.'

She tilted her head to one side, propped her elbow on
the table and ran her tongue over her bottom lip, torturing him. 'Sold, Montoya.'

'Call me Zane.'

'Yes, Zane.' The quick smile became astute. 'Tell me
something, do you date a lot of women?'

'Why do you ask?' That was a lot more direct than he
was used to.

'Because you're very good at it. And you haven't answered my question.'

'I never date more than one at a time,' he replied, not
wanting to tell her it had been six months since he'd
dated—and give this evening more significance than
it deserved.

'You're very cagey. Is that part of the detective code?
Not divulging personal information?'

'No.' He gave a half laugh, as if he didn't know what
she was talking about. But he knew he'd been busted,
and he wasn't sure how to deal with it. Women generally
enjoyed it when you made them the focus of the conver-

sation. He'd sure as hell never had one turn the tables on him this fast.

'I'm an open book,' he lied smoothly. He leaned back in his chair—the picture of relaxed indifference. 'What do you want to know?

'Why *did* you ask me out tonight?'

'For all the usual reasons,' he said carefully. Was that a trick question? No way was he going to tell her about his recently acquired butt-fetish.

'Which are?' she prompted.

The confusion cleared and he relaxed for real. She was looking for a compliment. Not surprising, given her recent association with Demarest. He leaned forward, happy to oblige.

'You're cute and tenacious. I admire your spirit— even if you do need a keeper when it comes to your personal safety—and I wanted to get to know you better.'

Truth was, he wanted to get to know her a lot better, but no need to go there yet.

Instead of her looking pleased with his answer, though, the light in her eyes dimmed and the colour in her cheeks bloomed. She stared out to sea for a moment, her smile pensive and more than a little sad. And he wondered where she'd gone.

'You're really a nice guy, aren't you?' she said at last. 'I'm sorry I was so rude to you yesterday—you didn't deserve that.'

Nice? What the hell?

Zane bristled, the spurt of irritation catching him off guard. No one had ever called him nice before. But before he could think of how to respond, a huge hand clasped his shoulder, and he glanced round to find his *primo* Manuel—the last person he wanted to see—standing by the table.

'Great to see you, *compadre*,' Manuel boomed, the hearty smile making Zane tense even more. 'Welcome back to my humble cantina.'

Cute!

Wasn't that what Brad had once called her? And she'd despised it even then. Why couldn't she be sexy, or, better yet, irresistible?

Iona let the grudging disappointment melt away as she listened to Zane's friend Manuel wax lyrical about the blackened catfish enchiladas, which she already knew were Zane's favourites. Her stomach rumbled loudly and the excitement of the evening seeped back.

Enough with the pity party. If you didn't want to know, you shouldn't have asked.

And cute was better than what she'd begun to fear. That the only reason he'd asked her here was to interrogate her about her association with Brad. As long as the man sitting opposite never found out the truth about that, she could live with cute.

'They sound ravishing, Manuel,' she said, smiling when the proprietor's warm mahogany eyes lit with enthusiasm. 'But I already know how good they are from Zane's sales pitch.'

Manuel beamed at Zane. 'You like them? I didn't know that.'

'It's hardly a secret how much I like the food here. I come here often enough.'

The statement was brusque, and lacked Zane's usual charm.

'And I appreciate your custom, cousin,' Manuel replied.

Her curiosity was piqued. How odd—why did Zane seem so tense if Manuel was his cousin?

'Enjoy your meals.' Manuel pasted the smile back on, smoothing over the discomfort. 'I'll see you Saturday, Zane, at Maricruz's *quinceañera.*'

A muscle in Zane's jaw jumped. 'Yeah, sure.' But from the look on his face as his cousin left, Iona didn't think he was looking forward to it at all. Which only piqued her curiosity more.

'Who's Maricruz?'

Zane watched Iona lick the salt from the rim of her margarita glass and tried to focus on the question, instead of the coil of desire descending south.

Their enchiladas had come and gone, and he'd discovered that watching her eat was as erotic as it had been last night. He'd never given it much thought before, but far too many of the women he'd dated in the past had picked at their food, or worse insisted on ordering nothing more exciting than a salad—usually because they had some dumb idea they were fat.

But not Iona. She'd closed her eyes and hummed with pleasure while swallowing her first bite of the spicy enchilada. The husky groan had arrowed right through him, and he'd been struggling to keep his mind on their conversation ever since.

'She's my cousin, like Manuel,' he clarified. 'And most of the rest of Santa Cruz.'

'How many cousins do you have?' She put down her margarita, her voice hushed in awe.

'Last count? Twenty-eight.' Or was it twenty-nine? It wasn't something he kept abreast of.

Her eyes widened. 'But that must have been fabulous

growing up,' she said, the words overflowing with enthusiasm. 'Having such a huge family?'

Not especially, he thought, annoyed to feel the old anger and resentment resurfacing.

'It was just me and my dad growing up,' she added, and he remembered what she'd told him about her mother. 'Do you have lots of brothers and sisters too?'

'No. There's only me,' he said, the soft brogue of her accent wrapping around him like a caress. 'My mother married a great guy ten years ago. They wanted more kids, but—' He stopped abruptly, astonished he'd let that piece of information slip out. 'But it didn't happen.'

Maria had never blamed him, never even mentioned it, but he knew having him had screwed up her chances of having more children. So he always avoided the subject.

'That's a shame,' Iona murmured, the genuine sympathy in her tone soothing, even though he'd cauterised the wound years ago. 'But I guess at least you had all those cousins.'

'We didn't see much of each other as kids,' he said, careful to stop short of explaining the reason why this time. He'd let go of the anger a long time ago, when his grandfather Ernesto had finally been forced to admit that Maria's *gringo* son could amount to something. But that didn't mean he wanted to talk about it.

'So what's a *quinceañera*?' Iona swirled the straw in her margarita and then placed it in her mouth.

Plump lips sucked on the thin plastic. 'It's a girl's fifteenth birthday party. In the Mexican-American community, that's when her family celebrates her coming of age.'

'And Maricruz's *quinceañera* is this weekend?'

'Yeah, I guess so.' How come they were talking about Maricruz and her party? He jerked his gaze off her lips, which had mesmerized him again. And struggled to get the conversation back where he wanted it. 'So how did Demarest get so friendly with your old man?'

Her smile faltered and then disappeared. 'That's a bit of a non-sequitur.'

'I'm curious.' He forced himself not to care when she stiffened. She owed him. He'd already told her more than he would usually tell a date about his mother's family, but she had a way of questioning him that made him forget to be cautious.

His gaze strayed to the snug bodice of her dress. Not to mention her other distracting qualities. He took a swig of his *cerveza*.

Behave.

'Why don't you want to tell me? Have you got something to hide?' he asked.

'He came into our gift shop,' Iona replied, her face a rigid mask.

'You told me you were the one who worked in the gift shop,' he said, and knew he had her when she flushed. 'Why didn't you tell me about you and Demarest, Iona?' He pressed his advantage, despite the tremble in her fingers as they clutched the stem of her margarita glass.

It was what he was trained to do. And he wanted to know. Suddenly it seemed vitally important to hear the truth from those lush lips.

'Why didn't you tell me about what Demarest did to you?'

She remained rigid in her chair, her eyes glassy with shock.

'Did you think I would judge you?' he added, softening his voice.

A lone tear spilled over her lid, shocking him.

Hell. Had it been worse than he thought?

She brushed the tear away with her fist and stood up.

'You can go right to hell, Montoya,' she whispered, her whole body vibrating with tension.

The show of temper was a relief after the moment of anguish. But his relief was short-lived, when she threw her napkin on the table and rushed off through the crowded tables towards the exit.

'Hey, come back here,' he shouted, making the nearby diners turn and stare at him, but she didn't even slow down.

Tugging his wallet out of his pocket, he threw a wad of bills on the table and headed after her.

Where the hell was she going?

Iona burst out of the restaurant into the night, ignoring the queue of people staring at her and Zane's shouted demand to slow down.

She wanted to throttle him. She would throttle him, if he so much as touched her.

'*Madre de Dios.*'

She heard the muffled curse only moments before a hard forearm wrapped round her waist, halting her getaway as his lean body butted against her back.

She swung round but he grabbed her bunched fist in his hand, and stopped her from socking him on the jaw.

'Calm down, damn it.'

'No,' she shouted, the word whipping away on the wind as the fury rose up to mask the pain and humiliation.

She'd let her guard down, had started to believe that this might be more than just a pity date. That he'd actually meant what he said about wanting to get to know her better—which only made the humiliation worse. 'Don't touch me,' she said yanking her hand out of his.

The tightening in her breasts, and the slow pulse of arousal in her belly that she had no control over, only added insult to the injury.

'Miss, is everything all right?' The tentative question had both her and Zane turning to stare at the older man who had come to her rescue. 'Is this man bothering you?' he asked, not looking quite so confident about the gallant impulse when Zane glared at him.

'She's great,' Zane ground out, before she could think of what to say. She knew she wasn't in any physical danger from Zane Montoya, but didn't emotional danger count? 'I'm a cop.'

'Okay.' Her Sir Galahad nodded quickly. 'Sorry to bother you, Officer.' He hurried back to join his wife in the queue—the impulse to rescue her hastily abandoned.

'You're not a cop,' she snapped as Zane hauled her into the car park, away from the ocean and out of sight of the other customers. 'You're a fake cop, remember.'

She kept her voice down. She was perfectly capable of fighting her own battles. Especially now she'd got a good head of steam.

'I used to be a cop,' he shot back, sounding as furious as she felt. 'Now shut the hell up before you cause any more trouble.'

'*Me?*'

He'd ambushed her, when she hadn't been prepared for it. She should have guessed he'd been a cop—he certainly had one hell of an interrogation technique. He'd let her think she mattered, that even though this might be a pity date, it had potential. She'd been flirting with him, the buzz of the margaritas making her bold as they devoured the food and she lapped up all that focused attention. And then he'd shown his true colours and ruined it all. And for what? So he could get information out of her that she hadn't wanted him to know. That he had no business knowing. The case was over, Brad was in jail where he belonged—what had been the point of humiliating her further? Had he wanted to punish her? Who gave him the right to do that?

'Yeah, you,' he snarled. 'You don't see me trying to punch anyone, do you?'

She wrestled her arm out of his grip, but as she turned to face him he backed her against the sand-washed brick of the restaurant wall.

'You deserved it.' She hurled the words at him, angry that her shiver of reaction had nothing to do with the chilly sea air and everything to do with his nearness. She raised her arms to shove him away but he captured her wrists, held her hands easily by her side to hold her still.

'Let go of me.'

'Not until you settle down,' he said in that firm, domineering voice that made her feel like a six-year-old.

'How could you do that?' she asked, her voice breaking on the accusation and making blood surge into her cheeks.

'Do what? Ask you about Demarest?' he replied, his face shadowed by the moonlight. 'Because you lied to me last night.'

'So what? I knew this was a pity date. I knew it,' she ranted, determined that he would never know how easily he'd primed her with his let's-get-naked hormones. She yanked her wrists free, wedged her hands against his chest.

'A pity date! What the hell...?'

'Oh, come on, Montoya. I knew you were patronising me. I figured you had an ulterior motive.' How could she have lost sight of that so easily? 'But I never thought you'd stoop that low.' The more she thought about it, the more outraged she became. He'd taken advantage of her inexperience and her vulnerability. Just like Brad. 'Did you learn that in cop school? How to flirt women into a coma, and then go in for the kill?'

'What the hell are you talking about?'

'I'm talking about how you played me.' As if he didn't know. 'All those smouldering looks. All the flirtatious words and clever little touches—as if you wanted me. When we both know all you really wanted was to question me about Brad.'

'Are you nuts?' The rising fury and frustration in his voice made her pause for a moment. 'You think I was faking that?'

'I know you were,' she shot back—not prepared to fall for the soft words and flirtatious tricks all over again. Even if the tone wasn't all that soft now.

He swore under his breath. Then murmured, 'To hell with this.'

Grasping her cheeks in callused palms, he slanted his lips across hers.

Shock came first, the gasp of surprise giving him the access he needed. His tongue delved into her mouth, firm and seeking and hungry. The shudder of arousal bolted down to her core. She squirmed, easing the ache against the hard wall of his chest. Rough palms trailed down, his thumb stroking the pounding pulse in her throat as he framed her face and angled her head, to take more.

The blast of need burned through her system as her tongue tangled with his. And the fast, furious exploration turned to slow, insistent strokes. He tasted delicious, the hot spice of heat and lust and man making her head spin. She reached for him, her fingers fisting in cool linen and feeling the flex of muscle beneath.

He lifted his head at last, his breathing as harsh as hers.

His hips trapped hers, and the ridge in his pants prodded her belly. 'You think that's fake?' His eyes glittered in the streetlight.

She shook her head, unable to speak as her tongue had gone numb.

'I've been sporting that most of the night,' he continued. 'Ever since you licked the salt off the rim of your first margarita.'

Iona blinked, desire unfurling in long ribbons of need.

'It appears I may have misconstrued your motives,' she choked out in a husky whisper.

His eyebrows shot up and then he laughed, the sound amused and arrogantly male. 'Yeah, just a little.' He dropped his forehead to hers, let out an unsteady breath, his thumb tracing the line of her collarbone in an absent caress. 'I shouldn't have made this about him. Because it's not,' he murmured. 'I screwed up and I'm sorry.'

'I accept your apology,' she replied breathlessly, the magnificent erection cradled against her belly.

He stepped back and her eyes darted down to the bulge of their own accord.

Oh, my!

Her tongue wasn't numb any more; it had swollen to twice its normal size—along with a few other parts of her anatomy. 'I stand corrected. That certainly doesn't look like pity,' she murmured.

He let out a strained laugh as he led her to the Mustang and opened the door. 'I better take you home.'

She climbed into the car. Home? He was taking her home? Now?

He climbed into the driver's seat, switched on the engine and crunched the gear shift into reverse.

'Excuse me for asking,' she protested, having found her voice at last as the car trundled down the access road, 'but why are you taking me home?'

He sent her another of those penetrating stares as the sheen of something dark and dangerous lit up those striking blue eyes.

'Because no way in hell are we ending this date in a parking lot.'

FIVE

_____

A pity date!

Zane kept his eyes locked on the road, the headlights slicing through the dusky dark.

'What made you think this was a pity date?' he asked over the rushing wind. Had Iona really been that clueless about how much he wanted her? How was that even possible?

'No particular reason,' she said, but he could hear the lift in her voice that signified she was lying.

'Sure there is.'

She glanced across the console and he slowed the car, so that he could divide his attention between her and the road.

A long-suffering sigh gushed out. She crossed her arms over her waist in a defensive gesture that would have been cute, if it weren't so distracting. 'You called me _cute_.'

'Only because you are.'

'No, I'm not. Babies are cute. Puppies are cute. I'm a grown woman and I'm not cute.'

He smiled. He couldn't help it—the snippy tone only made that do-or-die accent all the cuter.

'Puppies, huh?' he said, not quite able to resist the urge to tease. 'Have you ever owned a puppy?'

She slanted him a quelling look. 'It's not funny, Montoya.'

'I'm guessing that's a no, then,' he continued when she maintained a stony silence. 'Because if you had, you would know that puppies are not cute. I rescued a six-week-old lab cross from the pound a year ago. She ate a six-hundred-dollar pair of shoes, peed in my closet, drank from my john and tried to lick me to death. And that was all in the first day.' He pictured the love of his life, who'd nearly killed him this morning by sticking her wet snout in his ear while he was in the middle of his morning reps on the bench press. 'Not cute at all.'

'You didn't send her back, did you?'

The concerned tone tempted him to tease her some more. He resisted.

'Nah, we came to an understanding. Now she only chews her toys and she knows peeing in the closet is out unless it's on fire.' He looked her way, enchanted by the smile edging her lips. 'We're still working on the other two.'

'What's her name?'

'C.D.'

'You called your dog Compact Disc? What a dreadful name.'

'It's not short for Compact Disc. It's short for Cookie Dough.'

'You're joking.' She giggled, the sound light and so sexy he began to wonder how they'd ended up talking about his dog.

'Hey, it's my favourite flavour,' he said in his defence. 'And C.D.'s kind of the same colour, so it fit.'

'Now it all makes perfect sense,' she replied, the tentative smile turning into something warm and appealing.

Time to change the subject. And get this seduction back on track.

'The point is,' he began, because there had been a point in there somewhere, 'when I called you cute, I wasn't picturing you peeing in my closet or drinking from my john.'

She snorted out another laugh. 'That's a relief.'

He chuckled back, despite the heat now pounding in his abdomen like a nuclear reactor. He swung the Mustang onto her street, pulled into the driveway next to the tiny vacation rental and switched off the transmission. 'But I could probably live with the puppy analogy.' He slung his arm over the back of her seat, touched his knuckle to her cheek and watched her smile falter. 'If you had the sudden urge to lick me to death.'

Her pupils dilated and the freckles on her nose stood out against the flush of colour. He ran his knuckle across the soft skin, hooked a curl behind her ear.

Her tongue flicked out to moisten her bottom lip as those big almond eyes dipped to his mouth.

Cradling her cheek, he leaned across the stick shift and pressed his lips to hers. Determined to keep it slow this time, and easy.

She gasped, a soft sob that filled the air with the sweet scent of margaritas and desire. He swept his tongue across her lips, tempting her to open her mouth—knowing her taste was more intoxicating than that first sip of cherry cola on a sweltering summer day.

'Or I could just lick *you* to death,' he murmured, finally letting go of the pretence that he didn't want to devour her in a few greedy bites. 'Your call?'

Iona dragged herself back from the warm touch of his

fingers on her cheek, transfixed by the low murmur of his voice. She sucked in air past the constriction in her throat and got a lungful of his light spicy cologne tempered by the salty sea scent in his hair.

He wanted to lick her to death.

The hot ball of desire plunged, sending ripples of sensation radiating out.

'What do you say, Iona?' The husky tone made the desire ignite. 'It's your choice, no pressure. But I'd like to take this further.'

Yes, please.

The thought shot into her mind and spilled out of her mouth. 'Me too.'

His quick smile made her breath catch. Then he kissed her again. The press of lips hot and firm, the lingering touch of his tongue brief, subtle and not nearly enough. 'Let's take this inside.'

She nodded. But as she stepped out of the car and he clasped her hand and led her to the postage-stamp-size porch her mind began to race through all the things that could go wrong. She fumbled to find her keys as his palm rested on the slope of her back and rubbed.

Zane Montoya was hot and sexy and a bit too overwhelming What if she tensed up? What if, beneath that seductive charm, he was as rough and impatient as Brad?

She rushed ahead of him into the dark interior, heard the door close behind him, the thrum of purpose and possibilities tempered by the shot of panic.

His footsteps followed her into the galley kitchen. She dropped her keys and purse on the table, crossed to the sink and poured herself a glass of water. Her fingers trembled on the tumbler as he wrapped warm hands round her waist and enveloped her in that delicious scent again.

His lips traced the arch of her neck and she tilted her head, instinctively giving him access despite the tangle of nerves.

'You taste great, *querida*.' Hot breath nuzzled her neck as the forceful imprint of his erection pressed into her buttocks. 'As great as cookie-dough ice cream with extra chocolate chips.'

A desperate little laugh came out at the silly compliment, but then his large palms settled on her waist. She stiffened as the heat spread.

He moved his hands to her hips, turned her gently to face him. Lifting the forgotten tumbler out of her numb fingers, he placed it on the countertop.

'Iona, if you've changed your mind, you only have to say so.' The words were tight, a little strained, but there was no edge to them.

She raised her gaze and what she saw made her heart ricochet. The dramatic planes and angles looked even more breathtaking gilded by moonlight.

She shook her head. 'I haven't changed my mind. I'm nervous, I guess.'

He rested his hands on her hips, caressed the cotton. 'Why nervous? Is it too soon? After Demarest?'

She heard the controlled anger in his voice. And realised he thought she'd been a victim. That Demarest had traumatised her. When the truth was a lot more sordid.

'He didn't force me, Zane...' She felt the furious blush set fire to her scalp but soldiered on. 'We only did it a couple of times and then he got bored with me.' She stuck her chin out, made her gaze meet his. She had to stop feeling ashamed about this. 'Turns out, I'm not a natural at this.' She coughed, reached for her glass and took a quick sip to swallow down the frog that had lodged in her larynx.

'Not a natural at what? Sex?'

He sounded so incredulous, she got a little peeved. Was it really so hard for him to understand? Surely she wasn't the only woman he'd ever met who wasn't that into sex? But then she thought of the giddy rush that she'd been struggling to suppress most of the night—and realised she probably was.

'Yes…I get tense and flustered and I can't relax and then the moment's gone.'

His forehead creased. And the arousal fizzled and died.

Terrific, Iona, that was way too much information. Why not kill the mood completely?

'And Demarest made you think that was your fault?' he asked in a stiff voice.

She hitched her shoulder in a non-committal shrug, determined not to be defensive. Not every woman could be multi-orgasmic. 'Possibly,' she said, the hairs on the back of her neck stinging with humiliation.

'And you believed him, why exactly?'

'Because I don't exactly have a lot of other testimonials,' she blurted out, getting more peeved by the second.

'What are you saying—that he was your first?' He sounded incredulous again.

'Maybe.' She looked down at the floor, her humiliation complete. 'That's not to say I haven't had boyfriends. I've had lots of boyfriends.' *Two.* 'But it never… It never quite… There isn't a big array of possible… Kelross Glen is a small place and…' She trailed off.

Great, now he knew just how pathetic she was.

Warm hands still on her hips, he tugged her close, nudged her hair with his lips. 'That really sucks.'

'Don't I know it.'

He tucked a finger under her chin, lifted her face. 'So

I'm assuming you've never had an orgasm while making love?' The question was asked in a gentle coaxing voice that belied the intensity in his gaze.

She bit into her lip. Good Lord, how had they ended up talking about this? 'I'm really not comfortable discuss—'

'I figured as much.'

'I never said—'

'Shh...' He touched his thumb to her lips. 'No more talking, Iona. You talk too much anyway.'

Indignation flared. 'Now wait a—'

His lips covered hers, silencing the protest, and the need raged back to life, the dance of lips and tongue so erotic she could scream as he held her head and explored in slow, deliberate strokes.

He eased back and clasped his hands round her waist. He hauled her up as if she weighed nothing and deposited her on the countertop. Her bottom landed on the cold formica.

She clung on to his shoulders for balance, felt the bunch of muscle and opened her mouth to say something. Anything. But nothing came out as hot palms edged up her thighs under the dress, shocking her into silence.

'You know what we're going to do now, Iona,' he said slowly, his fingers drawing tantalising circles on her naked thighs.

She shook her head, having lost the power of speech for the second time in one night, which had to be a record.

'We're going to forget about him, undo all the bad stuff he did—and make this your first time.'

Something tight banded around her heart. 'I'm not sure that's entirely necessary—'

'It isn't hard to bring a woman to orgasm,' he interrupted. 'Not if you pay attention and take the time and trouble to do it right. If he didn't do that, it was his fault not yours.'

The blush crept up her throat. She'd known that, of course she had. She'd known as soon as she'd lost her virginity to him and he'd laughed at her inexperience that Brad was a selfish lover as well as a nasty man, but she'd been so desperate to believe his lies she'd allowed herself to bury her growing dislike of him. And that had been her fault, not his. Even if he had been a liar and a thief.

Wiggling out of Zane's hands, she jumped down from the countertop. Maybe if the cracked linoleum could swallow her whole, she could get out of this situation without making it any worse. She grasped her glass from the countertop, took a fortifying gulp and kept her back to Zane.

'Do you mind if we take a rain check?' *At least until the turn of the next millennium.* 'I'm not really in the mood any more.'

Instead of his taking the hint all she heard was a low chuckle. And then his thumb cruised under her hairline. 'You really want to give him all the power? Even now?'

She swung round, dislodging his thumb—which unfortunately did nothing to dispel the sizzle of sensation. 'This has nothing to do with him.'

'Uh-huh.' A sceptical eyebrow rose up his forehead. 'Then why don't you prove it?'

'And how exactly do you propose I do that?'

He braced his hands on the countertop, caging her in, and making her breathing accelerate. 'It's real simple, Iona. Stop blaming yourself—and get back on the horse.'

'You're not serious?' She propped her forearms against his chest, wanting to be outraged at the offer—but the surge of sensation as his hands came around her waist and he nudged her closer made it kind of hard to muster the required indignation.

'Try me.' The smile in his bright sapphire eyes twinkled with mischief.

'What? So you're offering your services, now.' She paused for effect. 'As my personal stallion?'

Instead of his looking affronted or even abashed, the smile only got naughtier—the slow twist of his lips as disarming as it was amused. 'Stallion might be overselling myself a bit. But, hey, I can go with that analogy if you want. I'm not as picky as you.'

A laugh choked out without warning as her eyes dipped to his pants and she spotted something that made her think stallion would not be overselling him one bit. 'You're incorrigible.'

'Well, hell, Iona.' He edged closer, his hands firm on her hips, the impressive erection nudging her belly as he smiled. 'That's the nicest thing you've ever said to me.'

The full-bodied laugh bubbled out, breaking the tension. She didn't know how he'd done it, but she didn't feel self-conscious any more, or guilty. She felt relaxed and sexy, desire pumping through her like a heady drug.

'Here's the way it plays for me,' he said, angling his head to nibble kisses under her chin. 'We take it slow. And we focus on pleasure. Your pleasure.' He lapped her collarbone with his tongue. 'No conditions. And no talking allowed.'

'Why no talking?' she asked, trying not to let her mind snag on the rough cadence of the word *pleasure*. And the riotous sensations shivering up her neck.

'Because you talk too much.'

'You are so cheeky.'

'Guilty as charged.' He chuckled, his fingers edging

under the strap of her dress to send sensation skittering across her shoulder blade. 'So no talking, except to tell me what you like and what you don't like.'

'Considering there are supposed to be no conditions,' she teased, 'there seems to be an awful lot of them.'

He hoisted her into his arms. 'Put your legs round my waist,' he demanded, strong hands gripping her bottom.

'See, there's another one!' she said, clasping her arms round his shoulders as her legs hooked his waist.

'Stop being so damn literal,' he said on a rueful laugh as he carried her into the shoebox-sized bedroom.

'And yet another condition, already,' she said, amusement loosening the flood of heat.

'Enough, woman,' he announced, surprising a laugh out of her as he dumped her on the bed. 'I forgot this bedroom's smaller than my closet,' he added, glancing round the room. 'Next time we do this at my place.'

The offhand mention of a next time had warmth wrapping around her chest, followed by the pinch of regret. There wouldn't be a next time. This was strictly a one-night fling. She wasn't going to make the mistake of thinking this meant more than it did. She wasn't that needy, insecure girl any more.

He stripped off his shirt, kicked off his shoes and climbed onto the bed beside her. Her vision blurred, dazed by the glorious display of muscles and sinews and bronzed skin in the moonlight. He looked magnificent, the masculine perfection of his chest almost as arresting as that incredible face. She placed her open hand on his sternum, explored the dark nipples nestled in the sprinkle of hair, and then let it drift down to the ridges of his six-pack.

He quivered beneath her palm and his hand covered hers, halting the descent. Her gaze rose, and she marvelled at the cleft in his chin defined by the hint of stubble, the dramatic slash of his cheekbones—the dark intensity of those sapphire eyes.

Thank you, God.

She whispered the silent prayer in her head as her heartbeat sped up to dizzying speeds. If one night was all she could risk with this man, she intended to make the most of it.

'I'm feeling kind of underdressed here,' he murmured.

She laughed at the wry note as his hand skimmed over her shoulder. He propped himself up to lean over her and she heard the sibilant crackle of the zip releasing. The bodice of the dress drooped and he nudged down the straps, revealing the pink lace of her bra.

'Cute,' he murmured, amused, and she huffed out another chuckle. She certainly didn't feel like a puppy dog any more.

'I thought I told you not to call me that.'

He tumbled her back onto the bed, straddling her before his hands swept down her body peeling the dress down to her waist. 'And I thought I told you not to talk.'

She wriggled but he held her still, hoisting her arms above her head, then pinned her wrists to the bed in one hand as he bent to press his lips to her collarbone. The trail of kisses dipped to her breasts, and he teased the edge of her bra cup with the rough stroke of his tongue. Her cleavage heaved against the confining lace, her body bucking against his hold.

'You like that, huh,' he said, gruff and amused.

It didn't sound like a question, but she answered anyway. 'I'm not allowed to talk.'

The wicked grin had the fire igniting. 'Now she remembers.'

He released her arms, but as soon as she dropped them sure, steady fingers slipped the bra straps off her shoulders, and her breasts spilled out. She moaned as he cupped the heavy flesh, flicked his thumb across the beaded nipple. He grappled quickly with the hook, stripped away the pink lace and moulded both breasts in his palms, then bent forward to take one straining nipple into his mouth.

She groaned, the sound deep and primal, as his lips suckled and the melting sensation became a hot, hard yank of need.

She arched into his mouth, her fingers clutching the bedspread, the riot of sensation new and overwhelming. How could so little make her feel so much?

He lifted his head, blew on the wet nipple, watching intently as it puckered even more. 'Good?'

'Hmm,' she rasped, her throat dry.

His gaze stayed transfixed on her naked breasts. 'They're gorgeous,' he said, and warmth flooded through her. 'Especially when they're begging for attention like that.'

Then the exquisite torture continued.

He licked at the areola, nipped and teased the tender tip, sending a new shockwave of need hurtling down to her core. Desire built as he feasted on first one breast then the other, the blinding pleasure warring with a foolish wave of gratitude. She felt powerful, important, irresistible, the need flooding between her thighs and making her sex ache. She curled her fingers into the short hair at the sides of his head, pulled his face up. The harsh look of arousal only made her more grateful. 'That feels so good,' she said. 'Thank you.'

Lifting up, he took her chin in his fingers. The kiss was hard, fast and demanding. 'You're welcome, Iona. Now stop distracting me.'

She laughed, delighted with the strain in his voice. Then gasped as he turned his attention back to her breasts while knowing fingers slid up under her dress, the heel of his hand pressing against the mound of her sex.

She launched off the bed, the sudden contact shocking as he cupped her through the silk of her panties.

'Easy, *preciosa*,' he murmured, his thumb brushing against the tight bundle of nerves at her centre in deliberate circles.

She writhed, seeking the exquisite touch and yet scared of the force of her need.

She gripped his forearm. 'Please...that's...too—' The words choked off on a sob as his fingers dipped beneath the gusset and found the hot wet heart of her.

Pleasure gripped like a silken fist, and her body bowed as his fingers played.

'There?' he asked as his sure, steady touch triggered a sharp, painfully exquisite sensation.

She nodded, cried out as he rubbed, circled, stroked her clitoris. Pleasure rippled and zapped across her skin in a billion sparkles of light—and then pulled hard. She sobbed, teetering on the high ledge for one tantalising second and then cried out—the cascade hurtling her over.

'Oh. My. Goodness.' Iona panted as she drifted back to full consciousness. Gradually she became aware of the cramp in her fingers as they dug into the sinews of his forearm, and the large, rough hand trapped down her knickers.

She released his arm instantly, worried she might have left bruises, and clamped her knees together as quickly and discreetly as possible.

He eased his hand out of her knickers, and grinned down at her as she shivered, still a little shocky from the strength of her climax.

Good Lord, the man has magic fingers.

'What did I tell you? Not hard if you pay attention.'

The smug, almost boyish look of satisfaction on that too-handsome face had her coughing out a laugh.

'That was...' *Awesome.* The word echoed in her head, but she stopped herself from saying it—and fought the sting of tears. This was only sex, she shouldn't make too much of it. 'Thank you,' she managed at last, not sure what else to say.

His grin widened and he placed a possessive kiss on her nose. '*Querida,* the pleasure was all mine.' He let his hand settle on her stomach, and she felt the outline of his erection against her hip. 'You look real cute when you come.'

She gave him a playful slap on the arm. 'Stop it.'

'And so damn sexy, I almost came myself.' He kissed her, the smile on his mouth as potent as the soft, sure touch of his lips.

She shifted as he raised his head, and, feeling bold, caressed the hard shaft through his trousers.

He tensed, let out a strained laugh. But when she reached for the zip to release him, he covered her hand, and stopped her. 'Don't...' He touched his forehead to hers. 'We can't take this any further.'

'Oh, okay.' She tugged her hand out from under his, the sudden sense of failure so intense it hurt. 'I'm sorry.'

'Why are you sorry?' He slipped a knuckle under her chin. 'I'm hoping like hell we can still take a rain check.'

She shook off his hold, gathered her dress to cover her breasts and sat up. 'All right,' she said dully, knowing a charity case when she saw one.

'Damn it...' He gripped her shoulders, dragged her round to face him, the spark of anger confusing her. 'I don't have any protection with me,' he said, his voice hoarse with exasperation.

'That's the reason you wanted to stop?' she asked, the fury in his eyes more exalting than the feel of his rigid flesh moments before.

'Damn straight it is. If I had a condom with me, I'd be inside you right this second.' He cursed viciously. 'I want you so badly I'm in agony here, and trying real hard to be smart about this, so don't you dare look at me as if—'

'There are condoms here,' she cut in, deciding to intervene before he got any madder. While the sound of his frustration was boosting her fragile ego into the stratosphere—she didn't want him to explode before they got to the main event. 'In the bathroom. I saw them yesterday.' She bounced off the bed, buoyant with pleasure that the moment of rejection was nothing more than a stupid misunderstanding. 'I'll go get them, shall I? Put you out of your agony,' she finished unable to resist the urge to tease him.

'No, wait.' He grasped her arm, drew her back. He wrapped his arms around her waist, buried his face in her hair. The deep breath he blew out brushed against her nape and sent awareness skittering down to her toes.

'I shouldn't have lost my temper,' he said, sounding serious. 'I apologise.'

'If you think that's losing your temper, you ought to meet a Scotsman.'

'Yeah?' He gave a rough chuckle, as she'd hoped he would. 'It's just you've got me so...' He sighed, the hesitation so endearing, and so unlike him, her heart pounded heavily. He let go of her waist, rubbed his open palms down her upper arms. 'I'll get the condoms.'

'But you don't know where they are,' she said, chewing on her lip to stop the smile as he climbed off the bed. Affection bloomed alongside her lust. She didn't know why it felt so good to see that super-confident mask of his slip. But it did.

He glanced over his shoulder on his way to the door. 'I shouldn't have too much trouble.' He winked. 'I'm a trained detective. Detecting stuff is my profession,' he said as he left the room.

She collapsed onto the bed, her hands still clasping her dress, and took in a shuddering breath.

His head popped around the doorframe, making her jolt upright. 'But while I'm gone, lose the dress and panties.'

She gasped at the audacious command as excitement and anticipation soared. 'Well, really!'

'Well, really,' he purred in a surprisingly good imitation of her Scottish accent. The roguish smile came back full force. 'I want you ready for round two when I get back, lady.'

She scrambled out of her clothes as his bare feet padded down the corridor, and shouted after him, 'Conditions! Conditions!'

SIX

Not cool, man. *Not cool at all.*

Zane glared at the cracked bathroom mirror, taking in the dull colour on his cheeks, and the crater-like furrows on his brow.

He'd almost lost it, again.

He released his death grip on the sink and glanced at the pounding erection confined in his pants, which had been so hard for so long it was starting to hurt. And had his answer.

He adjusted his pants to ease the ache. Something about Iona had really got to him.

Her honesty, her openness and the ease with which he could read every single expression on her face, made her more vulnerable than any other woman he'd ever seduced. And when you added what she'd revealed about her run-in with Demarest, he felt responsible for her in a way he never had before in a relationship. The guy had taken her virginity and given her nothing in return. Less than nothing.

But instead of her inexperience putting him off, which by rights it should have, it only made her live-wire response to the simplest of caresses seem that much more irresistible—bringing out the hunger he'd thought he'd satisfied years ago.

Tonight, he'd been less in control of himself than he'd been since he was a teenager, banging pretty much anyone who offered, and as a result he'd almost blown the stringent rules he'd imposed on his sexual appetite ever since.

When she'd come apart in his arms, the soft sobs of her surrender spurring his own arousal to fever pitch, and then held him through his pants, her face flushed with arousal, for one brief agonizing moment he'd almost snapped, consumed by the need to thrust deep inside her.

Thank God that burning need had only lasted a split second, and he'd come to his senses in time. But it had still been deeply disturbing. His control had almost shattered—giving him a connection he didn't want to contemplate to the man who had fathered him.

How could he be entirely free of that legacy, and even for a second have considered taking a woman without due care and attention? Without even the proper protection? Simply to satisfy his own lust?

He took two deep breaths, let them out as steadily as he could.

Don't overreact.

He rolled his shoulders, pulled on the mirror to check the bathroom cabinet and spotted the box of condoms, still wrapped in cellophane, on the top shelf.

His breathing slowed as the insistent ache subsided a little.

The thing to remember was, he hadn't snapped—he'd held it together. And he'd apologised to Iona. From her sweet, funny reaction it was clear she hadn't had a clue how close he'd come to losing it. Which was great, because now he had the chance to make it up to her—to finish what they'd started and do it right. The way he'd promised her he would.

He lifted the box off the shelf, ripped the seal.

Only three! Who the hell buys condoms in boxes of three? That's not even enough for...

He clamped down on the thought, let out another calming breath.

Hold it together.

Three was good. Three was enough. Three was more than enough for them to take the edge off their hunger and have a good time, before they went their separate ways.

He closed the cabinet, dumped the box in the trash and stuffed the condoms in his back pocket before splashing some water on his face, determined to be grateful for the three condoms if it killed him.

But as he walked into Iona's bedroom, and she smiled at him, the sheet stretched across her breasts, her dress and panties by her bra on the floor and her face flushed with anticipation, the hunger coiled hard, taunting him.

'Did you find them?' she asked, the eagerness in her voice making the erection pound.

He slung the condoms on the bed. 'I told you, I'm a trained detective.'

He eased the zip down on his pants and her gaze followed the movement. He shoved his pants and boxers off, and her upper lip curled into her full bottom lip, her gaze now riveted to his groin.

'That's impressive,' she whispered, the Scottish burr low with fascination.

He tore open the first foil package as his erection hit

critical mass—and admitted there was no freaking way three condoms was ever going to be enough.

Goodness.

Iona studied the long thick erection jutting out proudly from the dark hair at Zane's groin as he rolled on the condom with practised efficiency. Heat swelled in her abdomen, her heartbeat ricocheted into her throat and her breathing sped up.

She let her gaze drift back up his body, past the ropes of muscle that defined the V above his hip bones and up the thin trail of hair that bisected the flat ridges of his six-pack and then bloomed around his pecs.

She reached his face at last, her heart pounding so hard now it was practically choking her. 'You're gorgeous all over.'

He laughed but it sounded strained as he lifted the sheet and tugged it off. She lay still, the heavy beat of her heart plunging into her sex. Her skin tingled and tightened as his gaze roamed in return.

Just when she thought she couldn't stand the intense scrutiny a moment longer, his eyes finally lifted to her face. 'Not as gorgeous as you.'

Climbing onto the bed, he settled beside her, his flesh hot where it touched her thigh as he swept his hand over her in a tender caress, following the curve of her body to her breasts. He stroked the underside, then rolled the engorged tip between his thumb and forefinger. He bent to flick his tongue across the swollen peak and she jolted in his arms.

'Sweet,' he muttered, then suckled hard.

The choked sob of pleasure was almost animalistic as the prickle of need arrowed down. He took one breast then the other into his mouth, gorging himself on her and making the heat and pleasure race across her skin and tug hard in her sex.

'You're so responsive, you're killing me,' he rasped in her ear as he grasped her leg, lifted it over his hip and brought her sex into sudden contact with the large head of his erection. 'I'm not sure I can wait much longer.'

She gripped his shoulders, clinging on to sanity, and arched into him. 'Don't wait.'

He muttered something in Spanish, then grasped both her thighs and rolled, holding her open, until he was poised above her. Then he sank into her in one long, slow, all-consuming thrust.

She tensed at the shock of penetration, her body shuddering as she struggled to adjust to the invasion.

'Shh,' he soothed, his voice tense with the effort to hold still. 'Just breathe—it'll take a moment. You're so tight.'

Then his thumb traced across her hip and found the place where their bodies joined. She bucked beneath him, cried out as he touched the sensitive nub. Then he started to rock inside her, pulling out, thrusting back, gradually at first, and so gently. Then faster. And harder.

The full-stretched feeling gathered and intensified, the incendiary stroke of his thumb radiating outwards and shooting like lightning through her body. She moved with him, instinctively angling her hips to take him deeper, racing towards that glorious oblivion that beckoned just out of reach.

The brutal orgasm hit in a bright, beautiful, neverending wave, crashing over her and then rising up to crest again. She heard her thin cry of desperate pleasure matching his harsh grunt of release as the wave crashed through that final barrier, hurtling them over together.

Iona couldn't seem to keep her eyelids from drooping to half-mast as he tucked her under his arm and gathered her close. She settled her head on his shoulder, breathing in the spicy scent of his skin and the clean musk of fresh sweat—the slight soreness between her thighs nothing compared to the slumberous afterglow of spectacular sex and the sweet, serene feeling of achievement.

He brushed a strand of hair off her forehead and smiled. 'Good?'

She smiled back. 'Very.' And ignored the rush of tenderness as her heartbeat evened out and her eyelids grew heavy.

'Get some sleep, *querida*.' His lips brushed against the top of her hair. 'We're not finished yet.'

'We're not?' she asked, around a huge yawn, trying to keep a lid on the rush of excitement, and the swell of longing.

'Of course not. We've got two condoms left.'

She huffed out a laugh, and snuggled against him as she drifted into sleep—refusing to regret the fact that once they'd used those two condoms and the night was over, he would be gone.

SEVEN

Iona blinked at the business card perched on her nightstand. Sitting up in the empty bed, she picked up the card and flicked it over, to find a note scribbled in black ink.

Hey Sleepyhead,
I had to go let C.D. out before she starts figuring my closet is on fire!
Call me.
Zane
PS. You look real cute when you're sleeping—even when you snore.

'I do not snore,' she whispered, sputtering out a half laugh. She rubbed her thumb across the embossed writing on the front of the card and felt the lump lodged in her throat sink to the pit of her stomach and land like a lead weight. She stared at Zane's name and his contact details framed next to the geometric drawing of an office building—which was probably his firm's headquarters in Carmel—and then concentrated on the 'call me' scribbled in his looping scrawl on the back.

She set the card on the nightstand. Their fling had been amazing, but now it was over and mooning over him, or thinking they could take this any further, would be silly.

She needed to find gainful employment and a cheap place to stay—not get mixed up with a sex god like Zane Montoya. The man was way too distracting.

Getting out of bed, she stretched, feeling all the little aches and pains and tender spots Zane had left behind to remember him by.

He'd woken her twice during the night, both times bringing her expertly to orgasm before finding his own release. He'd located and exploited every erogenous zone she had, with the focused, thorough precision of a man who knew his way around every inch of a woman's body.

But each time she'd reached for him, eager to explore his magnificent body and exploit his limits in return, he'd distracted her, by swirling his tongue or stroking his finger across some super-sensitive part of her anatomy, or simply insisting that he'd never last if he let her have her way with him. And while that might very well have been true—she certainly hoped so—the last time she'd collapsed into his arms, dawn peeking through the pretty gingham curtains, she'd fallen into an exhausted sleep feeling sated and sexy—and the tiniest bit disappointed.

She examined her face in the bathroom mirror, the reddened patch of whisker burn under her chin and the sleepy afterglow still making her eyes shine.

Get away with you, woman.

How typically Celtic of her, somehow managing to find fault with the most stupendous sex she'd ever had.

She should be thanking the man, and rejoicing in the generosity of his lovemaking, not criticising him for his perfection. If it hadn't been for Zane she would have continued to believe that her experience with Brad was as good as it got.

Reaching into the shower cubicle, she turned on the tap full blast, set the temperature a notch below scalding and stepped under the stream.

And anyway, she was never going to see Zane again, so none of this mattered... She'd made a promise to him, and herself, to be out of the cottage today and the quicker she packed her stuff and got going, the better.

But as she shampooed her hair and soaped the scent of Zane Montoya, Latino-Lover Extraordinaire, off her skin she knew in a tiny part of her heart what he had done to her, and for her, all through the night, would always matter—even if she hadn't been able to do the same thing for him.

By mid-afternoon she'd showered, made herself a hearty meal—most of which she hadn't eaten—laundered the bed linen, scrubbed out the kitchen and phoned her father to tell him she was great and everything was going brilliantly. At least that wasn't as much of a lie now as it had been in the last few weeks.

And now she was ready to move on. Almost.

She flipped Zane's card over in her fingers. And stared at the phone. Should she call him? To say goodbye, and thanks? It seemed like the polite thing to do.

The heavy weight that she'd been busy ignoring all day rose up her throat. She placed the card by the phone, pulled the sketch she'd made of the hummingbird the morning before out of her rucksack and scribbled a note on the back in pencil. She then counted out twenty dollars from her purse and placed it with the sketch beside his card, her fingers trembling.

She stared at the meagre offerings, and knew she was taking the coward's way out, but she simply couldn't afford the luxury of a goodbye. It was always better to be self-sufficient. The blockage in her throat already felt suspiciously like an emotional involvement that had snuck up on her when she wasn't looking—and she mustn't pander to it.

Zane wasn't responsible for her, she was responsible for herself—and while last night had been wonderful, it wasn't only the sex that had been spectacular. The feeling of safety and security as she'd fallen asleep in his arms had been even more seductive, but she couldn't afford to count on it, or him.

Hefting the rucksack onto her shoulders, she turned to leave, when the loud rap on the door startled her.

Zane. Bugger.

She debated pretending she'd already left, but decided that was too cowardly, even for her. She dropped the rucksack, and opened the door.

Her heart thundered as she stared at the man leaning casually against the doorframe, wearing dark trousers, a pristine white shirt and a seductive smile she knew only too well. The lead weight in her throat expanded alarmingly.

'You didn't call,' he said.

'I know. I didn't have time.'

'Yeah?' He pushed away from the frame, his eyes fixed on her face for several potent seconds, before his attention strayed to the rucksack—and the sketch and money she'd left by the phone. He brushed past her, the spicy scent she remembered doing strange things to her insides.

'What's this?' he asked, picking up the sketch and then flipping it over.

She closed the door—and realised her clean getaway was history.

After reading the note, he glanced at her rucksack and the small pile of crumpled bills again. Then the narrowed gaze returned to her.

'Thanks for the picture—it's really cool,' he said, the tone measured, but she could see the muscle twitching in his jaw. 'But you're gonna have to explain the rest.' He held up her note. 'Were you about to run out on me?'

Shame mixed with the hormones raging in her belly, making her voice come out on a husky whisper. 'I told you I was leaving today. I didn't think you really wanted me to call you.'

His brow shot up, the muscle clenching tight. 'After what we did last night? What kind of jerk do you think I am?'

She flinched at the show of temper, but worse was the shadow in his eyes. Had she hurt his feelings somehow? She hadn't intended to, hadn't even thought she could. But the truth was, she hadn't even considered his feelings.

'I'm sorry, I didn't think...' She stared at her toes.

'Damn it, Iona.' The words came out on a soft sigh, the anger gone. 'Just because one guy's a deadbeat,' he said, 'it doesn't mean we all are.'

She nodded, feeling about two inches tall.

He cradled her cheek in one rough palm and her thoughts scattered.

'Where were you planning to run to?' he murmured

as his hand tugged through her hair and brushed the curls behind her ear.

She shrugged, trying to gather the will to pull away from his touch—and that piercing blue gaze. 'I figured Monterey? I need to find a cheap place to live and a job.'

'Accommodation in Monterey's not cheap. And why would you go looking for a new place to stay, when I told you that you can stay here for free?'

'But that was before…' The blush crept up her neck as his hand trailed down and settled on her collarbone.

'Before what?'

She pushed out a breath. The yearning to stay and take him up on his offer was so intense it was almost painful. But with the intense yearning came the kick of panic. She shouldn't want this, and certainly not this much. They weren't a couple, they weren't even an item, they were a one-night fling and wanting it to be more than that was dangerous—because it implied an intimacy that went way beyond sex. 'Before last night.'

His hand dropped to his side. 'You figure because we slept together, you can't stay here? Why not? One thing hasn't got a damn thing to do with the other.'

'It wouldn't feel right.' She felt her own temper kicking in. Why was he making this so hard? 'It would feel like I was taking advantage of you.'

'You…? You're kidding, right?' The incredulity was bad enough but the rough chuckle that followed had her glaring at him.

'What's so funny?'

'You are, Iona. How would staying here be taking advantage of me? This place isn't even mine—it belongs to a friend of mine.'

'Then I'd be taking advantage of your friend, wouldn't

I?' It all seemed perfectly obvious to her. Why was he being so obtuse?

'Settle down.' He grasped her wrist, drew her back towards him. 'The guy owns half of central California, so you staying here rent-free for a few weeks isn't going to bankrupt him.' He rested his hands on her hips, the confident, sexy smile firmly back in place—and having a predictable effect on her hormones. 'And you didn't sleep with him, you slept with me, so it's kind of beside the point.'

She pulled out of his arms. 'I fail to see why you—'

'Iona, I want you to stay here,' he interrupted, the determination in his voice neatly cutting off her tirade.

'Why?' she asked, wrapping her arms round her waist as her belly churned with a confusing mix of need and panic. They were strangers, despite what they'd shared last night—couldn't he see that?

'Because it's important to me.'

'Why?'

Her arms tightened, the churning getting worse. How could she be terrified that he was going to say she mattered to him—and equally terrified that she might not?

Zane saw the puzzled arousal and confusion in her caramel eyes and felt the answering pulse of heat, but steeled himself against the urge to scoop her up, carry her down the shack's corridor to her bedroom and show her just how important it was to have her nearby.

He wasn't here for sex. Or not only for sex.

She was probably dealing now with the same misgivings he'd wrestled with all day. When he'd wanted to call, but convinced himself it would be better to let her make the next move. But after a long torturous morning of

waiting for the phone to ring, he'd had enough of waiting. Although he still couldn't quite believe she'd been
about to skip out on him.

Seeing her backpack by her feet, and the guilty flush
on her cheeks had been more than enough to have his
temper straining, but it had taken a Herculean effort of
will not to start yelling when he'd read the note she'd
written on the back of her drawing:

Zane,
Please accept this sketch as a small thank you for
all your help. The money is to pay for the groceries
and the phone call I made to my dad in Scotland. I
hope it's enough?
All the best, Iona

Not one mention of last night. He'd had her sobbing
out her release in his arms less than eight hours ago and
now he didn't get a decent goodbye?

Cool it, don't get too worked up.

He didn't want to spook her. Or give her the idea this
was more than it was. So he needed to be careful.

He lifted both palms up, and kept the nonchalant
smile in place. 'Because I need to know you're safe. I used
to be a cop, remember.'

'That's the only reason?' Her cheeks turned a charming shade of magenta and he felt the answering spike of
lust. Damn, he'd forgotten how much that easy blush
turned him on.

'Yeah, what else?' he said, more than happy to oblige
if she suggested she wanted a little more than that.

It occurred to him in that moment that this would be
the perfect opportunity to give Iona The Speech.

The one about how he wasn't a good bet for the long haul, how he wasn't looking for anything too heavy, but how he really liked her in the here and now. He'd given The Speech to every woman he'd ever dated since leaving high school, usually long before they slept together, so it was already overdue.

But as he waited for her reply The Speech sat on the tip of his tongue like a bad taste—and he realised he didn't want to give it to her.

Not that he wanted anything heavy with her. He didn't. Exposing yourself to that kind of commitment simply wasn't in his make-up. He enjoyed the chase way too much, the challenges and the flirting and the non-stop sex that came at the beginning of a relationship—and the cooling-off period afterwards, when he had discovered all of a woman's secrets and she started nagging him to return the favour, a whole lot less.

He'd had some sticky moments in his twenties, when he'd been less aware of who he was and what he wanted, and he'd made the mistake of lingering too long. But since then he'd become an expert in reading the signs, getting his timing right and letting the women he dated down gently before they got the wrong idea.

But then Iona had thrown his usual dating routine totally out of whack right from the start and not one single thing had gone according to plan since. When was the last time he'd slept with a woman on a first date, or effectively been a woman's first lover? Because he wasn't counting what had happened with that deadbeat Demarest.

And then there was yesterday night. When was the last time he'd had to stop a woman touching him, simply so that he could keep a lid on his own desire? Not since he was a teenager.

But last night, he'd had to practically tie her down to stop her from tipping him over the edge.

She'd confused things again today, by not calling—leaving the need for her burning hot and hard, and forcing his hand. And now, for the first time ever, The Speech felt kind of redundant.

With all the whys and why nots and what the hells fogging up his mind as he waited, he didn't hear her muffled reply.

'What was that?'

She lifted her head and stared straight at him. 'I think you're right, Zane.'

'About what?'

'That it's better if we don't sleep together again.'

'Huh?' *When did I say that?*

He stared at her, dumbfounded, The Speech forgotten.

'I had fun last night,' she continued in the same steady serious voice. 'You were...' her blush brightened '...completely amazing.'

'Thanks,' he said flatly, more irritated than flattered. He'd been praised before for his skills in the sack, and it had always given him a nice little ego-boost, but it didn't feel like much of an achievement now. Did she think she owed him something, because the man who'd taken her virginity had been such a selfish jerk?

'But I don't want to complicate things,' she continued as he tried to concentrate on what she was saying and not the low level irritation grinding in his gut. 'Especially if I'm going to stay here.'

Okay, that did it.

'Sex doesn't have to be complicated,' he said. 'Not if we keep things casual.'

'But it doesn't feel casual, if you feel responsible for me.'

'Iona, it feels casual to me.' Or it would, once he'd made certain she was safe.

'Are you sure?'

'Sure I'm sure. Look, why don't you unpack, get settled, check out the job situation in Monterey and then give me a call in a couple of days when you're ready?'

The suggestion tasted like ash on his tongue. He didn't want to leave—or stay away until she was ready to call him. But he needed to get this fling back on track. And this was exactly how he would have played things in the past.

'I'd like to see you again,' he continued. 'And I've got the weekend free.' His first in months, he thought, looking forward to the chance to see her again already. 'But it's your call, okay?'

Iona was right; last night had been spectacular—but neither one of them wanted this to be anything other than casual. Which meant he needed to back off, and get over the urge to take her to bed right this second. This had to be her choice. Not his.

'Okay, that would be lovely,' she said, the smile in her eyes turning the caramel to a rich chocolate. 'And you're sure it's okay with your friend for me to stay?'

He sent her a long-suffering look.

'All right, great. And thanks.' She gave a little sigh of relief, the movement making her breasts move under her T-shirt.

The desire to cup the ripe flesh in his palms and tease the nipples into tight buds with his teeth was so acute he could taste her. He forced his gaze back to her face and watched the lids on her sultry golden eyes go heavy with the same longing.

'Good luck with your job hunt,' he murmured. 'But don't forget to call me this time.'

Three days, Montoya. You can last till Saturday. Then she can call you, and there won't be any more confusion about just how casual this is.

He picked up her sketch, but left the crumpled bills beside the phone as he crossed to the door.

'But what about what I owe you?' she asked as he opened the door.

'We can settle up once you've got a job.' Or more like when hell froze over, but that was an argument for another day.

'Okay, if you're sure.'

'I am.' Cradling her cheek, he gave her a light teasing kiss, but forced himself to pull back when her lips parted, inviting him in.

Not yet, but soon.

He brushed his thumb across her chin, enjoying the look of stunned passion. 'I'll see you Saturday.'

Her lips curved, the smile quick and spontaneous.

'I'll be looking forward to it,' she said, the burr of her accent smoky with need.

Not as much as I will be, querida.

EIGHT

_____

'Zane, you're here.'

Zane's gut tightened as he lifted Iona's fingers to his lips and buzzed a kiss across her knuckles. 'I thought we had a date.'

Colour flared in her cheeks and he grinned.

'Oh, yes, now I remember,' she said, the coy words somewhat contradicted by the dancing light in her eyes.

What the heck had possessed him to suggest they go for a drive? After three torturous days of waiting to have her again?

'I'll get my coat,' she said.

He watched her collect the denim jacket. She'd added gloss to her mouth, and there was something dark and sultry smudged around her eyes. Beaded sandals, a vivid pink scarf tied round her shoulder-length hair and a thin gold ankle chain completed the outfit. She looked chic and sexy and cute enough to eat.

But it wasn't until they'd climbed into the car, and he got a lungful of her scent, that the hunger really started to eat at him.

'So where do you want to go?' He laid his arm across

the back of her seat, and played with the curl that had escaped from her scarf.

'You decide? I'm easy.'

He laughed. 'I certainly hope so. I've been in agony for the last three days.'

She giggled; the light flirtatious sound had the heat twisting and turning. 'Haven't you ever heard of deferred gratification?'

'I've heard of it,' he said as he backed out of the drive. 'I've discovered I'm not real wild about it.'

Her smoky laugh drifted on the wind but when he stopped the car to lean across the console, ready to suggest they give in to instant gratification—and leave the drive till later—his cell phone buzzed.

Iona touched her finger to his lips. 'Uh-oh, saved by the bell.'

'Not really.' He nipped her finger. 'I'm gonna give the caller some deferred gratification. See how they like it.'

But when he touched his lips to hers, she wriggled out from under him. 'You should answer it. It might be important.'

He sent her a long-suffering look, but lifted the phone off the dash, stabbed the caller ID. Seeing his mother's number, he sighed. Maria rarely called him, and, although it was unlikely to be life or death, if she wanted to speak with him she'd only call back—better to get this over with.

'Hold that thought,' he said as he took the call.

It was only when his mother's voice rang out in his ear at top volume that he realised he'd forgotten to take the cell off speaker phone. 'Zane, where are you? The *quinceañera* started two hours ago. You promised you'd come this time.'

He stabbed the button to turn down the volume, but one glance at Iona told him the damage had already been done. She'd heard that loud and clear.

'I can't make it. I'm sorry.'

'Why not?' his mother asked in her typically pragmatic way.

'Something came up at the last minute.' He shifted, stupidly embarrassed by the double entendre he hadn't intended—and had to bite down on the flicker of annoyance when Maria continued to harass him about the party. She knew he didn't like spending time with her family. Why couldn't she let this drop?

'How about if I get Maricruz a present, make it up to her later?' he asked, trying to get out of the situation gracefully. He would do pretty much anything for his mother, but not this.

'It's not enough. You need to come. Why is it so hard for you to be a part of this family?' He flinched at the accusation—and the knowledge that he could never tell her the reason why.

He felt the light touch of fingers on his arm, and turned to find Iona looking at him, her eyes bright with sympathy. She mouthed something to him.

'Just a minute, Maria,' he said, and covered the handset.

'Is this your cousin's party? You should go,' she said as soon as he turned his attention to her. 'You can come back afterwards,' she said, the sincerity in her eyes crucifying him. 'I'll still be here.'

No way.

Everything inside him rebelled against the idea of leaving her alone for the evening. After waiting three days to see her, it wasn't just the sex he'd been anticipating.

But then she said, 'I don't feel right about keeping you away from your family,' and he knew he was sunk.

'Okay, great,' he said grudgingly. 'I'll go, but you're coming with me.' If she was going to guilt him into this, he didn't plan to be the only one suffering.

'Don't be silly. I can't go, I hardly know...'

Ignoring her protests, he put the phone back to his ear. 'We're on our way,' he added, blanking the gasp of annoyance from the passenger seat.

'We? Who's we? Are you bringing a date?' His mother sounded so surprised, and pleased, it suddenly occurred to him all the ways in which this could go wrong.

He never talked to his mother about his love life, to avoid any awkward conversations. And she hadn't met any of the women he'd dated since he was sixteen. 'I'll be there in about half an hour,' he replied, deliberately ignoring the question.

He switched off his cell. And raked his fingers through his hair.

Hell, the evening he'd had planned featuring some flirting, a little foreplay and lots of hot sex had already taken a turn he didn't like. But if Maria met Iona it could get a lot worse. His mother would be bound to overreact—totally screwing up the whole 'casual sex' vibe he'd just spent three days of abstinence to establish.

'Buckle up,' he said to Iona, who still looked mutinous about the invite. 'You wanted deferred gratification. You've got it.'

'That's enchanting.' Iona sighed, feeling more than a little overwhelmed by the dazzle of lights as the car approached the huge estate on a hill carpeted by rows of ripening vines.

The sun was slipping behind the Santa Cruz mountains, haloing the majestic hacienda on the brow of the hill in the golden glow of twilight. As they approached she realised the lights were lanterns, suspended from the porch railings and shining in the red, green and white livery of the Mexican flag.

What looked like fifty cars were crammed in the driveway, parked on the verges and squeezed under the towering oaks that edged the fields. Ornamental rose bushes and showy oleander vied for attention with wild flowers and ferns in the flowerbeds that framed the house. A band of teenagers hung out on the porch, the girls looking like beautiful peacocks in their elaborate ballgowns and the boys lanky and uncomfortable in matching tuxedos.

'I think we're a little underdressed,' Iona murmured as they walked towards the house, tugging down the hem of her minidress. As if it weren't bad enough that she'd been forced into coming, now she felt like a hooker. 'You could have mentioned the dress code.'

'Why? It's not like we had any time to change,' he replied, holding her hand as he led her towards the house.

She felt herself starting to pout. Hating the fact that he had a point. What had she been thinking suggesting he come? It was just that the woman on the phone had sounded so upset, it had made her feel guilty for thinking prurient thoughts about him, while he was supposed to be at a big family event.

But she was so over that now.

'Hey, don't sweat it.' Zane squeezed her hand, taking pity on her. 'The Queen of England would look underdressed at this thing. We won't stay long.'

The romance of fiddles and guitars played energetically in the background competing with the lively hum of conversation as they mounted the steps to the house. Someone shouted a greeting in Spanish to Zane as he led her past the group of teens. Her hand felt clammy in his wide palm, the nerves buzzing in her stomach like hyperactive bees as dark eyes settled on her, most staring with open curiosity.

Zane didn't pause, but led her round the deck to a huge landscaped garden at the back of the house festooned with more lanterns. The remains of an elaborate banquet lay on trestle tables while suited waiters dispensed sparkling wine and beer to the groups of guests crowded into every corner. A band of musicians played in front of a dance floor set up beside a glorious infinity pool. Numerous people in their finery waved at them or shouted greetings at Zane, which he returned with a perfunctory salute.

Then the crowd parted and a young woman dressed in beaded white lace like a Disney Princess raced towards them.

'Zane, you came!' She grasped the tiara on her head under the waterfall of artfully arranged curls before throwing her arms around Zane's neck.

Iona stepped back as he held the teenager for less than a second before depositing her back on ice-pick heels. *'Feliz cumpleaños, Maricruz.'*

She did a twirl, making the fanciful tiers of white lace shimmer. 'What do you think?'

'You look great,' Zane replied. 'All grown up.'

She grinned, her face flushed with excitement and the blush of pleasure. 'Maybe now you'll stop treating me like a *niña*.'

The flirtatious sparkle in her glorious brown eyes was unmistakeable and Iona wondered if Zane knew his fifteen-year-old cousin had a crush on him. Was that the reason he looked so uncomfortable?

'Maricruz, I want to introduce you to my date, Iona.' Reaching behind, he grabbed her wrist and dragged her forward, tucking her against his side.

'Oh, hello.' Maricruz looked stunned for a moment— and not particularly pleased to see her.

'It looks like a wonderful party,' Iona said, grateful for the weight of Zane's arm round her shoulders.

'Thanks,' the girl said a little sulkily, then beamed another winning smile at Zane. 'Will you dance with me, Zane? Later, there are going to be some more waltzes.'

'Sure, if we're still here,' he said.

'You will?' The sulkiness disappeared as quickly as it had come—and Iona felt a little sorry for the girl, guessing she hadn't heard Zane's qualification.

'Yeah.'

She sent Iona an impish grin that suddenly made the beautiful young woman look like an excited child. 'I love your dress. Where did you get it? It's so funky.'

Iona felt the tension in her stomach ease at the girl's open expression. 'From a little shop in Edinburgh.'

'What's your accent? It's way cool?'

'Scottish.'

'Awesome, like *Braveheart*.'

Iona grinned back. At last, an American who knew a little about her homeland—even if it was based on Hollywood folklore. 'Uh-huh. Among other things.'

'Do the men really wear skirts there?'

'Kilts,' she corrected. 'And yes, sometimes, although

usually only for special occasions. They can be a bit draughty.'

Zane tightened his arm round her shoulders. 'Enough with the questions. Iona's from Scotland, not the moon.'

'If you think I'm bad, wait till you introduce her to the family. Forget questions, it's going to be the Mexican Inquisition.' Maricruz sent Iona a conspiratorial smile. 'Zane never brings dates to family events.'

The startling announcement had the bees buzzing back to life in Iona's stomach.

'You are gonna be the hot topic of conversation for months,' the girl added.

'We need to go get some food,' Zane cut in. 'We'll see you later, Maricruz,' he said, deliberately steering them away from the inquisitive teen.

'I'll save the next waltz for you,' she called after Zane before being swallowed up again into the gaggle of teenage girls preening by the pool.

'That's not true, is it?' Iona whispered above the music from the Mariachi band. She'd just started to feel a tiny bit more relaxed about coming, and now this?

Taking her hand, Zane led her around the edge of the dancers towards a long table laden with food. He passed her a china plate and a cloth napkin. 'Let's grab some food before it goes—and then get out of here.'

'I'm serious, Zane. I'm not really the first date who's ever met your family, am I?' she asked, holding the plate limply as he proceeded to heap it with food from the tureens.

'Ignore Maricruz—she's teasing you.'

'That's not an answer,' she countered.

He sent her a deliberately sexy smile, and her heartbeat skipped into her throat. 'I don't bring dates because I don't usually come to these things if I can avoid them.'

'Why would you want to avoid them?' she asked, the panic replaced by confusion. Maybe the party was a little overwhelming, for a stranger. But he wasn't a stranger, he was part of this family and, from what she'd seen so far, everyone seemed very warm and welcoming.

He scooped up a generous helping of a fragrant rice and chicken dish. 'Because I usually have a lot of other stuff I'd rather be doing, like tonight,' he said, those striking blue eyes promising all sorts of heady excitement later in the evening.

The heat that was never far from the surface flared to life. 'I see.'

He chuckled, the sound rich and confidently male. Then leaned close, and let his lips linger over the sensitive spot below her ear. 'Now stop asking dumb questions and eat your *arroz con pollo* so we can get out of here.'

As it turned out, getting away from Zane's family was easier said than done. Before the two of them had managed to finish the delicious banquet leftovers, they had already been accosted by a parade of his relatives.

The succession of *tias* and *tios, primos* and *primas* ranging in age from teens to pensionable age whose names and places in the Montoya family tree Iona would need a wall chart to keep straight soon began to blur into one. But two things became obvious very quickly—every one of them was overjoyed to see Zane at the party, and Zane was a lot less than overjoyed to be there.

After close to twenty minutes of non-stop introductions, Iona was exhausted from all the attention they'd received—but also enthralled by Zane's close-knit and affectionate family, and his place within it. Why was he so tense and uncommunicative with people that obviously loved and cared for him?

Both questions she planned to ask him, the minute they managed to escape from their latest interrogator— his statuesque Tia Carmen, who if Iona's memory was correct was married to Zane's uncle, Carlos.

When Carmen finally paused for a breath, Zane grasped Iona's hand and butted in. 'We need to go, Carmen. I'll see you around.'

Carmen's mouth opened, as if she wanted to say more, but Zane was already dragging Iona away.

'Shouldn't we stay a little longer? We've been here less than an hour,' Iona asked above the swelling music as the smooth strains of a waltz began and couples flooded past them onto the dance floor.

He paused, quirked an amused eyebrow. 'Hell, no. I think we've handled enough of the Mexican Inquisition for one night, don't you?'

'It wasn't that bad. They've all been very sweet and very polite.'

He gave a harsh laugh. 'You call Roberto's interrogation about where your family come from polite?'

'I didn't mind. He obviously cares about you—they all do.'

He cupped her elbows, drew her towards him. 'Will you stop being so damn earnest? It just makes me want you more.'

She frowned at the deliberate evasion. 'I'm serious. It's nice to have people care about you that much. Why wouldn't it be?' How many times as a child had she gone to bed at night, wishing that her own mother could have given that much of a damn about her?

The thought of all those unanswered prayers made her a little sad, even a little annoyed that Zane seemed determined to shun the family he had.

He kissed her nose, gave a rough chuckle and then whispered against her ear. 'Maybe because my life is none of their damn business.'

He rubbed her arms, then took her hand in his. 'We've only got a small window of opportunity. Let's go.'

But as they headed for the deck Iona noticed Maricruz, standing by the edge of the dance floor, watching them leave, her hands clasped in front of her and a defeated expression on her face.

'No, wait, Zane.' She yanked on his hand to stop him. 'Maricruz's waltz, you promised. And I think she's waiting for you.'

Raking his hand through his hair, he looked over her shoulder and swore softly, obviously spotting the girl—and her anxious expression.

'It's her special day—you must.'

His gaze locked on hers and she could see that he was fighting a losing battle with his conscience. 'Fine, I'll do it,' he said at last. Then gripped her upper arms. 'But wait for me here, and don't move a damn muscle. I'll be back in ten minutes. Twenty tops? And then we're leaving.'

'Yes, Zane, although not moving a muscle may give me a cramp,' she teased, stupidly touched that he'd opted not to break the promise he'd made to his cousin, however reluctantly.

'Ha ha.' Cupping her cheeks, he planted a hot, firm kiss on her lips—her insides churned with a potent mix of heat and embarrassment. 'Stay put,' he said, the command in his voice unequivocal. 'Or there will be trouble.'

'I certainly hope so,' she chirped as he left.

She wrapped her arms round her waist, her lips lifting as she saw him stop in front of Maricruz. The girl dropped into a low curtsy in her ballgown, her forlorn expression turning to one of unadulterated glee. The girl laughed, her joy painfully transparent as he led her onto the dance floor and her Court of Honour cheered.

Iona sighed as she watched them together. Zane in his white shirt and dark trousers looked tall and impossibly dashing despite the fact that he was the only man on the floor not wearing a tuxedo. Perhaps it was his height—at six feet two or three he had several inches on the legion of teenagers dancing with their dates. Or maybe it was the tanned, chiselled features shadowed with stubble marking him out as a man and not a boy. Or maybe it was simply the effortless way he glided across the floor, his steps perfectly matched to Maricruz as he led the beaming girl in a series of perfectly executed twirls and dips. But as the romantic music swirled around her Iona realised it was more than Zane's height or his looks or his dance skills that made him stand out so much: it was that aura of tension and distance that he wore like a cloak.

No wonder Maricruz had a major crush on him. Iona could just imagine herself at that age. There was an air of danger about Zane, that lurked just beneath the surface of that lazy charm.

'Hello, I'm Juana.'

Iona jerked her gaze off Zane and his dance partner at the softly spoken interruption, to find a pair of astute coffee-coloured eyes studying her. 'I'm one of Zane and Maricruz's *primos segundos*. A second cousin,' she clarified. 'You're Zane's *novia*?'

'Yes, that's right, my name's Iona. Iona McCabe,' Iona replied politely, and offered her hand in greeting, even though she figured *novia* was a bit of an exaggeration—but she could hardly tell a girl who didn't look much older than Maricruz that she wasn't Zane's girlfriend, she was simply his casual-sex fling. 'Nice to meet you.'

The girl grinned, then turned her gaze back to the dance floor. She held a palm to her chest and sighed. 'Zane's so awesome. What's it like dating him? Is it really cool?'

So Juana was another of Zane's fan club.

'It's...' Iona stumbled—cool didn't quite cover what they'd done on their one date. 'Yes, it's pretty cool.' *And way hot.*

'I'm so glad he came, Maricruz would have been heartbroken if Zane didn't show.' The girl gazed at her. 'So thanks for letting him.'

'You're welcome,' Iona mumbled, confused. 'Although it didn't have much to do with me.'

The girl smiled and shrugged. 'It's still nice that you're not as stuck up as the rest of them.'

'The rest of who?'

'We think Zane only dates spoilt stuck-up women who don't want him to mix with his family.' The contempt in the girl's voice spoke volumes. 'Not that you're one of those. You seem really nice,' Juana added, her eyes widening as she realised she might have insulted Iona.

'What makes you think those are the only women he dates?' Iona asked, more curious than insulted. Juana was turning out to be a font of all knowledge.

'Because of his father.'

'What about his father?' Iona asked, realising he'd never mentioned the man.

'He was a rich *pinche gringo*.' Iona had no idea what *pinche* meant but, from Juana's hiss of disapproval, she didn't think it was complimentary. 'Not that any of us know who his father is. No one's allowed to talk about it. *Abuelo* gets mad at anyone who even mentions Zane is half-Anglo—you won't say anything, will you?'

'No, of course not,' Iona murmured, her mind spinning. It wasn't that much of a stretch to guess that Zane might be mixed race, not with those pure blue eyes. But why, when the Montoya family seemed to have embraced multi-culturalism—at least half of the guests at the party were 'Anglo' as Juana put it—was his parentage considered such a scandalous secret?

But as she opened her mouth to quiz the girl, Juana hummed with pleasure. 'Oh, look, Maria has cut in on Maricruz. That's so sweet.'

Iona shifted her gaze and her thoughts back to Zane and his dance partner, to see his hands resting on the waist of a statuesque vision in scarlet. All the air rushed out of her lungs.

Sweet wasn't the word she'd use. The woman oozed a stylish and classic sex appeal. Lush dark-chocolate hair tumbled down her back in a cascade of corkscrew curls, her hourglass figure spotlighted in a stunning red dress that hugged impressive curves but somehow managed to look demure rather than revealing.

Maria? Who was she?

But as she watched them together Iona knew exactly who she was. She had to be a past, possibly even a present lover—the familiarity and affection between them apparent in their co-ordinated dance moves, and the way Zane looked at her with none of the chill he reserved for members of his family.

So that was the real reason why he hadn't wanted to come tonight.

As Juana continued to wax lyrical in hushed tones about how sweet they looked together, the sick sensation of betrayal gripped Iona's stomach like a boa constrictor—and her vision dimmed. Why couldn't he have told her that this woman would be here? And why had he insisted on bringing her along?

A red haze began to descend over her eyes.

Was this why he didn't bring dates to family events? Because he knew *she* would be here? And yet he hadn't thought to spare Iona that humiliation.

Okay, maybe they were only a casual fling, and they hadn't mentioned exclusivity, but she'd simply assumed that was a given.

The waltz finished and both Zane and the bombshell turned towards the band and clapped politely. Then Iona watched, the boa in her stomach rising up to constrict around her chest as the woman leaned up on tiptoe, placed a hand on his shoulder and kissed him on the cheek. The love in his gaze was clear and unequivocal even from this distance, the two of them appearing to be in their own private little world as the other guests milled around them. And the boa squirmed and writhed, turning into something more than sickening, more than humiliating.

'Excuse me, Juana,' Iona murmured before threading her way through the crowd at the edges of the dance floor.

She should just go home, forget about him. They had no investment in each other. Just because she'd spent the last three days thinking about him, and the night they'd spent together. This was casual. Less than casual really. And clearly his relationship with Maria was not. She shouldn't care if he had a hundred former girlfriends, a thousand that he cared about more than he cared about her.

But somehow her feet kept moving forward, the boa rising up her throat. And she justified the confrontation she could feel racing towards her.

She couldn't go home. She was stranded here without a car. He'd introduced her to his family as his date. Didn't he know how humiliating this was for her? To have him pawing another woman, while she was expected to stand on the sidelines and watch?

She reached them just as the goddess threw back her head and laughed at something Zane said to her in Spanish.

His eyes met Iona's, the blue depths full of humour and not a trace of guilt or remorse.

No, he didn't know, she realised. Or he simply didn't care. Because her thoughts, her feelings, her pride were of no importance to him.

'Hey, Iona,' he said, but she could hear the tension in his voice.

'Could you take me home, please?' she said. 'Now.'

'Is there a problem?' he replied, the flash of guilt replaced with confusion. Did he really think so little of her that he couldn't guess what the problem was?

'I'd like to go home and I need you to drive me there,' she said through gritted teeth, determined not to raise her voice. 'Or take me to the nearest bus station.'

'Why would I drive you to a bus station?' he said, sounding annoyed now too. 'We've got plans for tonight, remember?'

The red haze went purple. How could he mention that here? In front of his other woman? It insulted them both. 'Not any more we haven't.' Her voice rose despite her best intentions. 'I'm leaving and if you don't want to take me, I'll find someone who does.'

'Think again.' His fingers closed around her upper arm. 'You came with me, which means you're leaving with me.'

She struggled against the iron grip. 'I'll do what I damn well please.'

'Zane, let her go, you're making a scene,' the goddess remarked, her voice calm but her warm chocolate eyes alight with interest.

Zane let her go, but ground out, 'I'm not the one making the scene—she is.'

Iona's chest puffed up with indignation, but before she could give it to him with both barrels the goddess intervened again. 'Iona, it's a pleasure to meet you.'

The snake coiled, but she refused to let it strike. She mustn't lash out at this woman. It wasn't her fault. It was Zane. He was the one who had brought her here under false pretences.

'Look, Maria, I'm sure you're a very nice person.' The venom she didn't want to admit to dripped from her tongue. 'Zane certainly seems to think so. And it's not your fault that he brought me along and then made us both look like fools.' She shot her best squinty-eyed look at Zane to telegraph her anger. 'But I'm not in the market for a threesome.'

The woman's eyebrows launched towards that glorious tumble of curls.

'And I'm sure you're not either,' Iona continued, diligently ignoring Zane's muffled oath and the shocked laugh that choked out of the woman's lips. 'Unfortunately, though, I'm stranded until he gives me a lift. But as soon as I get to the nearest bus station, he's all yours.'

Iona swivelled her head at the hissed exclamation from Zane, whose temper seemed to have dissolved in shock. 'Iona, you've got this all wrong.'

'I don't think so,' she whispered furiously, finally noticing the absence of music, and the sea of watchful faces currently fixed on their little tableau. The sound of muffled laughter rippled through the crowd, making her mortification complete. 'What?' She glared at Zane, who simply thrust a hand through his hair and swore again.

'Actually, Iona, it probably is my fault,' the goddess announced as the laughter finally began to die down. 'As I'm Zane's mother.'

'I beg your pardon?'

She gaped at the goddess. She had to be going deaf, or blind, or both. She simply could not have heard that correctly. This woman looked gorgeous, and glamorous, and not a day over forty. She'd never asked Zane how old he was but he had to be at least thirty? Didn't he?

'Maria Montoya, Iona.' The goddess held out an expertly manicured hand. 'Zane's mother.' She let out another little laugh, her expression friendly and giving, as if she were willing Iona to share the joke. 'And believe me, it really is a pleasure to meet you. My son has always needed a woman with the courage to stand up to him.'

Iona stared at the offered hand, sick waves of nausea hitting the rice and chicken and salsa she'd consumed. 'But that's... That's not possible,' she mumbled, the words barely discernible through the chainsaw buzzing in her eardrums. 'It's not. You're too young.'

'I wish that were true. But I'm flattered you think so.'

The woman's humour and the kindness in her gaze made the churning increase. Iona covered her mouth. What had she done? What had she said? How could she have insulted Zane's mother that way? In front of his whole family? This wasn't humiliating—it was practically certifiable.

'I'm so, so sorry,' she said, then turned and darted through the crowd, who parted before her like the Red Sea—or, rather, like people trying to avoid a certifiable nutjob.

'Iona, wait up!'

She accelerated, staggering past the Red Sea of amused, or astonished or simply stunned faces. These were people he and his mother knew, people who loved and respected him—even if he didn't seem to share the sentiment—and she'd just made that situation even worse.

She raced round the side of the huge house, having to push past those people who hadn't witnessed the freak show she'd put on in the garden, eventually making it to the front lawn and stumbling down the stone steps. The driveway wound through the fields of dark vines plump with grapes, but she headed down it, her panicked mind deciding she would walk all the way back to Pacific Grove rather than ask Zane for a lift again.

She got as far as the last car, when footsteps pounded on the gravel behind her and strong fingers grasped her arm.

'Damn it, where are you going?' he said, hauling her round to face him.

She squeezed her eyes shut, desperate to hold back the tears, but unable to look him in the face. 'I'll be fine. It won't take me long to make it to the road and I can hitch-hike from there.'

'No way are you hitch-hiking anywhere. And it's three miles to the road. And dark.'

'Please, I'll be fine, if you'll just please, please, please, tell your mother how sorry I am.'

He probably hated her now. And who could blame him? She'd made a laughing stock of them both.

'My mother is tickled pink you think she's in her thirties when she hit the big five-oh a couple of months ago.'

'Your mother is fifty!' What was one more shock in so many? 'But how old are...?'

'I'm thirty-four. She was sixteen when she had me.' She could hear the sting in his tone—as if he'd been asked the question a thousand times and was tired of answering it.

'Okay.' Although it wasn't. 'That explains my mistake, but it still doesn't make what I said any less mortifying.'

'Iona, this is dumb. You're overreacting.'

'I said the word *threesome* to your mother!' she yelped. 'It's horrific. Inexcusable. I made a terrible scene in front of your whole family.'

He tucked a knuckle beneath her chin, forced her gaze to his, but the concern she saw made her stomach hurt.

He probably pitied her now. And who wouldn't? Why had she said those things? Why had she even cared that much? Why did she always make such an idiot of herself where men were concerned?

'Iona,' he said, his patience almost as painful as the pity she thought she saw. 'Nuclear war is horrific. The famine in Africa is inexcusable. This is neither one. You made a mistake, that's all. And my family is Latino— and full to bursting with drama queens. As scenes go, this doesn't even register a two-point-five on the Richter scale of family drama.'

She heard the distance in his tone, and while his observation made her feel a little better about the biggest faux pas in human history, she didn't understand it. She'd just humiliated him in front of them. How could he not be mad as hell about that? Did their good opinion really mean so little to him?

NINE

___

'Zane, is Iona okay?"

Iona's stomach revolted at the sight of the goddess—his mother—hurrying towards them down the driveway.

'Yeah,' Zane said bluntly. 'But we're leaving. We've both had about as much as we can take for one night.'

Iona saw his mother flinch a little at the hostile statement and her stomach heaved. He shouldn't talk to his mother like that.

'I'm so sorry,' his mother soothed, looking genuinely apologetic, which only made Iona feel worse. 'I'm frequently mistaken for Zane's sister, but this is the first time I've ever been mistaken for his lover.'

'Please don't apologise to me.' Iona closed her eyes, not sure she could bear this woman's kindness now, after the hideous way she'd behaved. 'You didn't do anything wrong.'

'Of course, if Zane had had the good sense to introduce me to you when you both arrived this would never have happened.' Maria rounded on her son. 'And don't think I didn't see you trying to leave early.'

'I didn't much want to come in the first place,' he protested. 'So don't blame me for this, Maria.'

Iona listened to the conversation in a trance, so mortified she figured the safest option was to keep her mouth shut.

'Zane, isn't it past time for you to let the anger go?' his mother asked, cradling his cheek.

He jerked his head back 'We have to go,' he said, and Iona saw the shadow of hurt in his mother's eyes.

'Zane, please...'

'I'll give you a call during the week sometime.' He cut off her plea, then placed a quick kiss on her cheek, but the gesture was more guarded than giving.

His mother nodded, her sadness and confusion making Iona's chest ache. Why was he being so cruel? It wasn't his mother's fault that she'd made an idiot of herself—and the woman had a point: why hadn't he made any effort to introduce them?

'*Adios*, Iona,' Maria said. 'I will see you again, I hope.'

Iona watched her walk back towards the party, the lingering magnolia of her scent adding a sultry glamour to the earthy perfume of the vines.

'Your mum seems like a really nice person. It must have been great having her around as a kid,' Iona murmured, the wistful observation popping out unguarded. 'You shouldn't have been angry with her. It wasn't her fault.'

'I know that,' he murmured, giving a tired sigh before guiding her to his convertible. 'Come on, let's get out of here.'

His dark hair shined black in the evening light as he opened the passenger door, those spectacular features cast into shadow by the glow of lantern light from the hacienda. But Iona could still see the unhappiness in his face, and felt the sharp stab of compassion. His mother, it seemed, wasn't the only one hurting.

She climbed in, wanting to ask him what had caused the distance between him and his mother, because she had the distinct feeling it had very little to do with her meltdown on the dance floor, but stopped herself. She'd done enough damage for one night.

He settled in the seat beside her, but as he switched on the ignition there was one question she couldn't resist asking.

'Why *didn't* you introduce us when we arrived?'

He slung his arm across her seat as he backed the car down the driveway. Finding a place to turn round, he executed a perfect three-point turn before finally replying. 'No particular reason. I just didn't spot her until she joined me on the dance floor.'

He was lying, she knew it, but was afraid to call him on it. Had he maybe regretted bringing a virtual stranger to the party once they'd arrived?

As they powered down the driveway the rows of vines cast lengthening shadows on the tarmac as full dark fell.

She sank into the car's bucket seat, the leather scent a pleasant accompaniment to the freshening wind, and studied his profile. He really was the most beautiful man she'd ever seen. And so many things about him fascinated her.

Now she'd met his family—and especially his mother—he only fascinated her more. She wondered about him, what it had been like for him growing up. He was clearly close to his mother. When they had been dancing together in the lantern light, it had been obvious how close they were. But where did all the tension come from? Maybe it had something to do with his father? The *pinche gringo* Juana had talked about so disrespectfully. What had this man done that meant that no one in his family was even permitted to talk about him? That couldn't be healthy surely? And was that where the distance between Zane and them came from?

All questions she had no right to ask him. But she simply couldn't resist satisfying a little of her curiosity.

'Why do you call your mum by her given name?'

He didn't answer for a long time, and she wondered if he had heard her, but then he shrugged. 'I used to call her Mom when I was a little kid. But as I got older, it got easier not to.'

'Why?' she asked, only more intrigued by the non-explanation.

How the hell had they gotten onto this topic?

Zane glanced across the stick shift at the sleepy question. Iona's wide brown eyes blinked owlishly. She looked exhausted.

'I'm not sure I want to tell you,' he said, hoping to stall her until she fell asleep.

'Why not?'

'Because it'll make me sound like a jerk.' Which was exactly what he had been as a teenager. Selfish and volatile and immature. But there was another reason too, which he had no intention of sharing.

'How so?'

He huffed out what he hoped sounded like a relaxed laugh. 'All right, if you really need to know. At high school, she was much younger than the other moms, and well...' he rapped his thumb against the wheel '...built.' He stiffened at the description, and the memory of the wolf whistles and the catcalls she'd endured whenever she'd come into George Wallace Memorial High. 'She got a lot of attention. I'd lose my temper, get into trouble and I couldn't tell her why, because I didn't want her to know what they said about her.'

He pumped his foot on the gas remembering the constant fights, the swollen knuckles and black eyes and split lips, and the endless journeys to the principal's office, where he'd be forced to sit, sometimes for hours, refusing to defend or apologise for his actions. The impotent anger had boiled inside him for years—at the injustices his mother had suffered, simply because she was young and beautiful and had been forced into a life she had never wanted. But deep down there had been another anger, much blacker and more damaging, that seething, pointless self-loathing that he'd been unable to control then and didn't want to acknowledge now.

'Pretty damn dumb when you think about it with the benefit of maturity,' he said. 'If I'd been less proud and less stupid I would have ignored what they said.'

'You were protecting her in the only way you knew how,' Iona said, her voice thick with sleep. 'That's not proud or stupid. It's very gallant.'

Zane shrugged, the pleasure at her support making him feel uneasy—and exposed. 'Not exactly, because then I started calling her by her given name, so the other kids would think she was my older sister instead of my mom.'

Iona sighed gently. He looked across the console as the car eased to a stop at the end of the vineyard's driveway.

'So in answer to your question,' he continued, 'that's how I came to call her Maria, and now I'm a grown man it seems kind of dumb to call her Mom again.'

He couldn't make out Iona's expression in the low light, but she looked straight back at him.

'It's astonishing, isn't it, how cruel other kids can be, if there's something a bit different about your family set-up?' she murmured and he detected a note of wistfulness that made him realise she knew how it felt. 'We're all such horrid little conformists when we're young.'

His shoulders relaxed at the lack of censure. 'Yeah, I guess. But it must have been tougher for you when your mom left?' he asked, keen to steer the conversation away from himself.

'Aye, well, it wasn't great.' He felt the pinch in his chest at the weariness in the words. 'But we got over it.' She snuggled into the seat and yawned. 'I guess the hardest part is the not knowing why. When you're ten you're just egocentric enough to naturally assume it has to be your fault.'

He took his hand off the stick, the need to comfort her surprising, but he went with it. She sounded so hopeless. He squeezed her knee. 'But you know it wasn't, right?'

Was that why she had fallen victim to Demarest so easily? And why she'd jumped to the conclusion this evening that Maria was one of his lovers? Because of some seed planted years ago in her childhood? Being unwanted was a bitch. It could play hell with your self-esteem; he ought to know. He figured he should probably say something reassuring... But then the scent of her, fresh and sultry, drifted across the car, and his gut tightened.

Better not go there. He wanted her and all this serious talk was casting a spell over the evening, making them both reveal more than they probably should.

'I'm sorry I made things so uncomfortable between

you and your family,' she said around another jaw-breaking yawn.

Uncomfortable? His heart-rate did a quick skip at the perceptive comment. 'I'm the one who should be sorry,' he said, careful to keep his voice light. 'I had no business dragging you along.'

'I liked your family, especially your mother.'

He heard it then, the slight censure in her tone—and realised that she had noticed more than his uncomfortable relationship with Maria.

He rolled his shoulders, forcing himself to relax, and forget about it. Her observations, her opinion didn't matter, their fling wasn't serious—and she'd never have to meet his family again. He'd make sure of it.

'Do you mind if I have a nap?' she said, her voice groggy with fatigue. 'It's been an eventful night.'

'Sure, go ahead. It'll take about an hour to get back.'

He checked on her a few moments later as they hit Highway One. Curled in the seat, she'd drifted off into a sound sleep.

He'd forgotten to mention that they were headed back to his place and not hers. But he figured she'd find out soon enough. And he'd deal with any fall-out then. He wasn't going to push anything tonight, he could see how tired she was, but he didn't want her out of his sight for too long either. She'd been through the wringer at Maricruz's party. And that was mostly his fault. He should have introduced her to Maria, instead of running scared.

But as the car sped down the coast highway it occurred to him that, however casual their fling was supposed to be, something had changed tonight. Something about Iona pulled at him. Her honesty, her vulnerability, that prickly demeanor she used to hide her insecurities. It reminded him of the kid he'd once been a little too force-fully.

He stretched his neck from side to side as the muscles cramped. He felt protective of Iona—which probably wasn't a good thing. Because whenever he'd got protective in the past, it had generally been a disaster.

He shifted in his seat, the dull ache in his back reminding him of the two wounds that had signalled his exit from the LAPD five years before. He switched on the car's radio, let the pain and confusion from that time in his life slowly drift away on the seductive bass riff of the old soul song.

He was over-thinking. The only reason things had got heavy tonight was because he'd taken her somewhere he didn't feel comfortable.

And while he might feel protective of Iona, he didn't have to feel that way. She was a grown woman, who could take care of herself. She'd certainly proved that tonight. A wry smile lifted his lips at the intoxicating memory of her pale skin flushed crimson with fury as she stalked across the dance floor to confront him while he danced with his mother.

He pressed his foot onto the gas pedal, in a hurry to get home. This was still a casual fling—and he could prove it, because when they got back to his place he wasn't going to pounce on her like a starving man.

'Hey, *precios,* we're here. You want me to carry you in?'

Iona moved her head and caught the strong scent of sea air as the question drifted through the fog of sleep. 'Hmm?'

'Guess I'll carry you, then. Hold on.'

Her lids fluttered open as her stomach became weightless and she found herself being boosted into Zane's arms. The night air closed around them and she held on to his neck to stop herself from falling. The sound of surf and the cry of a nocturnal seagull had her squinting at the huge wood and glass structure that rose up out of a sand dune. 'Where are we?'

'My place. Figured it would be easier to stay here tonight.'

'But I...' she began, knowing she should probably object, but it felt good to be held.

'But nothing,' he said. 'You were exhausted. My place was closer.'

He shifted her in his arms to key a code into the door panel, then shoved open the front door and carried her through the darkened house.

'Relax, Iona,' he said, giving her a soft kiss on the forehead. 'This place has five bedrooms. I'm not planning on jumping you tonight.'

'Oh, okay.' Well, heck, she hadn't intended to object quite that much.

They passed the door to a vast open-plan kitchen, the low lighters illuminating dark marble surfaces and blonde wood cabinets, then entered a double-height living room that had a glass wall leading onto a wide terraced deck. A lighted pathway led off the terrace and out into the darkness.

'You live by the sea?' she said.

'Yeah, beach's just down there.'

The place was enormous and a little eerie, until the sound of claws scratching on wood broke the silence and a couple of excited yips were followed by the arrival of a big bundle of dirty-blonde fur that barrelled across the room towards them.

'Hey, C.D.,' Zane said by way of introduction as he stood Iona on her feet. 'Meet Iona—she's sleeping over.'

The delighted dog's tail wagged so hard its whole body vibrated. Careering to a stop in front of them, it plunked its butt down on the floor, and panted with delight. With a ragged ear, one squinted eye, and a misshapen head that made it look like an unfortunate cross between a lab and a bulldog, it had to be one of the ugliest mutts Iona had ever seen. But as it continued to vibrate with ecstasy, its tongue hanging out of its mouth in a doggie grin, she found herself completely charmed.

'Hello, Cookie Dough, it's nice to meet you,' she said, kneeling down to stroke the dog's head. It immediately flopped onto its back, and offered its tummy for a rub, surprising a laugh out of her.

'Great guard dog you are,' Zane said ruefully.

'You're gorgeous, aren't you, girl?' Iona purred, already in love and undeniably touched by the fact that Zane had chosen to rescue a mongrel pup that most other people would have rejected on sight. 'Pay no attention to him—you're just being friendly,' she cooed. The dog answered with a low growl of contentment as its tail thumped rhythmically on the floor.

'All right, that's enough, you little suck-up.' Zane snapped his fingers. The dog rolled back onto its legs, still shaking with excitement. 'Go on back to bed, Cooks. We'll see you in the morning.'

Iona gave C.D. one last pat and rub, before the dog sauntered off, back to its bed in the corner of the room.

'So that's the infamous Cookie Dough.' Iona chuckled. 'Eater of shoes and drinker of toilet water. She seems very polite to me.'

'Uh-huh, we'll see how that works for you when she

leaps onto your bed at dawn.' Taking Iona's hand, he led her across the room, to a wide metal staircase that curved up to the landing above. 'Let's find you a room. You and Cookie can get better acquainted tomorrow.'

Iona followed, her hand clasped in his, and tried not to let her disappointment show. If he wasn't that bothered, neither was she. She struggled to keep that thought front and centre when he pushed open a door on the first landing.

He flicked on the light switch, illuminating acres of thick blue carpeting, a king-size bed made up with luxury linen and the dark deck beyond.

'There's a spare toothbrush in the bathroom, which is through there.' He pointed to a door on the far wall. 'There should be towels too and anything else you need.'

She stared at the empty bed, the pillows piled high against the headboard, and heat flushed through her. She could smell him, that tantalising scent of spicy aftershave and sea air that was uniquely his—and more than anything she wanted him to climb in with her.

'Do you need anything else?' he asked casually.

He leaned against the doorway, his forearm propped against the frame, the cotton of his shirt stretched across that impressive chest. And she got a vision of that beautiful body naked.

Yes, you.

Her mind screamed, making the heat pound into her sex. 'No, that's great,' she heard herself say. 'I'll see you in the morning.'

His gaze lingered on her lips for the longest time. 'C.D. usually wakes me up at dawn to take her for a run, so if I'm not here, I'll be on the beach.'

The words sounded polite, distant, but the husky tone of his voice reverberated inside her.

How could he be so calm, so controlled? 'Right.'

He drummed his fingers against the doorframe, then straightened and let his arm drop.

She stood, unable to relinquish eye contact, her breath catching. Lifting one hand, he skimmed a knuckle down the side of her face. She tilted her head, leaning into his touch. Then his hand clasped the back of her neck and he hauled her against him.

'Just one more thing.'

She opened her mouth as his lips slanted across hers. Heat and awareness shot through her as his tongue delved. Firm, sure, wet and hot. The hunger built as she kissed him back, her knees shaking as if an aftershock had hit the San Andreas Fault. She flattened her palms against his waist, gripping his shirt.

A low moan issued from her lips as he pulled away.

'Get a good night's sleep, Iona,' he said, the rough demand matching the dark dilated pupils. 'I intend to keep you real busy tomorrow.'

Then he walked away, leaving her staring at his retreating back, her body battered by the need coursing through every pulse point.

'You have got to be kidding me?' she whispered as the sound of his footsteps disappeared down the hallway.

There wasn't a chance in hell she was going to sleep a wink now.

Zane slammed the bedroom door and leaned against it. He stared out at the night sky, and waited for the blood to stop pounding southwards.

Whose dumb idea was it to bring her here? And then not sleep with her?

Tugging the shirt off over his head, he wadded it up as he marched into the bathroom, and hurled it into the corner of the room.

Oh, yeah, his dumb idea.

Twisting the shower control, he guided the temperature down to frigid.

When was the last time he'd had a woman in his house, and not his bed? Never, that was when. He kicked off his shoes, dropped his pants and stepped under the spray. Then bit off the yelp as the cold water splattered his chest and hit the erection. Bracing his hand against the cubicle wall, he waited for the inferno to subside under the freezing deluge—it took a while, thanks to the succulent taste of her that lingered on his lips, and the soft sob of arousal that still echoed in his ears.

The woman was tying him in knots—tying them both in knots. She could have tonight, damn it. Because he'd promised himself this was going to be casual, and it didn't feel that casual after the night they'd spent with his family.

But tomorrow all bets were off. He wasn't holding back a moment longer.

He'd never been a pushy guy. Probably because he'd never had to be. But come tomorrow, that was all gonna change. She wanted him. He wanted her. End of story. She'd got back on the horse, now it was way past time for them both to enjoy the ride.

TEN

The blast of sunlight made Iona squirm as she opened her eyes and curled into the pillows. Yawning, she eased herself into a sitting position—and took a moment to orientate herself.

The glass wall on one side of the lavish bedroom framed a stunning view of rocks and sand and ocean as the events of the night before came tumbling back in a series of disjointed sights and sounds and scents.

The blank shock on Zane's face as she confronted him on the dance floor. The hurt in his mother's eyes as they left. The sense of connection that had made her chest hurt when he'd spoken about his high-school experiences, his knuckles whitening on the steering wheel—and the hot, firm press of his lips that had sent her into a frenzy of longing.

Iona let a slow breath out, and sucked another one in through her teeth. No doubt about it, it had been one heck of a night.

Flinging back the quilt, she climbed out of the bed and crossed the room. Placing her hand against the sun-warmed glass, she peered out. She could see the manicured lawns of a golf course in the distance, but Zane's house stood apart—its elegant modernism in direct counterpoint to the wilder, angrier edge of the bay. The sun hovered above the horizon. Seemed she'd managed a bit more than a wink despite the distractions of that goodnight kiss.

Working the kinks out of her shoulders, she made a beeline for the bathroom.

As she treated herself to a scalding hot shower she smiled, thinking of the sunny Sunday morning—and all the hot sex they had to catch up on from the night before.

But once she'd dressed and gone downstairs, she found no sign of him, or his dog, and realised he'd probably gone to take C.D. for a walk. She stepped out onto the deck, dismissing the odd little jump in her belly at the thought of how normal, how comfortable it felt being in his home and looking forward to a lazy Sunday together.

Despite a cloudless sky and the blaze of mid-morning sunshine, a brisk ocean breeze meant she was grateful for the denim jacket. She headed down the narrow stone steps that traversed a rocky outcropping to arrive at a secluded beach framed by gnarly Monterey Cypresses that separated the lot from the one next door.

Her heart bobbed into her throat as she spotted a tall figure jogging down the beach and the bounding hound next to him. She lifted her hand to wave, took several calming breaths to still the frantic thump of her pulse as they approached.

Zane's short hair spiked in the wind, the pair of jogging shorts speckled with water from the pounding surf. A gust of wind flattened the sleeveless sweatshirt he wore against his chest.

C.D. raced ahead to deliver an ecstatic greeting that involved launching herself at Iona, planting two huge sandy paws onto her tummy and nearly toppling her backwards onto her butt.

'Down, Cookie.' Zane's succinct command had the dog plopping heavily onto her backside. Iona grinned at the overgrown puppy and its expression of goofy enthusiasm, glad to be distracted from the silly swell of emotion at seeing Zane again.

'Sorry about that,' Zane said, picking up a piece of driftwood. 'We're still working on polite introductions.'

'That's okay. No harm done,' Iona said, wiping the last of the wet sand off her dress. Was it her imagination or did he sound a little tense too?

Zane lobbed the driftwood towards the tumbling surf. 'Go fetch, Cooks.'

C.D. gave an excited howl, before racing after the stick, arrowing her body into the shallows.

Iona pushed out a laugh. 'That's brave. It must be freezing.'

'More dumb than brave. Even I've got to admit, she's not the smartest dog in the universe.'

They watched the dog barking manically at the waves as it tried to retrieve the stick. 'No, maybe not,' Iona said.

'You sleep okay?'

Her chest compressed as she met the fierce blue gaze.

'Like a baby.' His gaze dipped to her lips and colour fired into her cheeks. 'I hope Cookie didn't wake you up too early,' she added.

'Early enough.' A smile lurked around the corners of his mouth. 'You hungry?' he said. 'I figured we could have waffles for breakfast.'

Her stomach contracted, but it wasn't hunger for food that gripped her. But how exactly did you go about jumping a guy at ten o'clock in the morning on a beach? Was there an etiquette to this sort of thing? Because if there was she had no idea what it was.

The dog came bounding back, pausing to shake out her wet fur and spraying them both with water. Iona leapt back, but this time neither of them laughed.

Zane wrestled the driftwood out of C.D.'s mouth, gave her a hearty rub and then flung the stick back into the surf. He watched as the dog headed out after it. 'Breakfast it is,' he murmured.

But neither of them made a move. She shoved her fists into the pockets of the jean jacket, the breeze making her shiver. She studied Zane's face in profile and felt the pull of connection and the tingle on her lips where he had devoured her the night before.

He swung round and caught her watching him. Then his gaze narrowed, the blue of his irises even more intense than usual. 'Unless there's something you'd rather do?'

The words came out on a gruff murmur, so quiet she almost didn't hear them over the rushing wind and the crashing surf.

Knuckles rough with sand brushed her cheek and then his open palm settled on the heated skin of her nape.

The shudder of awareness bristled down her spine. 'Well, actually, there might be something...'

It was all the encouragement he needed before his mouth swooped down, cutting off her protest.

He held her cheeks in cool palms and plundered, holding her still for the sure, hot sweep of his tongue, the hungry possession that promised so much more.

She couldn't resist, couldn't control the instinctive response, her body quaking with desire.

He lifted his head first, their ragged breaths mingling in the salty air. His pupils had dilated to black, his voice strained. 'You're sure about this?'

'Yes,' she said, knowing perfectly well there was no point in denying it.

His hands dropped to her waist, hauled her against him and she felt the solid ridge. Her centre melted, the need a wild thing burning inside her. But then he pulled away from her, his expression tense.

'You do understand, Iona, this isn't going to lead to anything else, right?'

She braced her palms against his chest, puzzled by the concern in his voice. Hadn't they already established this? 'Yes, of course I do.'

Emotion clutched at her chest, making her feel a lot less bold. Had he tired of her already? Was that why he'd left her in the guest room last night—because he was already bored? It should have annoyed her. The arrogance of the man. But somehow all it did was make her feel desperately insecure.

The dog returned and flopped onto her tummy, exhausted after all her sea-wrestling activities. Zane crouched down to greet her, and picked up the driftwood she'd dropped obediently at his feet. C.D.'s tail wagged like a metronome; the dog clearly oblivious to the tension that crackled in the air between them.

He took his time, rubbing the dog's head, praising her prowess, but his body language remained stiff and unyielding.

Iona's heart began to beat in double time when he stood to face her.

'If you're not interested any more, Zane, all you have to do is say so.'

She turned to go, but he grasped her arm. 'Hey, don't...' He tugged an impatient hand through his hair. 'It's not that at all. I just didn't want to be putting pressure on you. Giving you the wrong idea about what this is.'

His eyes remained fixed on hers, his hand absently stroking the dog's neck. He looked more frustrated than contrite, but the admission had her pulse rate slowing.

'I'm absolutely fine with it, as I've already told you, so what's the problem?'

'The problem is I shouldn't have kissed you last night, because I've been up half the night with a hard-on the size of Guadalajara, and it's made me cranky.'

She giggled, his frustrated response washing away her insecurity. 'Guadalajara, eh? That sounds impressive?'

'More painful than impressive.' His lips quirked in response. 'Especially when a two-ton hound leaps on top of you at dawn.'

She covered her mouth with one hand. The giddy rush of relief making it hard to suppress another giggle.

'Oh, you think that's funny, huh?'

Catching her round the waist, he bent over and hoisted her onto his shoulder.

'What the heck!' She rode the solid shelf, kicking and struggling, as he hefted her back towards the house. 'Put me down!'

'No way. We've got unfinished business.'

'And whose fault is that?' she yelped, trying to wriggle free as he hefted her up the steps and across the deck.

The dog leapt and barked playfully beside them, happy to join in the game.

Iona bucked trying to escape. But not trying very hard. Stepping through the sliding glass door into the living room, Zane shut the dancing dog out on the deck and dumped her unceremoniously onto her feet. She tried to dart off, but he caught her round the waist, then trapped her against the wall, his hands above her head, his body pressed into hers.

His lips covered hers, capturing the gasp of surprise. Their tongues tangled, and the relief was replaced by the hot shot of passion. His hands skimmed under the denim jacket, then pushed it off her shoulders, trapping her arms behind her back and drawing her close.

She moaned, her head dropping back, as his lips fastened on the pulse point in her neck.

'You taste so damn good, Iona,' he murmured, his breath hot against the sensitive skin.

She drew a much-needed breath, opened her eyes to find him watching her.

'I aim to please.'

'That's good.' The supremely confident grin coaxed another laugh to the surface—along with the rush of something she didn't quite want to identify. Zane Montoya made her feel good, he made her feel needed, but only in a purely physical sense. 'Because after the night I've had,' he added, 'you owe me one.'

'I don't see why,' she said, faking indignation. 'That goodnight kiss was your idea.'

Warm palms snuck up her sides. 'I don't remember you objecting.'

'Well...' She drew out the word, stretching into the caress as his thumbs brushed the underside of her breasts. 'I guess if you put it that way...' she lifted her arms, draped them round his neck and arched against him '...I might consider some payback fair.' He nuzzled her neck, sending the shot of arousal shooting down her abdomen. 'But purely as an act of mercy, you understand.'

It was all the encouragement he needed to grab her hand and head down the corridor.

Zane grabbed the bottle of maple syrup he'd left on the breakfast bar for the waffles as he dragged Iona through the kitchen towards the back staircase.

He had to keep himself from pushing too hard or asking too much. He wanted this to be good, to be fun, to be light and easy, casual, just like he'd promised, but he had a feeling that after the way he'd gotten himself going last night—and this morning—props might be a good way to remind himself of that.

He let the dog in the back door, and Cookie gave them a bark of greeting before settling into her basket.

'What's the syrup for?' Iona asked breathlessly as they mounted the stairs.

'Wait and see,' he said, anticipation making his hands tremble as they walked into his bedroom.

He kicked the door shut, flicked the lock, just in case C.D. didn't have her customary two-hour nap. As much as he loved his dog, he didn't want company.

He placed the syrup bottle onto the bedside table, the sharp crack reverberating round the room. Then went to the glass wall that looked out onto the beach, and dropped the shade.

He squeezed his fingers into fists, dismayed to feel the clammy sweat on his palms.

Get a grip, Montoya. You're acting like a nervous virgin, instead of a guy who popped his cherry a lifetime ago.

The wayward thought had the rushed, fumbled encounter and the crushing distaste on Mary-Lou Seagrove's face coming back.

'You're so handsome, but I guess you're more Mexican than I thought, because you screw like Speedy Gonzalez.'

He cut off the memory of the casual racism that had sliced him to the core, forced his fingers to release. That first sexual encounter might have been a total disaster, but he'd learned a lot since then—the first being, never pick your sexual partners according to their cheerleading abilities.

Iona stood in the middle of the room, her staggered breathing tightening the fabric on her dress as her breasts rose and fell in quick succession. The slatted blinds cast shadows on her face, but he could still read her mood with remarkable ease, her expression a gratifying mix of nervous and excited.

Forget Mary-Lou. You're not that overeager kid any more.

He sat on the edge of the bed, spread his knees and held Iona's waist. She stepped between his thighs and rested her hands on his shoulders. His pulse leapt as she took the initiative and bent to capture his mouth.

Her kiss tasted sweet and exotic, sugar and spice. He ran his tongue along the seam of her mouth, delved within, lifted the hem of her dress and cupped the firm cheeks of her bottom. Tracing the edge of lace, he slipped his fingers beneath the satin.

She shuddered and rocked against him as he found the slick moist heat, more potent than any aphrodisiac.

'You want to get naked?' he asked, determined to let her set the pace, but not sure he could wait much longer, the hard arousal pulsing painfully back to life in his shorts.

She let out a throaty laugh. 'That would be nice.'

Nice.

The husky burr of her accent made the word sound

rich and full this time, instead of insipid and vaguely patronising.

'Great,' he rasped. Finding the zip of her dress, he dragged it down.

She lowered her arms, and stood back to do a wiggle. The simple cotton dress flowed over her curves and drifted down to pool at her feet. The movement was quick, efficient and unbearably arousing.

She straightened, held her shoulders back, bold and determined. The bra was simply made but impossibly erotic in the shifting shadows drawn by the blinds, the dark outline of her nipples clearly visible through the delicate pink lace. He grasped her narrow waist, dragged her back, then, finding the fastening on her bra, he tried to unhook it, but she braced her hands on his shoulders to stop him.

'You'll not have me naked and you fully clothed,' she announced, the brogue much thicker than usual—and a little indignant.

'Point taken,' he said. Standing quickly, he gripped the hem of his sweatshirt, and tugged it off, flung it aside. But when he went to undo his fly, she placed a hand over his.

'Can I do it? Do you mind?'

Did he mind?

He barked out a tense laugh. 'Be my guest.'

Her fingers found the tab and eased it down. He heard her gasp as the straining erection sprang free.

'Oh, my,' she whispered.

He choked out another laugh, stripping off the shorts and his jockeys. The colour tinted her cheekbones, but she didn't hesitate as she reached out to hold him.

Oh, hell.

His flesh leapt as her fingers curled around him. He sucked in a sharp breath, calling on every reserve he had to stay still, stay focused and submit to the soft touch, the gentle exploration.

'Who says big isn't beautiful?' she said with a joyful laugh, and he thought he might actually die as the last drop of his blood pounded out of his head.

Don't lose it, Montoya, not now, or you'll screw everything up.

He took her shoulders in firm hands, knowing there was a limit to how much of this he could take and he was fast approaching it. He had to take charge, take control. He couldn't let her see how much she affected him.

Her hand dropped away, and her eyes lifted to his face. 'Is everything okay?' she asked, the hint of concern as sweet as the rest of her.

'My turn,' he managed, the words coming out on a croak, his mouth as dry as the Sahara after a fifty-year drought.

He used his hands, to turn her round. Unhooking her bra, he cupped her breasts from behind. The nipples poked into his palms as he nestled the rigid weight of his arousal against her buttocks.

She leaned back against him, arched into his palms as he traced the puckered skin, plucked at the hard tips. He splayed a palm across her stomach, ventured beneath the waistband of her panties. She bucked as he traced the plump lips of her sex, found the slick nub.

Damn, how could he want her this much again? So much he felt clumsy and raw and as if he were touching her for the first time, the only time.

Her hands reached back and gripped his thighs to steady herself, the soft moan almost more than he could bear as he circled and rubbed, beckoning the orgasm forth as he fought to keep the thin thread on his control from snapping. He buried his face in her hair, wrapped his arm round her waist to hold her still as he stroked relentlessly. Her body shook and then bowed back as her ragged sobs signalled her climax.

The scent of seduction surrounded him as she sagged against him. He picked her up, placed her on the bed.

She looked dazed, unfocused, her eyes round with wonder. 'Thank you, you're awfully good at that.'

He basked in the surge of satisfaction—and thanked God that she hadn't noticed his hands trembling.

She glanced at the bedside table, sent him a cheeky smile. 'Are we going to use the syrup now?'

He stared at it blankly. Then reached for it blindly, trying to get his mind to engage. 'Yeah.'

Fun, superficial, relaxed. Keep it light, damn it. Keep it hot. Keep it non-committal.

Twisting the top, he drizzled a drop onto the rigid peak of one breast, watched the areola tighten—then concentrated on adorning the other nipple. The hot blood pounding hard in his groin.

She laughed, shifted, letting the sticky sweetness trickle into the valley between her breasts. 'Watch out. We'll get your sheets all sticky.'

'Like I care.' He forced his lips to lift, then capped the bottle, stuck it back on the table. Gripping her hips, he dragged her beneath him.

He bent to lick off the amber sugar he'd been addicted to since childhood. But as his tongue swirled across the tight peak and she let out a soft sob of stunned pleasure all he could taste was the intoxicating essence of her.

* * *

Iona lifted off the bed at the sweep of his tongue over sensitive flesh, her mind still fogged with afterglow. He feasted on her, licking and suckling, until her nipples throbbed, sharp jolts of sensation shooting down to her still-tender sex. She lifted her hips, felt the head of his erection brush her inner thigh.

Holding his cheeks, she lifted his face. 'Please, Zane, I need you inside me.'

Power shimmered through her veins along with the passion as his eyes darkened.

Lifting up, he reached into a drawer on the bedside table, brought out a condom and sheathed himself.

Holding her hips, he bent her knees, positioning her so she was open to him and then surged inside in one devastating thrust. The fullness shocked her, so much more than before. She held on to broad shoulders, her fingers slipping on sweat-slicked skin. But then he started to move and the pressure built and intensified, turning to blinding, burning, all-consuming pleasure.

Her lids fluttered shut as the firestorm blazed through her, seizing her chest, rushing over her skin, making her breath hitch, her mind float, her centre throb.

'Look at me, don't close your eyes.' The words were harsh, demanding, but just beneath was the hint of desperation.

Her eyes flew open and she saw something wild and intense in the brilliant blue. He thrust harder, thrust deeper, stroking that secret place deep inside. Then reached down, expert fingers stroking her core.

'Come for me again, damn it.' The words ground out low and demanding as the wave of orgasm rushed towards her. Hard, fast and unstoppable.

Sensation exploded as her body broke apart, the waves of pleasure battering her. She sobbed, the cry of shock and exultation drowned out by his shout of release as he collapsed on top of her.

Iona drifted back to consciousness, his weight heavy on her, which had to explain the pressure on her chest. She could hear his tortured breathing and felt the hitch in her heartbeat.

Don't get carried away. Good sex. No, great sex. Is all about physical gratification. And nothing whatsoever to do with emotion.

But even knowing that, she couldn't resist the heavy beat of contentment as she stroked her hands over the long muscles of his back. Maybe this was only short-term, but however long it lasted, while it lasted, he would be all hers. The thought made her a little giddy.

She trailed her fingers over the bumps of his spine, smiled at his soft grunt of acknowledgement. And felt a little smug at the knowledge that she had exhausted him.

She stopped, her brows bunching, as her fingertips encountered two puckered scars high on his hip. 'What's this?' she asked.

He lifted up, rolled off her, dislodging her hands. Propping himself up on one elbow, he leaned over her. 'That was really something,' he murmured, dropping a proprietary kiss on her nose. 'For an amateur, you're awfully good at that,' he said, echoing her earlier compliment.

Her heartbeat kicked up a notch at the approval in his eyes and she forced herself not to care that he hadn't answered her question. She could always ask him again.

After all, they couldn't spend all their time together making love. If what had just happened was anything to go by, they'd end up killing each other. Funny to think, though, that she was just as excited about the time they would spend together out of bed as well as in it.

He placed one heavy palm on her midriff, traced the edge of her belly button with his fingertip. She felt the surprising jolt of arousal at her core, and wiggled out from under him. 'Now don't start that again,' she said, bending over to scoop her dress off the floor.

'Why not?'

She sent him a wry look over her shoulder. 'I need a quick shower, if that's okay? And then I need breakfast.' Her lips hitched. He looked so impossibly tempting with that puzzled frown etched on his brow. 'A girl can't live on great sex alone, you know.'

'This is true.' He got out of bed on the other side. She watched him locate his boxer shorts, admired the tight orbs of his backside flexing as he bent to pick them up.

No wonder he was so comfortable naked. Why would anyone so staggeringly good-looking ever have a reason to be self-conscious? But somehow the thought of his looks didn't feel intimidating any more. Maybe because of the memory of his face, harsh with desire and demand, as he'd climaxed.

He pulled the boxers up his legs, and the strips of sunlight rippled over the scars she'd felt on his back. And suddenly she knew exactly what had caused them. 'Who shot you?'

He twisted round. Glanced back. 'Huh?'

She pointed to the circular, puckered scars. 'There on your back—those are bullet wounds, aren't they?'

'Yeah.' He sounded nonchalant, but didn't offer an explanation.

'What happened?' she pressed—the distressing

thought of him being shot and in pain making the happy glow from their lovemaking dim considerably.

He shrugged. 'I messed up.'

'How?'

He glanced at her. 'You really want to know?'

'Yes, I really want to know,' she pressed some more, ignoring the shuttered expression.

He heaved a sigh, but to her surprise began to talk. 'We were on a stake-out. A low-level meth head. But we had intell he was in contact with the area's main dealer. When he turned up he had a girl with him. She was strung-out, looked no more than thirteen or fourteen and he...' Zane paused, shrugged, the movement so stiff it made Iona's breath get trapped in her throat. 'I broke cover, against orders and got shot for my trouble, and we didn't pick up the dealer.'

'You protected her,' she murmured, her chest tight.

He looked up, his gaze blank with memory. 'She was a kid. I couldn't sit by and do nothing.'

No, she thought, someone like him with such a strong streak of integrity wouldn't. No wonder she felt so safe with him. 'You did the right thing,' she murmured, impossibly touched by another tiny insight into his past and what it revealed about him.

He gave a harsh laugh. 'My commander didn't think so. He said the kid was collateral damage. I got suspended from duty and quit two months later.'

'You still did the right thing.' Did he doubt it?

He hitched a shoulder, his gaze sharp and intent. 'Maybe.'

He strolled round to her side of the bed, took her hand and hauled her up. 'Let's go grab a shower.' His hands strayed down to her naked behind, squeezed.

She wriggled out of his arms, her emotions suddenly too full to risk that kind of intimacy. 'I don't think so,' she said, keeping her voice light and flirtatious. 'If we shower together we'll get distracted. And it'll be midday before we have breakfast.'

'I've never known a woman to eat like you do.'

'Do you have a problem with that?' she said coquettishly, knowing from his admiring gaze that he didn't.

'Not at all. One of the things I love about you is your appetite,' he said, but she wasn't convinced he was still talking about food.

He grinned as the blush fired up her neck, but didn't offer any objections when she pulled her dress over her head. He might not be self-conscious about his nakedness, but suddenly she was.

Getting off the bed, he sighed. 'Okay, I'll shower in the guest bath,' he said. 'You can take this one. Then I promise to feed you.' He crossed his fingers over his chest. 'But in return I'm gonna expect lots of really dirty sexual favours.'

She scooped up the maple-syrup bottle on the nightstand, inspired by the mischievous look in his eyes and grateful that the rush of emotion had been replaced by the surge of lust. 'Watch it, Montoya, I am now in charge of the syrup bottle.'

He gave a low groan as she swirled her tongue around the neck of the bottle, then lapped at the drops of syrup that had dripped down from the lid. 'And I'm more than prepared to use it,' she finished before shooting off to the bathroom—with his pained shout of frustration echoing in her ears.

She closed the door, her heartbeat thumping with exhilaration and something she refused to address.

This affair wasn't a big deal. But why shouldn't she take pleasure in getting a peek behind that mask of devil-may-care charm he wore so easily—to discover the fascinating and complex man beneath? A man she would have the time to discover fully in the weeks ahead.

And if she had to use really dirty sexual favours to do it?

She laughed, the throaty chuckle filled with a sexual confidence she'd never felt before in her life.

Well goodness, it was a tough job, but someone had to do it.

ELEVEN

'Don't worry, girl, not long now.' Iona smiled at C.D., who gave her tail a lazy flap on the deck, keeping up her patient vigil for Zane.

Funny to think she and Zane had been having their casual sex-fling for nearly a month now. The time had passed in a blur of hard work, lazy dates and seriously hot sex—which had only got hotter when she'd moved into his place a week ago.

She'd had her misgivings at first, more than a little concerned about taking him up on his offer of a place to stay when his friend had got a vacation renter for the cottage. She knew she needed to be careful about coming to depend on him too much. But she'd been spending so much time at his place anyway in the weeks before that, he'd managed to make her objections seem like a childish overreaction. They were both adults, both completely clear about what this was and what it wasn't, and why should she go hunting up a new place when he was perfectly happy to have her stay here?

In the end she'd agreed, putting her mind at rest about the intensity of their affair by promising herself as soon as she had the required funds, she would book her return flight to Scotland.

She dabbed the ochre watercolour onto the pet portrait she'd been commissioned to do by one of Zane's clients—and ignored the flicker of dismay because she hadn't quite got round to booking the flight, yet.

It was simply because she was having such a good time here. Carefree and fun—and she'd also found a surprisingly fulfilling and lucrative outlet for her art.

Never having managed to find any seasonal work in Monterey, she'd been helped out of a financial hole when her neighbour in Pacific Grove, Mrs Mendoza, had asked her to paint a portrait of her Jack Russell, Zapata. Mr Spencer's cat Figaro was her tenth commission, the new cottage industry providing her with another practical reason to stay at Zane's. With all its natural light, his beach house was the perfect place to paint. She choked out a little laugh—and then of course there were the other, more exhilarating benefits of living here to consider.

Zane had looked so surprised when she'd joined him in his shower this morning, he'd dropped the soap. And risen to full attention so fast she'd been a little worried he might collapse from the loss of blood to his head.

For someone whose sex life prior to Zane had been spectacularly bad, the way he reacted to her never failed to thrill her. Hearing his heartfelt groan when she'd sunk to her knees and swirled her tongue over the head of that beautiful erection had been yet more proof that she now had the ability to make men weak at the knees. Or at least this man.

She loved the way he responded so readily to her teasing and her playfulness. Finding Zane's buttons, and pushing them, discovering his limits and then charging right through them had become as addictive as the man himself, and all the things he could do to her.

Iona dropped her brush into the turpentine, and stretched her spine, casting a critical eye on the portrait of the slightly moth-eaten but wise-eyed rescue cat.

She felt pleasantly fatigued and a little achy from standing in the same position while C.D. dozed beside her. She felt the answering ache tug her abdomen at the thought of Zane's imminent return, and grinned.

She rinsed the paintbrushes and packed them up ready for tomorrow. Drawing the easel up, she carried it and the half-finished painting into the house and stowed them in the alcove where Zane had suggested she keep her supplies. The dog's claws skidded on the wooden flooring as Iona slid the screen door closed and headed for the kitchen with C.D. at her heels.

As the weather was a little cooler than it had been the last two days, she'd put together a lasagne. She enjoyed cooking, had learned how as a young girl when she and her father had had to survive on their own. But she'd forgotten how much she enjoyed cooking for others. And now she could use Zane's state-of-the-art kitchen—instead of the tiny kitchenette at the cottage—it had become a real pleasure again. Of course, he'd moaned at first about her paying for all the grocery shopping, but she'd finally convinced him that if he wouldn't accept any rent he'd have to let her at least do this much to pay her way.

After ladling out C.D.'s chow and getting the dog a fresh bowl of water, she began searching for the salad ingredients in the fridge. Funny how after only a week in Zane's house, they'd settled so easily into a routine.

She glanced at the clock on the kitchen wall. Six o'clock. He'd be home in about an hour—and they'd be able to have a leisurely walk with C.D. before they had dinner. Or maybe they'd opt for sex first and dinner later.

The grin widened.

Quite apart from the empowering sex, she'd also got a surprising insight into the man in the last week. He still generally avoided talking about himself much, but their routine had allowed him to relax more and so she'd managed to weasel a few more details out of him, especially about his work.

It was so strange now, she thought as she sliced tomato and shredded lettuce, to think that when she'd first met him she'd been so critical, and more than a little suspicious about what he did for a living. Now she knew about the huge diversity of work his firm provided and how closely he supervised and controlled every aspect of it, she could see why keeping a similar rein on every other aspect of his personal life might be natural for him.

Zane exhibited a real dedication to duty in everything he did, which had made him not only a staggeringly successful entrepreneur, but also any woman's dream lover. But it was when she managed to shake that precious control that she enjoyed their time together the most.

C.D. sent up a series of exited yips, nearly making Iona slice off her thumb, before her less-sensitive hearing picked up the hum of a car engine in the driveway.

She was drying her hands on a dishcloth when the bell chimed. Excitement tickled her skin as she headed down the hallway. Was Zane home early?

Tonight might well be an evening for sex first, dinner later. Her lips twitched. In fact, she might have to insist upon it.

The excitement fizzled, though, when she spotted the silhouette through the glass bricks that framed the front door. That wasn't Zane. And then a white envelope popped through the letter slot.

She picked up her pace and opened the door, grabbing hold of C.D.'s collar to stop the dog barrelling after the woman already strolling back to a shiny red Beemer—with a baby perched on her hip.

'Hello, can I help you?' Iona called after her visitor, her disappointment turning to curiosity as she lifted the heavy envelope from the mat and spotted Zane's name in ornate lettering.

The woman swung round in a circle, making the baby giggle. 'Oh, hi,' she said. 'I thought there was no one in.'

She walked back and Iona felt the prickle of envy at the woman's tall, lithe figure. She exuded the slim, poised confidence of a supermodel with her short, classically cut blonde bob, which accentuated her amazing bone structure and a pair of stunning emerald eyes. The simple cotton summer dress that flowed around long legs and a cropped jean jacket only added to her funky glamour. The baby, who Iona would have guessed was about a year old, had soft curls of dark hair that framed a round face—and appeared to be blessed with the same easy smile and flawless petal-soft skin as his mother.

'I'm so sorry to bother you. Are you Zane's housekeeper?' the woman said, still smiling politely.

A panicked little flutter set up under Iona's breastbone. Okay, this was a little awkward.

The baby clutched a hand of his mother's hair in one fat little fist, and stared owlishly at Iona. As his mother laughed and extricated herself Iona got a much better look at the child. And the panicked flutter became a blast of astonishment.

The child had the same striking, translucent blue eyes as Zane, even down to the unusual dark rim around the irises.

Good Lord. Did Zane have a child he hadn't mentioned to her? She knew he was tight-lipped but that would be ridiculous, surely?

'Um, no, not exactly,' Iona stuttered. Not quite sure what the etiquette was in this situation. 'My name's Iona MacCabe,' she said, deciding that honesty was probably the best policy. 'I'm sort of living here, at the moment.'

The woman looked disconcerted, but gathered herself quickly, the curious smile staying in place. If she was Zane's babymama she seemed remarkably nonchalant about the new arrangements.

'You're Scottish,' she remarked.

'And you're English,' Iona replied, having been so preoccupied with the baby's eyes she had only just recognised the crisp cut-off vowels of her neighbouring countryman.

'How lovely,' the woman said, apparently sincere, and held out her hand. 'Hi, I'm Tess Tremaine. Oh, bugger...' she said, clapping her hand to her forehead as her smile became sheepish. 'Sorry, Tess Graystone. Would you believe it? We've been married for months and I can never remember to use his name.'

She shook Iona's hand with surprising vigour while the baby continued to stare, its fist now stuffed in its mouth.

'Nate thinks it's a Freudian slip because I'm secretly planning to run off with our estate manager, Manolito.' She rolled her eyes charmingly. 'As if! The poor man's seventy if he's a day...'

The husky chuckle at her own joke made Iona smile,

liking the woman. And Nate had to be her husband, so maybe she was mistaken about the baby.

'I think I owe your husband a debt of gratitude,' Iona said. 'I was staying in his cottage in Pacific Grove up until about a week ago.'

'That was you?' The woman's eyes lit now with a mixture of both excitement and curiosity. 'And now you're *sort of* living with Zane?'

Iona nodded, not sure why she was getting such an enthusiastic reception, but willing to go with it. 'Yes, that would be me.'

'How intriguing.' The woman jiggled the baby on her hip, making him giggle. 'I'm afraid I'm now going to have to invite myself in for a cup of tea and quiz you mercilessly. Because I've only ever met a couple of Zane's girlfriends and I've got to tell you—' Tess's gaze flickered over Iona, making her hopelessly self-conscious about her paint-flecked T-shirt, faded cut-offs and bare feet '—they were both boringly predictable in comparison to you.'

Iona huffed out a laugh, relieved at the woman's cheeky smile and her apparent candour, and desperately curious herself. 'You're more than welcome to come in for a cuppa,' Iona offered. But as she stepped back to let Tess into the house she got another good look at the toddler who stared at her with Zane's eyes and had to add, 'As long as you don't mind me quizzing you about Zane right back.'

'That seems only fair,' Tess said easily, bouncing the baby on her hip as they walked down the hallway towards the kitchen. 'Although I can't imagine I'm going to be much use. Even though Zane and Nate have been friends for ever, I'm afraid to say, ever since Brandon here was born, he's been a bit of a stranger. That's why I'm here, actually.' She nodded at the invite still clutched in Iona's fingers. 'To make sure he shows for the christening. I'm a little tired of us all pussy-footing around the issue of Zane's relationship to Brandon. So I was going to try to guilt him into making an appearance.'

Iona placed the invitation carefully on the countertop and filled the kettle. *Zane's relationship to Brandon?* So he was the baby's father.

The odd clutch in the pit of Iona's stomach made no sense, so she ignored it. She was just a casual fling—and Tess was the mother of his child. She had no call to feel possessive or resentful—or hurt. But as she pulled two mugs out of the cabinet she did feel she had a reason to be annoyed with Zane. Why hadn't he told her about the boy? The cup clattered onto the countertop as her fingers shook. Surely even a casual fling deserved that much information?

'Is something wrong?' Tess asked, touching Iona's arm. 'You look rather pale.'

'Yes, I...' Iona began, righting the cup and turning to Tess, whose inquisitiveness was now tempered with concern. Iona sighed, deciding it was probably best to just spill it. She'd never had much time for pussy-footing about either. 'You're being ludicrously reasonable about all this, Tess. And I don't know what the circumstances are surrounding the wee lad's birth.' For all she knew Zane might have donated sperm for his friend Nate. 'Zane didn't tell me about Brandon,' she continued, picking up the invite. 'Or this... But I guarantee you, I'm not the one stopping him from visiting his son.'

Tess's perfectly plucked eyebrows launched up her forehead, and then she let out a delighted laugh. 'You have no idea how priceless that is.'

'Why?' Iona asked, starting to feel as if she'd entered an alternative reality.

Tess gave her son a kiss on the nose. 'Brandon's not Zane's son. He's my husband's son. He's Nate's son.'

Iona stared at the boy again. And Zane's eyes stared straight back at her. 'But then how comes he has the same—?'

'Because that sky-blue colour and the dark ring around is a genetic anomaly,' Tess interrupted, clearly knowing exactly what Iona was referring to. 'An anomaly that runs very strongly through the male line in the Graystone family,' Tess added, her tone patient. 'Zane is Nate's brother. Or rather his half-brother. They have the same father.' The woman's smile faded. 'Not that anyone's allowed to mention it. Because as it happens, pig-headedness also runs very strongly through the male line in the Graystone family.'

Iona stared, having been given more information about Zane's father in a single sentence than she'd managed to prise out of him in a month. The one time she'd asked about his father, his reaction had been so cold and dismissive she'd never made the mistake of mentioning it again.

'Doggie,' the baby chortled and gestured wildly at C.D., cutting through Iona's thoughts.

'Why don't you go and give Cookie Dough a hug?' Tess said, letting the baby down and holding his hand as he toddled over to the dog's basket.

Iona's curiosity levels shot straight to fever pitch as she watched C.D. accept the baby's attentions with a patient thump of her tail.

So the *pinche gringo* was his best friend Nate's father too. And Tess seemed like a very nice, and very talkative woman, who was more than willing to be quizzed on the subject.

Iona depressed the switch on the kettle. 'How much time have you got, Tess?' she asked. 'I have a feeling this is going to take more than one cup of tea.'

Tess laughed and checked her watch. 'I'm at your disposal, for at least another half hour.'

Iona prepared the teapot, hunted up some chocolate cookies she'd made two days ago, and dismissed the twinge of guilt at talking about something behind Zane's back that he'd gone to great lengths to keep private.

The man had shoe-horned pretty much every detail of her personal life previous to the moment she'd met him out of her during their long walks on the beach and over dinner every evening, and ante'd up very little in return, despite Iona's concerted efforts in that direction—really dirty sexual favours included. Frankly, she was obliged to take Tess up on her offer—so she didn't expire from curiosity like the proverbial cat.

And anyway, this was what happened when you dated a detective. You were forced to get sneaky back.

'But that's ridiculous,' Iona remarked, dunking her second cookie into the now tepid cup of tea. 'How can they be best friends, know that they're also brothers and yet never talk about it? Or even acknowledge it?'

'It's beyond ridiculous.' Tess hugged her son, who sat on her lap busy gumming his cookie into a soggy mess. 'Especially now we have Brandon. Zane's his uncle and yet we're not allowed to say so.' She hitched her shoulders in an exaggerated shrug. 'All I know is that they did talk about it when they were kids. And as a result of what happened, Nate refuses to bring it up again, until

Zane says something first. And Zane never has. In fact, I have a suspicion that's why he's made himself scarce ever since Brandon was born. So now we're at this ridiculous impasse. You see what I mean about the pig-headedness.'

'What happened when they talked about it as kids?'

'To be honest, Nate doesn't talk about it much, because it still hurts, I suspect. He totally idolised Zane as a boy when he first went to live with his grandfather at San Revelle,' she said, mentioning the fanciful castle that Nate's great-grandfather had built near Half-Moon Bay and where Tess and her family now lived. 'Maria worked as his grandfather's housekeeper and she and Zane lived on the estate, so Nate spent all his free time at their cottage. Nate only found out years later that she'd gone to work there after Nate's parents had kicked her out.'

For getting pregnant by Nate's father, Iona thought, still disgusted by what Tess had already told her of Maria's past and the behaviour of a man who had seduced a teenager in his employ and then discarded her like so much rubbish as soon as her pregnancy started to show. Seemed Juana's assessment of Harrison Graystone was correct.

The Gallivanting Graystones, as the society press had dubbed Nate's parents, had both died in a light aircraft crash over a decade ago, en route to a party in Martha's Vineyard, but had left few people to grieve their parting, least of all their son Nate, who had been estranged from them both for years.

Iona thought it desperately sad, though, that the bad seeds Harrison Graystone had sown could end up destroying the friendship between his two sons. Why couldn't Nate and Zane be brothers, even if their father had disowned one and never acknowledged the other?

Especially as they had bonded so young—and had remained friends despite everything.

Tess sighed as she wiped Brandon's mouth with a tissue. 'All I know is that when Nate discovered the truth about Zane's parentage he was overjoyed. He'd always wanted a proper family and he already thought of Maria as a surrogate mother. So naturally, he raced down to the cottage to tell Zane without thinking about Zane's reaction...' Tess's voice trailed off, as if even she couldn't bear to recall what she'd been told. 'He was only twelve, for Pete's sake.'

'What happened?' Iona prompted.

'Zane went berserk,' Tess said softly. 'He punched Nate and kept on punching him until Maria pulled them apart.'

Iona gasped, her stomach hurting now, not only at the thought of what Nate had endured, but also at how angry and confused Zane must have been to react in that way.

He'd once told her he'd been wild as a teenager, but Iona couldn't imagine him being violent. It simply didn't jibe with the man she had come to know—because beneath Zane's lazy, devilishly sexy charm was a man who always strived to keep his emotions on lockdown. It was what made seducing him such a delicious challenge. But now she was beginning to wonder if his control wasn't a symptom of something painful and much more deep-seated than simply a desire to be in charge in bed.

'Do you think Zane might have been in shock?' Iona asked. 'And that's why he lashed out?'

'No, it's more complicated than that.' Tess shook her head. 'Nate's convinced he already knew who his father was. Which is why Nate refuses to mention it to Zane again. Zane rejected their connection once, in the most graphic way possible—so Nate reverted to the Guy Code to salvage their friendship.'

'The Guy Code?'

'Avoidance as the better part of valour.' Tess got up from the stool to bounce Brandon on her hip, who had become a little fussy now his second cookie had been demolished. 'They pretend it never happened.' Tess scoffed. 'Which is patently counterproductive, but Nate refuses to budge.' She pulled a multicoloured rattle out of her purse, and waved it in front of Brandon—who grabbed it and wedged it into his mouth.

'So you thought you might be able to persuade Zane to talk about it instead?' Iona said as realisation dawned. 'By making sure he comes to the christening?'

'Yes, Brandon's even named after him—Zane's his middle name—so I thought if he came he might...' Tess plopped back on her stool, her son now drooling contentedly over the chew-toy. 'It's a stupid idea, isn't it?' she said, resigned. 'Zane makes Nate look like an amateur when it comes to avoidance.' She pushed out a breath. 'But seriously, I'm desperate. I feel like there's this big elephant in the room every time we see him, and, while the two of them are busy avoiding it, I keep tripping over it. I want to know why they can't be brothers as well as friends. And I think Nate does too, although of course he won't say so. But it's worse than that. A week ago Nate asked Zane to be Bran's godfather and he point-blank refused—I think they had a bit of a row about it, in fact, but of course Nate won't talk about that either now.'

'When is the christening?' Iona asked, knowing she shouldn't be interfering, but not quite able to stop herself.

She liked Tess. Had warmed to her instantly, in fact, even when she had believed she might be the mother of Zane's son. And could totally sympathise with Tess's frustration—because she'd been on the receiving end of Zane's stone-walling too.

But more importantly than that, her heart ached for Zane. Why was he so determined to isolate himself, not just from Nate and his nephew, but also from his mother's family too?

Hearing Tess talk about his reaction to Nate's news had reminded her of the tense, distant way he had handled Maria's family at the *quinceañera*. The more people reached out to him, it seemed, the more he tried to pull away. What was it that made it so hard for him to let people get close?

Iona didn't think for a second that she had any special insight into the answer. But she knew it wasn't a good thing. Zane needed that in his life, she knew he did, because during their lovemaking, on those rare occasions when Zane's guard was down, she got a tiny glimpse of all those needs that he was busy pretending didn't exist.

Maybe it was foolish of her, but she wanted to help him in whatever small way she could. Surely that was the least she could do, after the many ways in which he had helped her?

'The christening's next Thursday, the twenty-fifth,' Tess said.

'Right,' Iona replied, trying to think of how she could bring it up with Zane.

'Do you think you could get him to come?' Tess asked, her eyes lighting with enthusiasm. 'I know it's a big ask—and I shouldn't really involve you in all this—but I'm all out of ideas.'

'I'll give him the invite.' She picked the envelope up. 'And make sure he reads it. I'm afraid that's all I can promise.' She didn't hold out much hope of persuading Zane to do anything, especially as she was only a casual fling. But surely it couldn't hurt to at least try.

'That's brilliant, Iona, and so sweet of you.'

'Do you want to give me your phone number, and I'll let you know if I have any luck?'

'Yes, of course.' Tess whipped out her mobile phone and they exchanged numbers. 'So now you need to tell me more about you and Zane.'

'Oh, there's really nothing much to tell. We're just a casual thing...' she said, the words oddly leaden on her tongue all of a sudden... 'It's no serious. Which is why I wouldn't get your hopes up too high about me being able to persuade Zane to come to the christening.'

She tried to shrug off the melancholy thought. She needed to keep a good firm grip on the fact that, however much she might want to help Tess, Zane's family wasn't her family.

'But that's...' Tess's mouth pursed into a thin line. 'That's silly. How can you possibly be a casual thing when you're living in his house?'

'It's not really significant,' Iona said, prevaricating deliberately. Even though she knew Zane and her weren't serious, had never been serious, she didn't want to tell Tess exactly how not serious they were.

'But you're sleeping together? Aren't you?'

'Aye, but only because...' God, why did their arrangement suddenly sound a little sordid? 'Well, it's fun and convenient.' And casual... Remember casual.

Tess blinked. 'Iona, now this is just me being nosey, and obviously I've only just met you. But did Zane ever mention his Golden Rules to you?'

'Golden Rules? No.'

Tess let Brandon wriggle down off her lap, and watched him crawl over to C.D., before turning her attention back to Iona. 'Okay, this is second-hand, because Zane told these to Nate and then I managed to shoehorn them out of Nate when I said how odd I thought it was that Zane had never been snared by some lucky woman. You know, because he's so available and so confident with women and so handsome and so ridiculously sexy—I mean, the man's practically got a sign on him that says "I can make you come till you pass out."'

Iona laughed, while at the same time feeling her cheeks heat.

Tess pointed. 'Bloody hell, I knew he would be phenomenal in bed. He is, isn't he?'

Iona coughed out a laugh as embarrassment warred with smugness. 'Well, I'm no a great judge, because my sex life sucked before I met him—but I will say that, for once, the advertising doesn't lie.'

'Stop right there, before I have to slap you.' Tess held up her hand in mock indignation. 'Do you have any idea how much a toddler mucks up your sex life? These days me and Nate have to make an appointment to have an orgasm. And foreplay? Forget it.'

Iona laughed. 'So what are Zane's Golden Rules?' This should be interesting.

'Okay, let me see if I can remember these correctly. First off, he never sleeps with anyone on a first date, because he doesn't like to appear too pushy.'

'Oh.' Iona felt her colour rising again.

'Ah-ha, I'm getting the impression from that lovely shade of pink that he broke that rule.'

'Well, I...'

'How about this one, then? Another of Zane's Golden

Rules is that he always gives his dates The Speech.' Tess did air quotes. 'Before he sleeps with them.'

'What Speech?'

'You haven't even had The Speech? About how this is strictly short-term and lightweight and not to get too attached.'

'Ah, well, yes, he did sort of give me that.' Hadn't he said something along those lines the first morning they'd spent here?

'Only sort of?' Tess gave a considering hum. 'That still sounds like a fairly significant departure from Zane Montoya's Golden Rules of Non-Engagement.' She did a quick check on Brandon, who was busy tugging on the ever-patient C.D.'s one good ear. 'Especially as we already know the last two are already toast.'

'What are they?'

Tess lifted her fingers to count them off. 'He doesn't let dates meet his family—and you went to his cousin's party, right? He even invited you specially.'

'But I think he only did that under duress,' Iona qualified, starting to feel very uneasy.

'Fine, but it's still breaking the rules, and, most important of all, he never lets women move in with him. Period.'

'What? Never?'

Tess shook her head. 'I think he had some live-in girlfriends back when he was a cop and he told Nate they would freak out when he did overtime or nightshifts and didn't mention it. In other words, they had the audacity to make demands on him like any normal person would. So these days anything beyond the occasional sleepover is too heavy for Zane. And yet here you are, living in his house.' Tess sniffed the air. 'Cooking him delicious din-

ners. Working on your art. Bonding with his beloved dog.'
Tess's grin widened. 'You may think this is casual, but all
the evidence suggests it's anything but for Zane.'

Iona felt the pit of her stomach swoop down to her
toes.

'Which brings me to my next question.' Tess leaned
forward, skewering Iona with a determined frown. 'What
exactly makes you think this isn't a serious relationship,
with serious potential?'

Iona opened her mouth, to say all the platitudes that
had come so easily a month ago. Because her real life was
in Scotland and she was buying a ticket home, soon. Because her arrangement with Zane was never meant to be
anything but temporary. Because they'd always agreed
that this was casual—and not serious.

But not one of them would come out of her mouth, because not one of them sounded true. Or at least not the
whole truth. Not any more.

'Th-there are a lot of reasons,' Iona stammered, and
heard how lame that sounded.

Tess's eyebrow arched. 'I'm sure there are, but aren't
there also some reasons to think this might be a lot more
than the casual relationship you say it is? Like Zane's a
fascinating, complex, intriguing and gorgeous guy—and
you seem to be the only woman who's ever got under his
guard?' Tess rocked back on the stool. 'Of course, if one
of those reasons is you're not enjoying being with him—'

'But I am,' Iona interrupted, only to realise she'd given
herself away big time when Tess's smile became a little
conniving.

There was a heavy clatter and both women turned to
see Brandon sitting on his butt on the marble floor, his
face screwed up in a horrified grimace.

Tess jumped off the stool and scooped him up before the wail let loose. 'Bran, baby, it didn't hurt that much.' She settled the baby on her hip, apparently unfazed by the decibel level as her son howled as if he'd been stabbed in the eye with a hot poker.

'I better go,' she said, cooing at him. 'He only had a twenty-minute nap this afternoon so this is merely the start of the meltdown.' Gathering up her purse from the countertop, Tess leaned in to give Iona a kiss on the cheek. 'It was wonderful to meet you, Iona. And I really, really hope this isn't the last time I see you.'

'I'll do my best to get Zane to Brandon's christening,' she said as Tess's long-legged stride took her down the hallway ahead of her.

Tess paused on the doorstep, Brandon's howls subsiding to choking sobs. 'If you can at least get him to consider coming, I'd be eternally grateful.' She took Iona's hand in hers and gave it a quick reassuring squeeze. 'But could you do me an even bigger favour?'

'What's that?'

'Don't run off back to Scotland too soon. Zane's an amazing guy for all his pig-headedness, and I think he deserves someone special who can shake up his life— and get past all that industrial-strength charm to the man beneath.'

The shot of adrenaline returned, accompanied by the kick of panic.

'But how do you know I'm that someone?' Iona asked, the panic starting to choke her.

Tess shrugged. 'I don't, but then neither do you. And if you leave without giving this relationship a sporting chance, you never will.' She bounced the baby on her hip, her voice sobering. 'I guess it boils down to whether you want to find out for sure?'

With those disturbing parting words, Tess headed off down the driveway. After loading the now hiccoughing Brandon into his car seat, she sent Iona a jaunty wave goodbye.

Iona stood on the doorstep, watching the shiny Beemer turn into Seventeen Mile Drive and disappear from view. Her heart galloped into her throat.

She pressed her hand to her shaky tummy...feeling a little nauseous.

She checked her watch. Zane would be back soon. And for once she wished he'd take his time. What if Tess were right? She already knew this wasn't as casual for her as it should be, or she would have bought her ticket home by now. But what if it wasn't casual for Zane either? And did she have the guts to find out for sure? To risk having him reject her?

And how the heck was she going to eat the lasagne she'd spent an hour preparing earlier, when her tummy was doing cartwheels?

TWELVE

───────

'That's great. Let's schedule a conference call tomorrow with your contact in Ocean Beach, then we can turn over the evidence to the San Diego PD.' Zane pushed a hand through his hair and ended the call to his detective.

They were within days of catching the scammer who'd been selling non-existent luxury cars on an Internet auction site, but the sweet rush that usually accompanied closing any big investigation was conspicuous by its absence. Probably because his mind had been less and less on work lately and more and more on what he was missing while he spent the long hours his business demanded away from Iona.

Iona. With her bright, teasing smile, her warm golden-brown eyes, her funny, forthright conversation and that lush full mouth that could drive him wild and scare the hell out of him at one and the same time.

In the last week, ever since she'd moved in with him, it had become a major struggle to leave her every morning, and harder still to stay tied to his desk until he could return each evening. And he knew why. Because every moment he was away from her he could feel the time they had left together slipping through his fingers. The last month had shot past in a haze of spectacular sex and scintillating conversation and easy companionship and he could already see the day when she would get on a plane and return home to Scotland racing towards them at breakneck speed.

Rising from his desk, he opened his briefcase to stuff in the papers he was supposed to be reviewing this evening, but knew he was unlikely even to look at.

It was plain dumb and illogical to be worrying about her leaving so much, when that had always been the plan. But the more time he spent with Iona, the more dumb and illogical he seemed to get.

He grabbed his suit jacket from the hook behind the door and headed down the corridor.

He'd had spectacular sex before and scintillating conversation, but it was the quiet times when he knew he didn't have to talk, didn't have to charm, didn't have to make her feel good because she was already there that he had become really addicted to.

This urgency, this need to have her, would eventually pass. But when? They were a month in and it was showing no signs of waning, yet. He rolled his shoulders, the muscles contracting at the thought of the fifteen-minute drive home before he could see her.

The last couple of evenings, he'd had to put in a titanic effort not to fall on her like a starving man as soon as he got home. He rubbed the back of his neck as he strode through the building. Hell, yesterday evening, when they'd been on the beach, C.D. barking at the surf, she'd laughed and the husky, smoky sound had arrowed right through him—and all of a sudden, he'd been hard as an iron spike.

He gave Jim an absent wave as he passed his office. His mind already focused on putting a stranglehold on the growing warmth in his crotch. How many times in the last few weeks had he driven home with a hard-on? It was a damn miracle he hadn't totalled the mustang on Highway One.

As he walked into the parking lot, the buzz of his cell phone cut the evening quiet. Pulling it out, he spotted his mother's name on the display. Unlocking the mustang, he dumped his briefcase on the passenger seat, and tossed the cell on top, ignoring the prickle of guilt as he waited for the call to go to voicemail.

He'd hardly spoken to his mother since the *quinceañera* a month ago, because when he had it hadn't gone well. For years his mother had tried to get him to talk about his father. And for years he'd never had too much of a problem deflecting her.

But in the last week, ever since he'd turned down his friend Nate's request to become his son Bran's godfather, he'd found it harder and harder to deal with his mother.

Zane's shoulders cramped as the cell stopped ringing. He'd have to call her soon, he knew that, but not tonight. Not when his addiction to Iona was already tying his brain in knots.

Avoidance *was* the answer and it always had been when it came to the question of his relationship with his father, and Nate, and his son Bran, because the alternative was unthinkable. And he couldn't risk going there again.

He flexed his fingers, his knuckles throbbing at the sudden memory of that morning when he'd been four-teen years old and he'd hit his best friend and kept on hitting him. Connecting with bone, feeling Nate's flesh tear, seeing the sticky blood splatter Nate's favourite Spiderman T-shirt, hearing the startled whimpers of pain, the thud of the blows as they landed—and feeling nothing, not even the smarting skin on his knuckles, until his mother's screams had cut through the rage.

The jolt of shame hit harder as he recalled the look on Nate's face last week when his friend had asked him to be Bran's godfather, and he'd come up with some lie about not being all that into kids.

Nate had been shocked and saddened but had remained silent. And Zane hadn't had the guts to tell him the real reason he couldn't be Bran's godfather.

He was into kids, especially Nate's kid; Bran fascinated him. He could still recall the staggering feeling, tinged with awe, when he'd arrived at the maternity hospital last April and this tiny perfect bundle of humanity had been cradled in Nate's arms. But as Bran had grown, seeing him had brought back echoes of the quiet all-consuming rage that had dogged his every step as a teenager and been kept so carefully contained as an adult.

Brandon was another child with Harrison Graystone's eyes. And that meant Zane couldn't bear to spend too much time with the boy.

He straightened, his shoulders screaming with tension. The sun beating down on him through the car window did nothing to melt the fury and disgust settling in his gut like a block of ice.

His mother didn't know, would never know, how much he already knew about his father, Harrison Graystone. And he would never let her know, because she'd already suffered enough. So until he found a better strategy for avoiding the conversation she seemed determined to have with him about Nate, and Bran and his father, he was forced to avoid her calls instead.

He turned on the transmission and cranked up the AC. But as the clammy sweat dried on his brow he pressed his foot on the gas, speeding back to his house on the bay. Because he knew only one thing would chase away the chill.

Iona.

Sinking into her hot, wet flesh, hearing her broken sobs as she fisted around him would make it all go away— for another day.

C.D.'s sudden barks from the hallway had Iona juggling the lasagne. Her heart rate jumped as she heard the low murmur of Zane's voice and the front door slamming.

And then her heart stopped completely as he walked into the kitchen. How could she not have noticed how seeing his face still took her breath away even now? But then she noticed the creases at the corners of his eyes as he slung his briefcase onto the countertop and the deep grooves around his mouth. He looked shattered.

'Hey, honey, I'm home,' he said with a grim smile.

The dog jumped to prop her paws on his waist, but instead of making a fuss of her, as he usually did, he gave her an impatient shove. 'C.D., will you quit that now?'

C.D. returned to her basket, her tail drooping almost comically. But Iona wasn't laughing. Seemed she wasn't the only one who'd had a disturbing day.

'What's wrong?' she asked.

Strong fingers curled around her wrist and he hauled her towards him. 'Nothing you can't fix.'

He wrapped his arms around her in a hard hug, buried his face in her hair and took a deep breath. But tension vibrated through him as his palms cupped her bottom.

The rush of lust stemmed the panic as she felt the familiar weight of his erection. She hugged him back, absorbed the delicious spicy scent.

Sex was easy. Simple. And it would make her forget her cartwheeling tummy.

The long firm muscles of his back rippled through his shirt as she ran her hands down his spine and felt the steady punch of his heartbeat against her ear.

'Supper smells terrific,' he murmured, framing her face in rough palms. 'But I don't want food right now. I want you.'

'Then we're in luck,' she said as she let all her worries about how attached she was getting be consumed by the insistent arousal. 'Because I know how to reheat it.'

The rumble of his laughter made her heart leap painfully and then his lips covered hers. Making her forget everything but the touch, the taste, the scent of him.

He plunged his tongue into her mouth, his fingers moulding her buttocks, then fumbling with the button on her shorts. He swore and the button released. Searching fingers cupped her sex through her panties, making her swell against his hand.

'Zane, wait.' She pressed her hand over his to still the exploration, more than a little shaky. Sex was simple, so why did this suddenly feel like anything but?

'Why?' he demanded. 'You're soaking wet.'

'I know, it's...' She glanced over her shoulder, looking for a way to slow him down until she'd got the foolish vulnerability under control. And saw the dog watching their actions with big soulful eyes.

'We should take this upstairs,' she said. 'C.D.'s over there.'

'She's a dog, not a child,' he said, the tone sharp, but he dragged his hand out of her shorts.

Kicking the door open, he clicked his fingers. 'C.D. out.'

The dog slunk out, giving them a disconsolate look.

Zane slammed the door shut. 'Okay?'

'Yes, but...'

Before she could raise any more objections, his mouth swooped down. He grasped her waist and lifted her onto the counter. Dragging her shorts and panties down, he flung them away. Her naked bottom felt cold against the marble. She braced her hands behind her, shocked when he hooked her legs over his shoulders, forcing her to lean back and open for him completely.

He bent to flick his tongue over the swollen flesh. And then concentrated on driving her wild. The hot, rough strokes had her sobbing with staggered pleasure—the last of her defences crashing down as he set his mouth on her clitoris and suckled.

She tried to hold on, to hold back, to stop the rush of sensation devouring her but the ferocious orgasm slammed into her. The glorious wave crashing as she cried out her release.

He raised his head, those sapphire eyes dark with arousal as he released himself from his trousers. She clung to his neck, tasted herself on his lips, as he held her thighs apart, and plunged deep.

The raw shock of penetration—so full, so stretched— was nothing to the visceral shock of renewed arousal as he began to thrust—hard and fast. Digging his fingers into her hips, he held her powerless to resist the depth and intensity of his thrusts, the onslaught sending her back over the edge with alarming speed.

The endless orgasm crested, retreated and crested again. Until at last she shattered, her ragged sobs echoing off the cold hard surfaces.

He shouted as his own climax hit, his forehead slick with sweat as he buried his head against her neck and emptied himself into her.

Iona's hands trembled violently as she clasped the damp hair on Zane's nape, her body caught in the aftershock of the climax, her heart beating so hard she could feel it hitting her ribs.

What had just happened? She felt as if she'd survived a war—just barely survived it.

She groaned, the large erection still firm as he shifted then withdrew. Readjusting his trousers, he cursed and walked away, leaving her limp and trembling and shaken on the countertop.

She could feel the sticky residue of his semen as she climbed down, her legs like wet noodles as she picked up her knickers and cut-offs and put them on.

He stood by the kitchen's picture window, his shoulders and back rigid, his hands braced on the sink and his head bowed. The tail of his shirt hung outside his trousers.

'I'm sorry,' he whispered, the tone raw with an emotion she didn't understand.

His head lifted as she approached but he didn't look at her. The shadows of twilight cast his profile into harsh relief—the lines of exhaustion on his face more pronounced.

'I'm no better than he is.' The words came out on a barely audible murmur as if he were talking to himself.

'What are you apologising for?' she asked.

He dragged his hand through his hair as he turned to face her. 'I behaved like an animal. I didn't even take the time to suit up.'

'I could have asked you to stop if I'd wanted you to,' she replied, confused by the shame in his voice. 'I didn't.'

'What makes you think I would have stopped?'

'Because I know you,' she said, stunned by the question. 'And I know you would never do something like that.'

He shook his head. 'Which proves you don't know me at all.'

She placed her hand on his back, felt the bunched muscles through the creased cotton. 'Zane, what are you talking about? We had rough sex. Rough, consensual sex, which we both enjoyed.' She stroked trying to soothe the tremble of reaction. 'You have nothing to apologise for. I had more than one orgasm. And I happen to enjoy it more when you don't hold back.'

He huffed out a weary laugh, but the muscles remained rigid underneath her palm.

'Who were you talking about?' she asked, although she was sure she already knew. 'When you said you're no better than he is?'

His eyes met hers, the expression in them so sad, so confused she felt her heart constrict.

'My father. He raped my mother.' He straightened, and shoved bunched fists into his pockets. 'That's how I was conceived.'

Shock came first, swiftly followed by sadness at the controlled contempt in his voice. Was that why he strived so hard for control? Always struggled to hold back a part of himself? Because he thought he was responsible for that?

'How do you know? Did your mother tell you that?'

He stared at her blankly for a moment, then frowned. 'Of course not. I've never spoken to her about him,' he said in a broken voice. 'Why would I? When it would only hurt her more?'

She doubted that. The Maria Montoya she had met was a woman who loved her son. Iona couldn't imagine Maria wanting to see Zane suffer like this, any more than she did. 'But then how do you know it was rape?'

'Because I saw them together at the house where we lived, on his father's estate, when I was twelve years old.' The bitterness had returned, tenfold. 'When he tried to do it again.'

'Oh, God.' Iona touched shaking fingers to her mouth, so horrified at what both he and his mother had endured she was momentarily speechless. Had he seen his father assaulting his mother? It was too hideous to even contemplate. 'Zane.' She stroked his arm, trying to offer what little comfort she could. 'I'm so sorry.'

'It's okay—I said he tried. He didn't get away with it a second time. I saw him pawing her through the cottage window.' He shrugged. 'I thought they were kissing. I'd never seen my mother kiss a man before that.' His eyes met hers, the pain in them so naked, she felt her heart tearing in her chest. 'But as I watched through the window, I saw she wasn't kissing him back, she was struggling. I wanted to help her, to stop him, but I couldn't move.'

'Zane, you were probably in shock—it's not surprising.' He sounded so guilty, so disgusted with himself.

'Don't you get it? I didn't do anything.'

'Did he hurt her?' she asked, praying that he hadn't.

'No. She slapped him really hard. And he howled something about what was she getting so pissy about, she'd enjoyed it before. And then I heard her say "I didn't enjoy it, you raped me—and you know it. Don't ever come near me again, or I will kill you." And then he said, "If it was that bad, why did you have the kid?" And then I turned and ran. And I hid. I heard his car leave a few minutes later and when I finally got up the guts to return, she was there, making lunch. Pretending nothing had happened. But I could see her fingers shaking. I wanted to say something. To apologise. To make it better. But what could I say when I was a part of the man that had done that to her?'

'That's ridiculous, Zane,' she whispered. 'Is that why you won't acknowledge your brother Nate or his son?' she asked, understanding it all now, and her heart aching for Zane and his misguided guilt and stupid gallantry. Had the disgust he felt for his father—and for himself—been the trigger for that too? 'Because you're trying to protect your mother?'

Couldn't he see how foolish that was? And how unnecessary? She refused to believe Maria would have asked that of him. So why did he ask it of himself?

He looked stunned for a second, then his brows slashed down in a furious frown. 'How the hell do you know about Nate and me? You've never even met the guy.'

She didn't flinch at the hoarse accusation.

'Tess called round this afternoon to bring you this.' She pulled the invitation out of her pocket. 'Because she really wants you to go to Brandon's christening.'

She held out the envelope but he only stared at it, until she lowered it again.

'She had Brandon with her and I...' She paused. 'I mistakenly thought he might be yours. So she explained about you and Nate and we had a cup of tea... And a wee chat.'

He cursed under his breath. 'What's a wee chat? Is that Scottish for "I grilled Tess about something that was none of my damn business"?'

The closed fury on his face made it very obvious she'd stepped way over the line. Her throat thickened, the brittle accusation almost as brutal as the dismissal behind it.

If she'd wanted proof that this had never been more than casual for him, she had it now. Unfortunately, seeing the desolation in his eyes a moment ago had also forced her to acknowledge the truth—their relationship had never been casual for her.

In the last month, she'd come to depend on him and the way he made her feel: cherished and important and desirable, but worse than that Zane had made her feel needed, in those moments when he'd let his guard down.

But now she understood he hadn't needed her at all, not specifically. Everything he'd done for her, even the spectacular sex, had been a symptom of his need to protect her, just as he had needed to protect his mother, and that young girl being brutalised by a drug dealer, and probably every other woman he'd ever encountered.

'No, it's Scottish for Tess and I had a mature conversation about a man who matters to me,' she said, refusing to let him see how much his dismissal had hurt.

'I matter to you? Then maybe you should butt out of this.'

She flinched but refused to let the uncharacteristic show of temper derail her again. This wasn't about her. She could see that now.

Clearly Brandon's birth and his christening had brought Zane's issues with his father bubbling to the surface in the last year—she'd never been the special someone Tess had talked about; she'd simply been a convenient distraction.

But even so, she didn't intend to be a doormat too.

'They love you, Zane,' she continued. 'Not just Tess and Nate and your mother, but her family too. Don't you see how insane it is for you to shut them out, because of some pig-headed idea that you're responsible for your father's crimes?'

She would be leaving as soon as was feasibly possible. And she could never tell Zane that she loved him—because it would only be a burden to them both—but she wanted to at least try and make him see how wrong he was about himself.

His damn head was exploding. He'd taken her on the sideboard—like a damn animal—without an ounce of restraint. So what if she'd had an orgasm? So what if she'd had twenty? He'd used her in the worst way possible, because his need for her had consumed him. He'd proved that he had the same sick flaw as his father, and she was acting as if it didn't matter.

And now she wanted to talk about Nate and Tess and his mother. Was she nuts? Couldn't she see what he was? What he had always been? Didn't she know he could never be Nate's brother, Brandon's uncle, because he didn't deserve to be? He didn't even deserve to be his mother's son. Any more than he deserved Iona.

She watched him now, those almond eyes wide with conviction. And the realisation that keeping her meant risking doing that to her again—made him want to punch his fist through a wall.

He thrust a hand through his hair, his fingers trembling, and heard the plaintive whine of the dog from outside the door.

He had to get out of here. 'I should take C.D. for her run,' he said, keeping his tone neutral, and plunging his hands into his pockets to stop from hauling Iona close and taking her again.

He didn't even have the right to ask her now if they could make this relationship more, not after what he'd done, the way he'd treated her. He had to find a way to make that up to her. To show her he could control himself. That she could trust him to be careful.

But with his nerves shot and his stomach raw, he couldn't think straight. He needed time to cool down, to figure a way to work this out.

'I won't be long,' he added, making it clear he didn't want company. Not this time.

He saw the shadow of hurt in her eyes, and felt the answering tug in his chest, but thanked God when she nodded. 'Okay.'

He opened the door and the dog bounded in. 'Hey, Cooks,' he said, trying to sound pleased to see the dog as she jumped onto him.

Iona gave the dog's head a rub. C.D. lapped up the attention, as always, but then Iona stepped back, and he saw the single tear slip down her cheek. It pierced his heart as she swiped it away.

'I won't be long,' he said, pretending not to notice her distress. He couldn't deal with this now.

Damn, he might even have gotten her pregnant, he thought, the panic returning. What the hell did he do about that?

She nodded, the wobble in her bottom lip crucifying him. 'All right.'

He placed a gentle kiss on her lips, felt the tiny tremor and hated himself even more.

He'd make it up to her. Tonight. And he'd fix this. Because he had to. Whatever he was, whatever he deserved, he couldn't let her go too.

He returned half an hour later, his suit pants ruined from walking in the surf, but with a course of action figured out that just might work. He'd never had to beg before. But this time, he figured it was the only option.

The house was eerily silent as he followed C.D. into the kitchen. The dog whimpered, as if something was wrong. And then he saw the lasagne dish standing on the sideboard and the note propped against it written in Iona's neat, precise script—and realised what it was.

You're a good man, Zane. Go ask your mum, she'll tell you. And don't forget to take care of yourself and that silly dog.
Iona x

The devastation came first, but the anger soon followed. How could she have left him, without even giving him a chance to make amends?

THIRTEEN

———

'Open the damn door!' Zane rammed his fist against the hardwood door of the pretty little colonial, having already rung the doorbell twice.

Iona had to be here; this was his last hope. He'd driven to Pacific Grove first to check in with Mrs Mendoza and her other neighbours. Then he'd called Nate. Maybe Iona and Tess had only just met, but Tess had always been a meddler, so it was possible she'd offered Iona a place to stay.

But he'd drawn a blank there too. Nate had been adamant. 'There's no one staying with us, I swear. But who is she? Is there a problem, cos you sound kind of weird, man.'

He'd made some dumb excuse and ended the call. There wasn't a problem. Or there wouldn't be as soon as he'd tracked Iona down.

He rang the bell again and the hall light came on.

'Hold your horses.'

The locks clicked and his mother appeared in the doorway. Her usually perfect hair was pinned up in tight curls as she wrapped her robe around her waist. He felt the shimmer of guilt at having got her out of bed.

'Zane, what on earth's the matter? Why are you beating down my door in the middle of the night?'

'It's important.' He strode past her into the house, deciding it was too late for guilt. 'Is Iona here?'

'Iona?' She blinked sleepily following him into the small kitchen that always smelled of fresh herbs and home baking, and switched on the overhead light. 'You mean the pretty Scottish girl you brought to Maricruz's *quinceañera*?'

'Don't act dumb with me.' He shouted at his mother, as all the frustration and panic of the last few hours—while he'd driven around trying to figure out where she might go, and prayed frantically that she hadn't already caught a flight home—made his chest feel tight. 'You know damn well who Iona is.'

The sharp slap cracked out, stunning him into silence and making his left cheek sting like a son-of-a-bitch.

'Don't you dare talk to me like that.' His mother propped her hands on her hips and glared at him. 'You ignore my calls for weeks and now you turn up in the middle of the night and use profanity in my house.'

His temper cooled rapidly as he cradled his cheek—which was on fire.

'That hurt—' He bit off a curse, before he ended up with two sore cheeks.

'That's because it was meant to,' she returned, not looking remotely apologetic. She gave a huge yawn, making the guilt return. 'Now sit down and tell me what's going on and what Iona has to do with it.' She indicated the kitchen table, the moment of temper gone as quickly as it had come.

He hesitated. He didn't want to stay and talk. He had to keep searching. But as the anger and desperation drained away, it was replaced with hurt and confusion. If Iona wasn't here, where was she? Watching his mother placing home-made cookies onto a plate, he suddenly had the overwhelming urge to take the comfort she offered. He slumped into one of the dainty kitchen chairs, absently rubbing his flaming cheek.

His hand dropped to the table, the pain from the slap nothing to the tearing pain in his chest as exhaustion and hopelessness overwhelmed him.

He couldn't keep looking, because there was nowhere else to look.

He waited for his mother to finish the tea-making ritual. Placing the freshly baked chocolate-chip cookies in front of him, she poured some tea into a china teacup and pushed it towards him. 'Now what's all this about?'

Steepling her fingers, she observed him with the firm but compassionate expression he remembered so well from his childhood and something broke open inside him.

He gazed at the cup of tea, the scent of fresh mint making his stomach leap into his throat and then become a huge brick that he couldn't swallow down.

If only she could fix this, as she had when he was little. Back in the days when she'd been able to make nightmares go away. But that had all stopped when he was twelve and he'd first found out the truth about his father.

Her warm hand covered the one he had fisted on the table and she squeezed. 'Talk to me, Zane. Don't shut me out any more.'

He raised his eyes and Iona's note came back to him: *You're a good man, Zane. Go ask your mum, she'll tell you.*

'I did something unforgivable.' The words tumbled out. 'And she left me. And I can't find her.'

His mother nodded. 'Is this Iona we're talking about?'

'Yes,' he said, humiliated when his voice cracked.

'So you've fallen in love with her.'

He stared blankly at her hand where it held his, noticed the solid gold wedding band Terry had put on her finger a decade ago, when Zane had given her away—and the abject panic he might have expected at her suggestion didn't come. Instead it all felt a little unreal. 'Maybe.' He shrugged. 'I don't know.'

'What did you do to her that was so unforgivable?'

He shook his head, tried to swallow past the brick in his throat. He couldn't tell her that, because then she'd know that despite all her efforts he was no better than the man who had sired him.

But then she cupped his chin in cool fingers and raised his face.

'Does this have something to do with your father?'

He jerked his head out of her grasp, so stunned he forgot to mask the emotion. She'd always been intuitive— but now was she a damn mind-reader?

'I don't want to talk about him.'

'I know you don't.' She sighed. 'But don't you think it's past time we did?'

'No. I can't.'

'Why can't you?'

He dragged his hands out from under hers, and blurted out the truth. 'Because damn it, I know he raped you. And I can't stand it. To know he hurt you. And that I'm the result.'

'What...?' Her face went white, with shock or pain, or quite possibly both. 'How do you know that?'

'I saw the two of you together when I was a kid. When he came to the cottage that time. I saw him try to hurt you again. And I heard everything he said.'

'Oh, Zane.' She took his hands in both of hers, clutched them hard. 'I had no idea you were there—if I had I would have explained it to you. Why didn't you tell me?'

'I couldn't. I couldn't tell you.' He pulled his hands away, all the anger and bitterness and self-loathing he'd kept hidden for so long threatening to choke him. Until finally he had to ask the question that had been lurking inside him for so long. 'How can you not hate me?'

'Stop that.' She stood up, and pulled him into her arms. The magnolia scent enveloped him as she held his head to her breast, ran her fingers through his hair. 'Now you listen to me.'

His whole body shook, but the quiver of emotion calmed as her sure steady voice drifted through him.

'Yes, he raped me, but it wasn't as black and white as you probably think. I was young and foolish and he was handsome and sophisticated and married and I had a crush on him. I knew he liked me and I flirted with him, encouraged him. It was only when he came to my room that I panicked. I asked him to stop and he wouldn't.'

She drew back, cupped his cheeks in gentle hands. 'I'm not saying what happened was my fault, because it wasn't. He was a ruthless, selfish and ultimately cruel man who took advantage of my naivety. But even though I hated him at the time, and for years afterward, I managed to find forgiveness for him. And do you know why?'

Zane shook his head, not sure he could bear to hear it.

'Because out of that horror, out of that cruelty and selfishness, I got you.'

He covered her hands with his, drew them away from

his face. 'You don't have to say that. I'm not a kid any more. And I know having me ruined your life.'

'Zane!' Her gaze became shadowed with hurt, and it cut into his heart. 'Don't say that. Don't ever say that. You didn't ruin my life.' She placed her hands on his shoulders. 'You are and will always be the best part of my life.' Her voice strengthened. 'I thought that after twenty-four excruciating hours of labour. I thought it when you were eight and broke a tooth in a fist fight that cost me three hundred dollars to fix.' She gave him a little shake as if trying to force the words into him. 'I thought it when you insisted on losing your virginity to that dreadful girl Mary-Lou who thought it was funny to call you a "wetback."'

'You *knew* about that?' he croaked as mortification engulfed him.

She waved her hand dismissively. 'And I even thought it when you beat up Nate, for no other reason than he wanted to be your brother.' A lone tear trickled down her cheek, and he ducked his head, humbled as all the shame and anger that he had held inside for so long was beaten into submission by his mother's love.

'Why on earth would I stop thinking it now?' she whispered. 'When you've become this big, strong, beautiful man who always tries so hard to do the right thing—even when he doesn't know how?'

She cradled his cheek. 'You may have come from a horrific act. But you're not responsible for it. Any more than I was. And just because he fathered you, it doesn't mean you're like him, any more than Nate is like him. Or Brandon. Think about it, Zane. Because if you're tainted by his blood then so are they and any child you might have. Surely you can see how foolish that is?'

He let out a heavy sigh.

Iona was right. He should have talked about this with his mother a long time ago. It would have saved them both so much heartache.

'That's some speech,' he said, at last.

'If I had known that you knew what you did, I would have given it to you twenty years ago,' she said, giving his cheek a gentle pat and returning to her seat.

He smiled weakly. 'I should have told you.'

'Yes, you should have, but you're a man, so it's not all that surprising you didn't.' She laughed, but then her gaze sharpened. 'Now, tell me all about Iona.'

His smile faltered.

'I knew there was something going on there,' his mother added. 'You seemed taken with her.'

He shrugged, more than a little uncomfortable talking about exactly how taken he had become with Iona. 'There's not a lot to tell.' Or not a whole lot he could tell his mother. 'We've been dating for a while. She's been living at my place this past week...'

What did he say? That he'd fallen in love with her? How was he supposed to know that? He wasn't even sure what the hell it meant?

'And...? What?' his mother prompted.

'And it's been good. Better than good.' That much he knew was true.

He'd never been so desperate to get home every evening, and so torn when he had to leave every morning. And it wasn't just the sex. He missed her bright aimless chatter. Her enthusiasm for home cooking and the little flecks of paint on all her clothing. Her kindness and her compassion and the easy no-nonsense way she handled C.D. The way she blushed like a blueberry whenever he teased her and then the smart, sexy way she teased him right back. He missed every bit of their time together and not just the time they spent in bed. In fact, better than good was probably an understatement.

'But then...' he began. Then he spotted the sparkle of interest in his mother's eyes and stopped again.

Okay, no way was he telling his mother about the kitchen-counter sex, or the fact that he'd failed to wear a condom. One whack across the face was enough for tonight.

'And then she ran out on me.'

'Hmm.' His mother lifted a cookie and bit into it, sending him a considering look. 'And you want her back?'

'Yeah. I do.' That much he was sure of. And after what his mother had told him, he also wanted an explanation as to why she'd run off, because it seemed he might have overreacted about his part in that.

His mother slung the cookie down. 'Then what are you doing sitting around my kitchen eating cookies?' She got up and hauled him out of his chair.

'Hey!'

'Zane, you've never spoken about any woman like this before. You need to go find that girl.'

'I know that,' he said, feeling exasperated himself when she shoved him down the hallway. 'But I don't have a clue where she is.'

His mother cocked an eyebrow as she swung the door open. 'Then go get a clue,' she said as he stepped out into the night. 'You're a detective, remember.'

FOURTEEN

———

Iona rinsed out the last of her underwear in the motel's tiny washbasin and began hanging them on the rail.

The dull pain at the memory of Zane's face as he'd left to take C.D. for a walk had her leaning heavily on the sink. She bit into her lip to stop the stupid flood of tears returning.

She'd cried far too much in the last week. And all it did was give her a headache. She needed to get over this now. It had been a fling, pure and simple. A fling that she'd taken a mite too seriously.

And if she had woken up an hour ago and stupidly remembered it was Brandon's christening today and spent the morning moping about hoping that Zane had gone to it, that only proved how delusional she'd become.

The knock at the door had her dumping the last of the wet underwear in the sink. Please don't let that be the piggy-eyed guy on Reception, who kept 'checking up' on how she was doing.

She gasped as she checked the peephole—her knees going to jelly—and opened the door on autopilot.

'Zane, what are you doing here?'

Am I hallucinating?

'What am *I* doing here?' he said. 'Shouldn't that be, what the heck are *you* doing here? Do you have any idea how many favours I had to beg, steal and borrow from my buddies on the force to find you?'

He strode into the room as her hand went slack on the door. Okay, she definitely wasn't hallucinating. The guy in the debonair linen suit making the small grotty room look smaller and grottier was certainly Zane; she'd recognise that devastating face and that lean, muscular build a hundred years from now.

He swung round, his brows drawing down. 'Most of which were borderline illegal.' He checked the time again. 'Do you have something fancy to wear?'

She stared dully at the knickers and camisole she had on to survive the heat—because the air conditioner hadn't worked since day one. 'Why do I need something fancy?'

'For Brandon's christening.' He checked the time again. 'It starts in an hour. So you better get moving.'

She shook her head, worried she might be hallucinating again, but determined not to start bawling. 'I can't go.'

Zane looked disconcerted, but then warm strong fingers wrapped around her forearm. 'No way are you skipping out on this. I spoke to Nate last night, after I finally found out you were here. And somehow got roped into being Bran's godfather.' The puzzled frown deepened.

'That's wonderful, Zane.' Her heart lifted at the news. 'I'm so happy, for you and your family.' But as pleased as she was for him, she couldn't get drawn in too deep again. Or she'd never survive.

'Yeah, it is kind of cool,' he said. 'And you're coming with me.'

'I can't come with you.'

'Why the hell not?' There was that edge again, so unlike the charming, charismatic man who had first seduced her, but so like the guarded, vulnerable man she had come to know and love. She sighed, the tears threatening again. And who didn't love her.

'Because I have no place there.'

She tugged her arm out of his grasp. It wasn't fair that he should come back and make her feel this way again. She'd been stupid and naive and had fallen for a man who wasn't interested, but he hadn't done a whole lot to stop her making that mistake.

He'd pursued her, right from the start. He'd made her feel special and important and safe, given her mind-blowing sex, and some tantalising glimpses of the man behind the facade. And given how well he knew women, he must have known how irresistible that would be, especially to her, a woman who had a few self-esteem issues of her own.

She'd never even got The Speech. Not properly. He could at least have given her that much, so she could have had some chance of protecting her heart.

After all the tears in the last week, the rare spark of temper felt good.

'Tess invited you, didn't she?' he said.

'That's beside the point. Don't be ridiculous.'

'I'm ridiculous!' he shouted. 'You run out on me without a damn explanation and hole up here for nearly a week without a word and I'm the one being ridiculous. When were you planning to tell me where you were?'

'I wasn't,' she declared.

'Why not?' he said, grasping both her arms this time and dragging her to him. 'What did I do that was so unforgivable?'

'Nothing, I just...' She braced her palms against his chest, not wanting to be this close, her limbs shaking and the inevitable heat building. She couldn't tell him, and have her last scrap of pride torn away.

'You could be pregnant and you didn't even give me a forwarding address.'

Pain and disappointment made her throat hurt. So that was the real reason he was here, the invitation to Brandon's christening nothing more than a ruse to finesse the truth out of her. Because Zane always had to finesse women, charm them. He could never ask anything directly, because that would give them the power, she thought, forcing her temper back to the fore to work through the hurt.

'I'm not pregnant. I had my period.'

'You're not pregnant? For sure?' She'd expected him to look relieved, but strangely he didn't, he almost looked disappointed.

'No, I'm definitely not pregnant.'

'Okay, then I want a damn good reason why you can't come home.'

'Home?' she said, the anger faltering.

'Yeah, home. I want you to come back to Seventeen Mile Drive. I want you to give me another chance.'

'I canny do that...' She shook her head, trying to pull away from him now. The tears welling in her eyes, closing her throat. 'Don't ask that of me—it isn't fair.'

'Why not?' he asked, his voice thick too. 'If this has to do with your father, we can go visit him...'

'That's not it. It's because I've fallen in love with you,'

she whispered, her throat raw. She hadn't wanted to tell him this, and now he'd forced it out of her.

To her astonishment, he laughed. 'Is that all?'

She struggled out of his arms, the tears falling now. 'Don't you dare laugh at me. My feelings are important.' She rapped her fist on her chest, believing it completely for the first time in her life. 'My feelings matter.' The sob burst out without warning. 'I'm not going to prolong our fling just so I can feel even worse when I have to leave.'

'Hey, hey, hey.' He folded her into his embrace, smothering her struggles. 'Iona, don't cry. I know your feelings matter.' He stroked a hand down her hair, cradled her cheeks, the sapphire-blue of his irises warm and unguarded. 'Because there's nothing more important to me.'

'That's not true,' she replied, shaking now. 'You told me I had no business talking to Tess. No business knowing about you and Nate. You never let me in, not really.'

'Because I was a jerk. And terrified of you finding out something I'd believed about myself for years and wasn't even true.'

'Your father?' she murmured.

'Yeah, my father.' He walked to the bed, sat down on it, the creak of the springs audible. 'You know what's ironic, when I was a little kid, I had this dumb idea he was a great guy. Back then, it was my mother who didn't want to talk about him. But I knew who he was. Because I'd seen the photos at San Revelle and it didn't take much to make the connection. Why my mom had gotten the job. Why the old guy who owned the place came by to ask how I was getting along from time to time.'

'You mean your grandfather?'

He nodded stiffly. 'But that day, before...' He swallowed. 'Before I saw him with her. I met him. It was hot and my mom had told me to stay away from the big house, because they had guests coming in a couple of hours for a weekend party and I shouldn't get in the way. But he arrived early and parked right next to where I was playing on my skateboard.' He shrugged, the movement defensive. 'He looked me over and grinned, and said, "You're Maria's kid, right?" I nodded and everything inside me stopped. I figured this was the moment I'd been waiting for. That he'd tell me he was my father and maybe he'd take me for a ride in his car.' He gave a sad smile. 'He had a really hot cherry-red Ferrari with white wall tyres.'

She sat next to him on the bed, and placed a hand on his thigh, her heart aching for that little boy. 'You had a passion for cars even then?'

He put his hand over hers, and nodded. 'You want to know the only other words my father said to me?'

She wasn't sure she did, but whispered, 'Yes.'

He gave a brittle laugh. 'He threw me the keys to his car and said, "Tell Mano to get this cleaned before I leave tomorrow."'

'Zane...' She placed her hand on his jaw and kissed his cheek, trying to transmit all the love she had. Not just for the man, but for the boy. 'He was a hideous human being, but that doesn't mean you're...'

He turned and touched his finger to her lips. 'I know. I took your advice and finally spoke to my mother about him.' He threaded his fingers through hers, and held on. 'I told her what I'd seen and...' He paused to stare at the ceiling. 'And you were right—it didn't matter.'

'But, Zane, I don't understand—how could you have ever believed it did?'

'I was angry and hurt and scared, I guess. And when I began to have sex myself, I had this burning hunger.'

He dropped his head back, let out a rueful sigh. 'Which I told myself I had to control or else I'd be no better than him.' His firm lips tilted into a sexy smile. 'Then you came along and changed everything, because I couldn't control it any more.'

She wanted to believe him, to bask in the approval she saw in his eyes. But she knew the truth. 'I didn't change anything. I'm just another of your damsels in distress.'

'You're... What?' He chuckled, looking bemused. 'Iona, what the hell is that supposed to mean?'

She pulled away from him, annoyed by the easy smile that sent the dimple into his cheek. And made him look even more adorable and even further out of her reach. 'Isn't it obvious, Zane? Why you were attracted to me? Why you seduced me? Why you were so determined to keep me safe? Why you asked me to move in with you?'

'No, it isn't, not to me.'

She wrapped her arms round her waist, feeling naked under that steady gaze. 'You rescue women, Zane. It's what you do. Ever since that day you couldn't rescue your mother.' She tightened her arms, the blank look on his face making her stomach hurt. 'I was just another one of your rescue projects. That's all.'

He shook his head, the puzzled frown becoming more pronounced, and it was like losing him all over again. Then he said, 'That has got to be the dumbest thing I've ever heard.'

'It is not!' she said. 'It makes complete sense if you look at the facts.'

'The hell it does.' Grabbing her wrist, he hauled her towards him, then tumbled her onto the bed.

'Get off me,' she cried, trying to buck him off. But he

simply straddled her hips, and held her captive with her hands above her head.

'Calm down,' he said firmly, ignoring her struggles. 'Because now it's my turn to talk and your turn to listen.' The sharp edge of frustration shocked her into stillness. 'You're right about one thing. I respect women, I want to protect them, and yeah, maybe because of what happened to my mother, I get so mad when I see a woman hurt— whether she's some sweet old lady who's been mugged by a gang member or a teenage hooker who's been beaten up by her pimp—that I have a hard time controlling it. But that doesn't have a damn thing to do with us.'

Bracketing her wrists, he pressed them into the mattress, the cold steel in his voice flatly contradicted by the warmth in his eyes as his gaze roamed over her face. 'Because that's not a tenth of what I feel for you.' The steel softened and her heart throbbed into her throat. He leaned close, the tender touch of his lips on hers bringing tears to her eyes. 'Now tell me you believe me.'

She nodded, her throat too tight with emotion to form words.

Letting go of her hands, he framed her face in rough palms. 'Now kiss me again, *querida*—and show me you mean it.'

His tongue tangled with hers and she strained upwards, flinging her arms around his neck to give him the proof he needed—the leap of joy in her heart as intoxicating as the hunger coiling low in her belly.

When he raised his head, she could feel the satisfying weight of his erection against the bare skin of her thigh, hear the ragged sound of her own breathing and see so much more than hunger in his eyes.

'So are you gonna stop messing around now and come home to me and C.D.?' he asked.

'I suppose so.' She grinned, the smile suffusing her whole face. 'If you insist.'

The quick grin sent a dimple into that chiselled cheek and took her breath away again. 'Damn straight I do.'

* * * * *

THE WEDDING DRESS DIARIES
Aimee Carson

ONE

———

'Can I get you a drink?'

The busty brunette behind the bar at the exclusive Manhattan restaurant was addressing the guy at the end of the counter. And, when Amber spied the man, she did a sharp double take that would surely leave her with a crick in her neck.

Parker Robinson.

Blinking, Amber adjusted to the sight as the sounds of Reese's engagement party faded.

When Parker didn't respond, the bartender repeated, 'Can I get you a drink?'

Attention finally caught, Parker drew the sexy smirk like a gun from a holster. No doubt he wasn't even aware. It was more like an automatic response, like most people would say please or thank you or mutter an excuse me when they accidentally stepped on someone's toe.

'Why, yes, you can,' Parker said.

The brunette puffed up her chest, clearly pleased she'd finally earned an attentive smile, and Amber resisted the urge to roll her eyes. Apparently Reese hadn't exaggerated; her half brother's attitude toward women hadn't changed much since adolescence. Amber had witnessed that grin directed at girls often enough, that knowing twinkle in his eye communicating that females liked what they saw, and he knew it.

A cocky confidence that, on Parker Robinson, was more endearing than annoying.

The sun-streaked blond hair of his teens was now a light brown with leftover golden highlights, like keepsakes from his childhood. He still wore it tousled with soft spikes up front, and the little-boy, rough-and-tumble look totally suited him, hair begging to be tugged. Years ago she'd longed to do just that, to pull him in for a kiss. Had fantasized about him teaching her how. And while his hair hadn't changed much, his masculine features were better defined, cheekbones and jaw now sharp enough to cut cold butter. Yet he straddled youth and maturity with an ease to be envied, that cocky teen housed in the bad-boy adult making a killer combination.

His gaze collided with Amber's and held, and a pit yawned wide beneath her stomach. The brilliant green eyes hadn't faded with time. Pulse pounding, she realized, belatedly, that he'd caught her staring, and the shameful memory barreled into her. The day when he'd called her out on exactly that. But she wasn't the besotted little preteen anymore, the one that had followed him around like an adoring puppy.

'You a friend of Reese's?' he asked.

Amber was proud she didn't laugh out loud. Amazing. Ironic that the guy she'd spent every summer in the Hamptons with from the ages of seven to twelve—the guy she'd loved from the ages of eight to fifteen—didn't even remember her.

Though, in his defense, she'd been in the sixth grade the last time he saw her.

In jeans and a leather jacket the color of burnt butter, Parker picked up his glass and came closer, moving with that easy earthy stroll that came with a confidence few could dream of. It had been captivating on Parker the teen.

On Parker the man, it was absolutely breathtaking.

He slid onto the bar stool next to hers and leaned his elbow on the counter, facing Amber. Parker cleared his throat and lowered his head a little to look up at her face—most likely a *stupefied* face—as if worried her lack of response meant she wasn't completely sane.

Parker seated this close was definitely threatening her sanity.

'Are you a friend of Reese and Dylan's?' he repeated.

It had been fifteen years since she'd seen him, had been close enough to *touch*. She gripped her glass and sipped her wine, hoping she looked more sophisticated than she felt.

Amber managed a nod of her head. 'I've known Reese a long time.' *I've known* you *a long time*. 'Why would I be at their engagement party if I didn't know them?'

'Could be a party crasher, here for the expensive food and free drinks.'

It was surreal to be having this conversation with her childhood crush, protected by her unknown identity. Because she had plenty to be embarrassed about when it came to Parker.

From the time Reese had asked her to handle her wedding, Amber had been dreading the moment she had to measure this man for his tux—an event that needed to occur soon. But she'd thought she could relax tonight because Reese had said Parker would never show. He hadn't attended any of the other parties for his half sister and her fiancé. So why had he come now?

'Is that why you're here?' she said with a smile. 'For the free food?'

Parker let out a bitter scoff. 'If only.'

He didn't want to be here.

The realization hit her with all the force of a sledgehammer on steroids. It fit with what Reese had told her, the man who refused to have anything to do with the Michael family anymore. Not that Amber could blame him. But ever since her engagement, his sister had been trying to pull him back into, well, if not into the fold, at least within touching distance.

He tipped his head with an almost boyish curiosity. 'Do I know you?' he said, and Amber's heart froze. 'I definitely think I know you.'

He pursed his lips contemplatively, and Amber wished her memory of his mouth hadn't been so spot on. He *did* have the most gorgeous lips in the world. Full. Sinful. Utterly kissable. Pretty savvy of a stupid twelve-year-old to notice, if she did say so herself.

Enjoying the rare sense of power in Parker's presence, she sent him another smile. 'Maybe.'

'A name would be helpful,' he said.

Amber let out an overly thoughtful *hmm,* as if she were seriously considering giving him the information. But suddenly, the moment she'd been dreading, her first meeting with Parker, was more about fun than fear.

'That would be too easy,' she said.

Parker's understanding smile at her tone set her pulse fluttering. 'Okay,' he said, settling in as if for a prolonged conversation, the light in his eyes sizzling. 'I'll bite.'

God, she wished he would.

'Do I know you through your work?' he said.

Amber bit back the smile. 'Could be,' she said with laughter in her tone. 'I used to be a seamstress, but now I own my own bridal shop.'

He actually recoiled as if slapped, and the look on his face as he backpedaled made her laugh. Clearly, Parker Robinson was offended at the thought of frequenting an establishment that dealt with weddings.

'Definitely not through your work,' he said gruffly. 'Maybe through mine?'

Amber pretended not to know. 'What do you do?'

He narrowed his eyes at her. 'I work Homicide down at the fifty-seventh precinct. Maybe I interviewed you as a witness before?'

'Maybe I was once a suspect,' she said as coolly as she could.

The roll of his eyes, that sarcastic 'yeah, right' expression made her suddenly sentimental. She remembered that look from her childhood, and a small part of her was glad he hadn't changed too much.

'Do I look too innocent?' she said.

'No,' he said bluntly. 'I just remember all my perps.' His face grew tight, and a harsh laugh escaped his mouth, and he slid his eyes to somewhere beyond her shoulders. 'And yeah, you look too sweet. But, trust me,' he said with a light tone that he didn't quite pull off. He took a sip of his drink and carefully set the glass down, his tone distant. 'No one is as innocent as they look.'

There was a hard set about his eyes, the crinkles at the edges more about experience than age. A bitter fatigue that had started in his teens and now was fully realized.

That bold green gaze was back on her, intrigued. *Interested.* 'Maybe we attended the same school?'

She shook her head.

'Did we meet at a party once?' he asked.

Enjoying his frustrated curiosity, she sipped her wine. 'Try again.'

His eyes narrowed in thought. 'Well, I know we haven't slept together,' Parker went on, sending her stomach plummeting to her toes.

God, only in her teenage dreams.

'Because, although you're certainly attractive,' he said, 'you're definitely not my type.'

Amber ignored the sudden surge in her pulse and maintained an even tone. 'Is that the *only* reason we couldn't have slept together?' she said. 'Because I'm not your type?'

The reflexive sexy smirk lit up his face.

And as the words finally sank in, she drew back a touch in surprise. 'Wait,' she said. 'What type do you think I am?'

His gaze traveled down her body, leaving her hot in places that normally...weren't. Her A-line dress was simple, with a classic cut. Nothing seductive. No overt 'I'm yours for the taking' in the way it clung to her body.

He hiked a brow dryly. 'You own a bridal shop, which means you believe in the institution of marriage.'

'And you don't?' she said softly, only pretending the statement was a question.

Sure enough, a bitter sound escaped those beautiful lips. Not that Amber could blame him.

'Hell, no,' he said.

Heart bleeding a little for him then, she remembered the day she'd found him by the dock, devastated by his mother's words.

You were a mistake.

Amber had grown up knowing she was wanted. Secure in the knowledge her parents had been devoted to each other, were devoted to *her*. Her dad had died when she was a child, and her mother had loved him so much she'd never remarried. And Amber's bridal store revolved around proving that love existed every day, with every client.

But Parker...

Well, Parker's experiences were opposite in every respect.

And the boy who'd given Amber her first taste of romantic love—*unrequited,* but love nonetheless—had grown into a man who mocked its very existence.

'You've made weddings your business,' he said. 'So, obviously you believe.'

'And that's how you've concluded I'm not your type?' she said. 'Because of the dress I'm wearing and what I do for a living?'

He sat back a bit to study her, no teasing, seductive tone now, but a kind of gaze that could see through your soul. 'No,' he said, shaking his head softly. The thoughtful look on his face was deep and, for the first time, he actually looked at her. *Really* looked at her. 'It's the light in your eyes,' he said with a simple shrug. 'You still believe.'

Her lungs slowly collapsed, forcing the air from her body. Believed in what? In love?

In *life?*

The thought instantly drained from her mind when he shifted closer, and the scent of his leather jacket drifted in the air.

'I can't remember who you are.' Simmering gaze on hers, he said, 'How about throwing a poor guy a hint?'

'Okay,' Amber said. After the years of crushing on Parker the teen, now that he was looking at her as a desirable woman, she wanted to work the moment for all she was worth. 'You once pressed your lips against mine.'

Parker's eyes widened, and he dropped his gaze to her mouth, pulling all the oxygen from the atmosphere. Amber's breathing increased in an attempt to suck in enough air.

'Awesome.' His voice slid lower, like heated silk. 'I approve of my choices.'

He leaned close, his eyes glowing, sparking embers she'd thought long dead—those secret pieces of a young girl in the throes of her first sexual attraction. Not really understanding the full extent of what she felt.

His teasing grin was hot enough to light the Christmas tree at Rockefeller Center. 'Did I get to second base?'

Skin vibrating at the thought, her smile was strained.

'Sorry, only first,' she said.

And technically, it was probably only *half* base, but she was having too much fun to clarify the exact nature of how their lips had touched.

'Did I slip you the tongue?' he said.

'No.'

'My loss,' he said, and his mouth parted a bit, as if imagining righting that previous wrong.

The tiny peek at his tongue sent a shot of adrenaline through her body, surely leaving her glowing. Fine hairs standing on end.

'And as first kisses went,' she pressed on, 'it could have been better.'

Mostly by being *real*.

The offended expression on Parker's face was comical. 'Could have been— Wait...*first* kiss?' He shot her a skeptical look. 'Either this was a really long time ago or you've confused me with someone else.'

'I definitely don't have you confused with someone else.' When he looked at her as though he was beginning to suspect she truly *wasn't* sane, Amber sent him a smile and gave up the pretense. 'I practically grew up at your mother's house because my mom worked as her personal assistant,' she said. 'Which was the fancy title for glorified gofer girl.'

There was a three-heartbeat pause that felt like thirty as Parker's expression remained blank.

'I'm Amber Davis.'

'Amber Davis,' he said slowly, as if pulling the name from a memory long buried. Recognition finally shot through his face, and his shoulders snapped back. 'Well, hell,' he breathed out. 'You're the one who tried to drown.'

TWO

——

Swimswimswim

Eyes fixed on the dock, the chant rang on and on in Amber's head. She'd lost sight of her paddleboard ages ago, swept away by the Sag Harbor current. Crap, she was *so* getting in trouble for this.

Mom's gonna kill me if I drown.

A fresh slice of panic surged. How was she going to marry Parker now if she died? At the stupid age of twelve. Jeez, she'd never even been kissed before! Frowning, she paddled harder. She should have played Spin the Bottle at Nancy Kruger's last month. Okay, so Amber probably would have been stuck kissing Jimmy Stevens, better known as lizard tongue, but at least she wouldn't be drowning with virgin lips. An epically lame end to the suckage that was her life.

All except for Parker.

Parker.

So what if he was in the eleventh grade and she was

only in sixth. She'd loved him since she was eight years old. He'd briefly been replaced with Justin Timberlake from 'N Sync, but even she knew that was pretty unlikely to happen. And Parker was cuter. She wanted to marry him so bad that she'd picked out her wedding dress ages ago. Course, it had taken her four months to whittle it down to her top five favorites. Her obsession with tulle and satin and lace was growing pretty strong. This summer, in a fit of boredom, she'd planned the whole ceremony. Reese would have been her maid of honor cuz she was Parker's half sister and Amber's sort-of friend.

Stupidstupidstupid

Sneaking off and forgetting the life vest. But she'd really *really* wanted to get better on the paddleboard. Mostly cuz she wanted to impress Parker. Last summer he'd taught her how to stand and maneuver a turn, but this summer he was more interested in kissing Susie Frances. Amber scowled. And he never helped her bait a hook or capture crabs anymore.

The current was scarily strong, and the dumb dock was slipping farther away. The chill from the water seeped deeper with every passing minute, despite how hard Amber swam. Teeth chattering, her arms and legs grew heavy. So much so it was a struggle to control them now.

A sob ripped from her throat, and she fought back the fear, closing her eyes.

Giveupgiveupgiveup

Her muscles screamed for a break, her lips quivering, the taste of salt a mix of seawater and frustrated tears. The furious pounding of her heart was now just as much about terror as tiredness, and she was sure her chest was gonna explode.

Her thoughts began to drift and grow foggy. She knew there was something she was supposed to be doing. Swimming? Finding Reese?

'Amber!'

The call shook her out of her daze. God, she really *was* drowning. Was she already in heaven? Now she was hearing Parker calling out her name.

The voice grew closer, the tone urgent. *'Amber.'*

Exhausted, she turned and spied Parker sprawled on his board, sleeves pushed to his elbows as he paddled toward her like a madman. She sucked in a breath, getting a mouthful of salt water that burned her throat, and she coughed and gagged, slipping beneath the surface. The cold closed over her head and she stopped fighting for a moment. It was peaceful. Quiet. And she was so, so tired; it was nice not to fight so hard to keep her head above water.

She drifted, floating, until an arm circled around her chest and heaved her up. She had a vague sensation of being hauled onto something hard, but she couldn't move. It took too much effort to breathe.

And then there were lips on hers and warm breath filling her lungs and she had an overwhelming urge to cough again. She rolled, gagged and then threw up a bunch of salt water that stung as much coming up as going down. Shattered, she collapsed again, drifting in and out, only half-aware as Parker paddled the board for shore and dragged her up on the beach.

That was when the shivering started for real. Water dripped down his nose as Parker gathered her close, fear making deep lines in his forehead. She gazed up at him, dazed, her heart pounding from the feel of his arms cradled around her. The feel of his breath, *Parker's breath*, on her cheek was awesome. But the close-up of his face was just...was just... And as she blinked, her mind clearing, it hit her.

Parker had kissed her!

Her heart fluttered like a hummingbird stuck in a cage. Okay, true, it was more like he'd given her mouth to mouth, but still... She closed her eyes, remembering the hard press of those soft lips she'd been obsessing about for years. Pressed against *hers*.

OMG...it was almost worth drowning for.

His dark blond hair looked brown when wet. A smattering of freckles bridged his nose, and thick lashes framed the prettiest pair of green eyes in the history of *ever*. Eyes that always did funny things to her stomach when they locked on hers. Used to be they'd look at her with patience and, when she was *really* lucky, a hint of fondness. Now that Parker had gotten older there was a lot of irritation. But it wasn't *her* fault his mother made him watch out for her and Reese when Amber's mom wasn't around.

She clutched his arm. 'You can't tell my mom,' she croaked out.

'Aw, come on, Amber.' Parker's face scrunched up tight. 'You nearly freakin' died.'

'I did not.'

He rolled his eyes in that ever-sarcastic 'yeah, right' way of his. 'What if you get sick or something?' he said. 'She needs to know.'

And be grounded? Amber had been looking forward to summer vacation for *months*. As the daughter of Ms. Michael's personal assistant, Amber had practically grown up in the Michaels' home. Parker never visited his mother in the city anymore, so summer at the Hamptons was the only time she got to see him.

She pulled harder, panicking now. 'If you tell, I'll— I'll—'

Her mind sputtered as she scrambled to come up with a good threat. And then a memory filled her mind. A vision of Parker, lids rimmed red, sniffing as she stumbled on him down by the dock. He'd yelled at her, of course, scrubbing at his face as he'd told her to scram. As always, her heart hurt when Parker got that look in his eyes. And the only person in the world that could make Parker that upset was his mother. It had been a long time since she'd seen him sad about his mom. Lately, his reactions more often resembled anger.

She straightened up. 'I'll tell Susie Frances that I caught you crying like a baby.'

His gaze flashed to hers. 'I was not crying,' he said. 'I got salt water in my eyes, is all.'

They both knew it was a lie, and she fought the temptation to look away. This was too important.

'Fine,' he said. And then he jabbed a finger in front of her face. 'But you have to stop the creepy stalker stuff.'

Heat flaring up her face, she was horrified by the words. Had she been that obvious?

Suddenly, she wished she'd been swallowed up by the waters of Sag Harbor. 'Fine,' she said, mimicking him. But then her bravery ran out, her voice growing small. 'I don't suppose we can find the paddleboard?'

Parker stood, and right away she missed the heat of his skin. He swiped a hand through his hair, leaving it spikier than usual. 'The board's long gone.'

Jeez, it all seemed so *unfair.* Blinking back the tears, she looked across the water. Petrified Parker would see her cry, she dragged her hand across her eyes and sniffed. Another shiver racked her body, and the rustle of clothing brought her attention back to Parker.

He'd taken off his hoodie. 'Don't worry about it, Ace,' he said gruffly, pulling his sweatshirt down over her head.

Her heart soared, both from the touch and the words and the protective tone in his voice. And she'd always adored his nickname for her. She jabbed her arms into the damp sleeves, savoring the heat from his body, the smell of *Parker.*

'I'll take the blame for the board.' Those too-beautiful lips flattened grimly. A dark look crossed his face. 'My mom already hates me, anyway.'

A needle pricked her heart, the sharp pain familiar. Ms. Michael was all *Reese Reese Reese,* spoiling her daughter rotten. But Parker? He barely even existed in the Michael household. No wonder he chose to live with his dad.

'Thanks,' she said, hoping she wasn't tearing up like a baby again.

His lopsided smile appeared, leaving her weak in the knees as he said, 'Let's get you home.'

Parker gripped his whiskey glass.

Amber Davis.

Discovering the redhead's identity had been like a cattle-prod shock to Parker's nervous system, his mind reeling with the memories of his youth. He struggled to ignore the beautiful woman who'd trailed after him as a kid, hanging on his every word. His every move. The one who'd witnessed his most humiliating moment.

You were a mistake.

Tossing back the rest of his drink, he tried to focus on his goals for tonight. Avoid his mother at all costs, speak to Reese and tell her no and then get the heck out of here.

Attention firmly on him, Amber asked, 'Do you remember—?'

'Yeah,' he said gruffly, fixing his eyes on his empty glass. No way was he letting her finish that question. 'I remember.'

He could feel Amber's gaze, but he needed a minute to adjust. Several of them, actually. Because he sure as hell wasn't ready to face the lady who, years ago, had found him sniffling like a wussy little girl.

Thank God for his cell phone.

Parker glanced at the incoming number flashing in time with the vibration, answering with his pat 'What's up, Robby boy?'

'Why aren't you at Rosie's Bar?'

Parker let out a discontented grunt, longing for the bar that was the watering hole for most of the fifty-seventh precinct. His gaze swept across the elegantly attired guests at the restaurant, the fancy venue most likely chosen for its bird's-eye view of Manhattan. The only bright spot had been the pretty redhead that he'd known was too sweet and *all* kinds of wrong for him. Resisting a little harmless flirting had been impossible.

But, man, was that ever a freakin' mistake.

'I'm busy,' Parker said to his partner as he shot a look at Amber.

Creamy skin, wide mouth and eyes the color of maple

syrup. Her auburn hair was pulled back in some sleek knot that looked more professional than dressy. If he'd known she was gonna turn into a stunning redhead, he might have actually paid more attention. But she had been all knobby kneed, gap-toothed, with gangly arms and legs. A quiet kid.

A lamb among wolves at the Michael household.

He'd always felt a little sorry for her, a bit protective. Some of that had been drilled into him, to watch over Reese and Amber when Amber's mother couldn't. And more than anyone, he knew how it felt to be an outsider in the Michael household.

Now Amber was gorgeous, but there was still a lingering sense of the innocent openness that she'd had as a child. He could see it in her clear, honest eyes, the face that left everything on display. Parker couldn't remember ever being innocent.

Had stopped *believing* in innocence long ago.

Gaze locked with the redhead's, Parker spoke to Rob, who was waiting patiently on the other end of the phone. 'Trust me,' he said. 'I'd rather be spilling a beer with my partner at Rosie's Bar than at this fancy restaurant.'

'Get your butt down here,' Rob said.

'Sorry, Robby boy.' *Christamighty* was Parker sorry he was here instead of there. 'Got something I've got to do first.'

There was a long pause on the end of the phone. 'This isn't about the Miller case, is it?' Rob asked.

Parker's insides felt as if they'd been hooked to two tractor trailers racing in opposite directions. Shoulders tense, he rolled them back. 'No,' he said, careful to keep his voice casual. 'I've done this job long enough that nothing shocks me anymore.'

He knew his partner thought the turn of events had affected him. Was worried, somehow, that Parker was burning out on all they dealt with day to day. But he was more disturbed by the fact that he *wasn't* affected. The latest case had taken a twisted turn that most people could never fathom and, yet, Parker hadn't felt a speck of shock. Zip, zilch, nada.

The hollow darkness surrounding his heart expanded, and Parker refused to admit how much it scared the hell out of him.

Rob cleared his throat on the other end of the phone. 'I hate that our number one suspect is a teen, especially given his parents are total dirtbags,' he said.

Parker huffed in agreement. 'Yeah, sometimes family sucks.'

Eyebrows tenting at his words, Amber frowned.

And as he said goodbye to Rob, Parker let out a sigh and addressed the redhead. 'You got something you want to say?'

'Just wondering if you've spoken with your sister yet,' Amber said.

'Haven't had the time.'

'Haven't *made* the time.'

As if on cue, a feminine voice called his name, and he turned to face Reese. She was crossing the hardwood floor in a cocktail dress, her blond hair in a delicate twist.

'Be nice,' Amber whispered.

Parker frowned. 'I'm always nice.'

As Reese drew closer, he slipped his phone in his jacket, bracing for the upcoming conversation. Confronting his sister and telling her no appeared to be the only way to get her off his case. Emails hadn't worked. The phone calls had been a failure. Seemed the only way to get her to accept his no was a face-to-face conversation.

You can do polite.

But when Reese went to hug him, for a moment he panicked. Freakin' *panicked*. A master at deflection, he shifted on his feet, subtly placing his shoulder forward, blocking her attempt. Fortunately she interpreted his body language accurately and abandoned her attempt.

He didn't do public displays of affection.

He'd learned long ago not to do affection *period*.

'I'm glad you came,' Reese said with a small smile. 'I hope this means you've changed your mind about the wedding.'

Parker bit back the urge to say *hell, no*.

Now that she was getting married to her supposed dream guy, Reese was suddenly all 'peace on earth, good will toward men.' More persistent in her insistence they pretend they were a real family. They lived in the same town and hadn't seen each other in two years.

Mostly his fault, sure, but *still...*

'I came to talk to you in person,' he said.

'And to catch up with old friends?' Reese said.

His sister shot the redhead at his side a curious look before addressing Parker.

'So...' Reese said. 'Are you and Amber setting an appointment time for you to get measured for your tux?'

Parker's lips quirked in surprise as he slid his gaze back to Amber. She was watching him as if assessing his every move, the beautiful woman's attention sending a thrilling shimmy down his spine. *Amber* was supposed to measure him for his tux?

Interesting notion, but not enough to get him to change his mind.

'Come on, Reese,' he said, trying to be the diplomat he wasn't. 'Can you really picture me in a monkey suit?'

How many more times did he have to say no?

He wasn't a part of the Michael family, had never been welcomed. And at the age of thirty-two he wasn't going to start pretending now.

'Of course we want you there,' Reese said. 'You're my brother —'

'Half brother,' he said bluntly, knowing he sounded callous and trying to care. 'With emphasis on the half.'

Amber briefly touched the back of his hand and flashed him a disapproving look, and he chose to ignore the warning and the stimulating warmth of her touch, the fleeting feel of soft fingers. Reese eyed him warily. As if, after knowing him forever, she was still trying to figure him out.

Yeah, well...good luck with that one. He was still working on that himself.

'Listen,' he said. 'I'm happy that *you're* happy that you and that fiancé of yours are finally tying the knot.' He did his best not to scoff out loud. 'Not that I believe in the whole marital thing. But you know, to each his—or her—own delusion.'

'Parker,' Reese said gently, and he hated the worried look in her eyes. 'Love isn't a delusion.'

'Oh, yeah?' Parker screwed up his face, hoping he looked more doubtful than like the caustic bastard that Jessica had called him before breaking it off. After four months, a real record for him, it was almost a relief to have her gone. 'If I remember right—' he studied his sister '—you've pledged 'till death do you part' before.'

Amber's fingers returned to his wrist, gripping him hard. The contact briefly short-circuited his brain, bringing to mind better reasons she could be holding on to him so tight.

Not your type, Robinson. Not your type.

He discreetly pulled his wrist from Amber's clasp. 'Mason was your ex's name, wasn't it?' Parker said, lifting a brow at his sister.

Pink staining her cheeks at the mention of her first husband, Reese ignored his comment. 'Being in the wedding doesn't mean you're endorsing the institution.'

He plowed a hand through his hair, not caring if it stuck out in all directions. 'Reese—'

'Please,' she said, her face the picture of sincerity. 'You're family.'

Every muscle in his gut tensed with the hit. As far as he was concerned, his family died the day his father had passed away.

And the void that had started with his mother's *you were a mistake* had grown through the years, only to expand to unbelievable depths the day his dad had died. Since then he'd felt numb, as if nothing touched him. Detached. A black hole that threatened to consume everything.

Amber shifted slightly on her feet, and his eyes went of their own volition to land, *again*, on the pretty tagalong from his youth. She pressed closer until their shoulders brushed, a distracting touch. But she was giving him an emphatic stare that screamed *Don't you dare break her heart*.

Because Reese didn't deserve it, not really.

It had taken him years as an adult to realize that his sister wasn't responsible for the way their mother had treated him. That Reese's precious-princess status in the Michael household was her parents' doing, and not his sister's. She'd been a clueless, pampered kid adored by her mom and dad. And wasn't that the way life was supposed to work?

But Parker Robinson wasn't a fake.

He puffed out a breath. At this point, he was just gonna have to let her be disappointed when he didn't show up for the Big Day.

'I told you,' Parker told his sister. 'Dylan needs to pick someone else for his fifth groomsman.'

Parker headed for the elevators, and Amber spied the crestfallen look on Reese's face.

'He's never going to say yes,' Reese said.

Amber hated seeing her so down. Helping her childhood friend plan her dream day—complete with a reunion with her three college roommates as bridesmaids—was vital. Because she'd watched Reese work hard at her marriage to Mason, had *seen* how devastated she was when it failed. It had been painful to watch her friend suffer. Reese deserved her happily ever after with Dylan.

'Parker will say yes,' Amber said. 'Because deep down he knows you care about him.'

'You care about him, too,' Reese said with a knowing look in her eye.

Her stomach lurched. 'That was a long time ago.'

'And you're both grown-ups now,' her friend said, tone riddled with subtext.

Shooting Reese a look, Amber said, 'Anyone who chooses to get involved with Parker is a glutton for punishment.' She cast an eye at the man as he waited for the elevator. 'And I don't chase men.'

'No,' Reese said with a sigh. 'You just sit back and let life pass you by.'

'Hey,' Amber protested. 'Romance will happen when it's good and ready.'

Her mom had always said loving her father had been easy. Reese and Dylan's relationship always looked effortless, too. They were the perfect couple. Amber's other friends chased love as if it were something to be hunted down and captured, torturing themselves in the process. Amber knew when she met the right man, love would happen naturally.

Until then, she'd help others plan their perfect day.

Reese let out a *hunh*. 'Maybe you should be more proactive in getting what you want.'

'Listen,' Amber said, changing the subject. 'I'll talk to Parker about the wedding.' Amber gave her friend a hug. 'You go find Dylan and enjoy the rest of the party, okay?'

Heart pounding, Amber followed in Parker's path. But who was she, really, to try to convince Parker Robinson of *anything*?

The elevator doors were beginning to shut, and Amber picked up her pace and slid inside just before they closed.

Tension bounced off the walls, making the space feel especially small.

Parker sent her an overly tolerant look. 'Did Reese send you to try to change my mind?'

'No,' Amber said truthfully. She knew she needed to ease her way into this conversation. Years of resentment weren't going to be undone with a one-minute elevator ride. 'I was hoping you could give me a lift home.'

He straightened up and stared at her.

'Are you coming on to me?' he said. There was no seductive tone. He actually sounded amused by the thought.

Amber sent him a disgusted look she didn't feel. And why did he find the idea *funny*? 'No,' she said. 'Will you give me a ride, anyway?'

'I'll give you a ride because you're *not* coming on to me,' he said. Before she had time to process the unsatisfying words, Parker pushed the button and went on.

'Where do you live?' he asked.

'In a loft above my shop,' she said. 'Down under the Manhattan Bridge overpass.'

An emotion she couldn't quite place swept up his face. 'I would have thought Reese wouldn't be caught dead in a shop anywhere other than on Fifth Avenue itself.'

Affection flared across her heart. Reese's wedding to Dylan Brookes was one of *the* social events of the year. The Michaels and the Brookeses were two of the most prominent families in the city. Handling the account was going to put her shop on the map, and she would forever be grateful for her friend's business and her trust.

'Reese has changed,' Amber said as they exited the elevator. She knew that better than anybody. 'I know she was a little oblivious as a teen...'

Parker chuckled at the understatement, though there was no malice in the sound.

They entered the lobby and Parker held the door open for her, and Amber passed through onto the busy, nighttime sidewalk. Traffic whooshed by, the smell of rain heavy in the air.

'Honestly, I don't care how much she's changed.' And as he gave his ticket to the valet, he shot Amber a sharp look. 'I'm not convinced this thing with her and Dylan is even real.'

'You're just cynical about relationships in general,' Amber said with a small scoff. 'Everyone knows they're perfect for each other.'

'Regardless,' Parker said. 'I'm not going to be in her wedding.'

Heart shifting lower in her chest, Amber curled her fingers in her hand, determined to change his mind by the end of the ride home.

No matter what it took.

THREE

————

'What is this?' Amber asked when the valet pulled up with Parker's car.

'This,' Parker said, unable to hold back his grin of affection, 'is a 1967 Ford Mustang Fastback with a 390 cubic-inch, V-8 engine.'

Face blank, she stared at him.

'She's fast and she's furious and she's as badass as me,' he said, knowing the response it would produce. And so what if he enjoyed the roll of Amber's eyes. He blamed the small slice of pleasure for the words that slid from his mouth next. 'It belonged to my father.'

A look of tenderness leaped into her eyes and his chest clenched hard, the black hole cinching tight around his heart.

Stretching out her arm, as if to take his hand, she said, 'I'm sorry—'

'Don't.'

He stepped back before he knew what he was doing. He wasn't sure where the harsh word had come from. But Parker also knew he couldn't bear to hear whatever she was going to say next.

And no way could he stand to have her touch him in comfort.

They settled into his car, and he was grateful for the distraction of merging with traffic. The misting rain turned into a steady drizzle and the *swish swish swish* of the windshield wipers filled the vehicle. Riding in silence, the awkward commute felt longer than it should have, and Parker was almost relieved when they drew closer to her turnoff and he had to ask her for directions.

Once he parked on her street and turned off the car, the rain began to come down a little harder. He slid off his jacket and turned to toss it onto the backseat, noticing her eyes on his chest. And the sharp stab of lust to his groin was unexpected.

'I'll walk you to the door,' he said, gearing up for a goodbye.

'No need,' she said. 'There's no sense in two of us getting wet.' She twisted in her seat to look at him. 'Parker, about the wedding—'

Stomach knotted with tension, he bolted out of the car and rounded to the passenger side, opening Amber's door. 'We're a block away,' he said. 'We should get moving.'

He closed the car door behind her with a forceful *thunk*, because the former stalker had lied to him. She was going to try to convince him to change his mind. And the last thing he needed were *two* females hounding him about an impossible task.

Amber frowned. 'It won't take long to get there, so we can—'

'We better hurry before the rain gets worse,' he said, taking her arm.

Leading her up the sidewalk, he glanced at the redhead from the corner of his eye. She had a nice figure.

Slim, but curvy enough in the right spots to capture a man's attention.

'Parker,' Amber said, sounding impatient. 'We need to—'

The skies opened up and began to release a load of rain as if it had grown too heavy to hold. Their mad dash to the awning wasn't fast enough, and, when they arrived, water dripped down their faces.

Parker turned to Amber, trying hard not to appreciate how good she looked wet.

'The last time I saw you that soaked you were trying to drown,' Parker said.

Sending him an overly tolerant look, she opened her mouth to speak again. But Parker had other ideas.

'There's something I gotta ask.' He narrowed his eyes at Amber with a curiosity that was genuine. 'Were you just pretending to be dead so I would do mouth to mouth?'

The shocked and offended expression on her face was instantaneous, and her mouth dropped open wider. 'I—'

She blinked and tried again. 'You—'

'Hey,' he said by way of protest. So far his choice of conversation had left her practically mute, which was exactly what he'd planned. 'You *followed* me around. I mean, come on, I couldn't seem to get rid of you.' A smile split his lips at the memory. 'I even caught you watching me make out with Susie Frances.'

Pink coloring bled up her cheeks. Parker would never forget the gaping look on Amber's face when he spied her peeking at them from behind the lifeguard house. He knew his gruff 'You got some kind of voyeur kink going on there, Ace?' had been totally out of line. But the expression on her face had been priceless. Poor kid didn't have a clue what he'd been talking about, but he remembered the look in her eyes.

From an awkward twelve-year-old it had been embarrassingly uncomfortable.

From a beautiful twenty-seven-year-old it made him embarrassingly uncomfortable in his jeans. Case in point, the way her eyes had skimmed over his chest in the car.

'I did not mean to spy on you while you were with Susie,' she said.

'Feel free to keep lying to yourself,' Parker went on. 'So...did you?'

She blinked. 'Did I what?'

'Pretend to be dead.'

'Yes,' she said with a huff of sarcasm that told him it wasn't true. 'And vomiting up seawater was part of my evil seduction plan, too.'

'Come on, you know you wanted to kiss me back then. It was hellaciously embarrassing, let me tell you,' Parker said.

The color climbed higher up her cheeks. 'Trust me, I didn't plan out almost drowning just so I could get your lips on mine,' she said. 'Which is a good thing, too, because it would have been a terrible disappointment.'

'You keep saying that.'

'Because it's true.'

'Awesome,' he said with a dry twist of his lips. 'My skills are being judged on a one-time incident of giving you mouth to mouth—' he paused, as if for emphasis '—while you were trying to, you know, *die.*'

'Sorry,' she said with a delicate lift of her shoulder. 'It's my only basis for comparison.'

In a fit of madness he wanted to wipe that look off

her face. 'Well,' he said as he stepped closer, hating how rough the word came out. 'There's an easy fix for that.'

Hands on her arms, he was vaguely aware goose bumps prickled her skin, and he wondered if it was from the chilling rain...or his touch.

No matter. He intended to be quick in his efforts, to dazzle her with his finesse. Get in; get out. Hopefully blow her mind. Or at least replace a stupid ten-second mouth-to-mouth moment with a kiss that was worthy of being judged. His pride was at stake here.

But when his lips touched hers, she let out a whimper that slayed him and canted her head up, opening her mouth beneath his as if she'd been waiting all night to do exactly that. And if he took advantage of the offer to sweep his tongue against hers, and instantly followed through on the crushing need to repeat the act, well... he was as weak as the next guy when faced with a beautiful woman in his arms.

He might have arched against her.

His breath might have caught in his throat at the glorious feel of her soft body.

Before he knew what he was doing he was shifting closer, his hands in the silk of her hair, and angling her head to increase the contact. To maintain the seductive slide of tongue against tongue. She tasted like maple and smelled like the syrup that matched the color her eyes.

For a heart-stopping moment he pushed aside the fact that she was too sweet. That she was the sort of woman that would expect more than he could give.

That she was the one person who knew the truth about how weak he'd once been.

The mood-killing thought hit like a jolt of lightning, and he tried to pull away. But her soft hand on his neck didn't allow him to escape too far, now only an inch of space separating them. Her breath was sweet, warm and moist on his lips.

Heart thumping harder than it should have from a simple kiss, he stared into the golden-brown eyes.

And then she feathered her mouth across his in a way that was so soft, so barely there, that Parker didn't know what to do with the moment. As lips ghosted across his, he frowned, frozen, adjusting to the foreign feel of something *not* focused on the act of sexual gratification. The barely-there touch of skin on skin that managed to gut him so thoroughly. Affect him more than any other more carnal action could have.

And an odd, soft feeling was seeping into his chest. A feeling he didn't quite know what to do with.

But he did not do sweet. Not in his relationships, not in his work, not in his *life*. Yet, for some unknown reason, he couldn't pull away. He didn't respond, but he couldn't move, either. Like a stupid deer in the freight-train-lights moment.

When she finally leaned back, her throat was flushed the same shade as her face, her fingers stroking against the hair at the base of his neck. Sending goose bumps, freakin' *goose bumps,* down his back.

What the hell?

Rain pounded the pavement around them, gushing off the awning and cocooning them in a rushing wall of water.

'So,' Parker finally said. He cleared his throat. 'I'd say that puts the kiss issue to rest.'

But, man, did it ever create a whole new set of problems.

Because he was staring at her face, still wet from the

rain. A drop dripped from her hair and slid down her cheek, slipping past the corner of her mouth, and Parker was struck by the gut-wrenching urge to lick the trail. The slender body in the dress that now clung to curves he hadn't *truly* appreciated without the addition of water. And, as if the *want* wasn't bad enough, the strand of hair that clung to her temple added an air of vulnerability that was far worse than the feeling of lust.

From this proximity he could reach out and brush the lock from her forehead. Not that he planned on following through, or that he longed to. At all.

Damn it.

'You seem awfully confident,' she said softly.

'I am.'

'Shouldn't I have a say?'

Lifting a brow, he waited.

'It definitely puts the issue to rest,' she said.

And the smile on her face left him wanting to kiss her again, and he fisted his hand.

He worked in a world of bitterness and darkness and death and she dealt with joy and lightness and happily ever after. He couldn't bear the thought of being the one to snuff out those good feelings. And he would, too. Every woman he'd left behind him had been just a little more jaded, a little less innocent. Had believed a little less.

He didn't want to...

No, he *wouldn't* do that to Amber.

'Take care, Ace,' he said as he set her back.

And then he headed out into the night and the rain, before she could say something they'd both regret.

Focusfocus*focus*

Amber clutched her purse as she trotted up the steps leading to Rosie's Bar, hoping Parker was here. Three days after she'd set out to get him to change his mind and gotten so deliciously sidetracked, she'd finally recovered enough from his devastating kiss to face him again. It had been all she'd imagined and more.

And after years of fantasies, that was a supersize order beyond belief.

The beautiful lips had been softer than she remembered, the slide of his tongue electrifying. The smell of the leather jacket clung to his T-shirt in its absence. Hands hard on her head, he'd held her still as the kiss had quickly shifted from a teasing joke to something more, until he was nearly mauling her mouth with an intensity that had sapped the air from her lungs.

She pushed aside the swirl of heat in her stomach. No more getting distracted by her memories or the way he made her feel. She'd followed Parker into the elevator that night with every intention of convincing him to agree to be in Reese's wedding. But once she'd climbed into the car and been enclosed in the small space, his enticing smell, those captivating eyes and that finely honed body had derailed her plans.

And of course, then there'd been the leftover strain in the air from the mention of his father....

No, that wasn't right. The tension had come when she'd tried to show him how sorry she was for his loss. All she'd wanted was to offer a bit of sympathy. She might have been small when her father had died, but she still felt the loss acutely. And she'd been overwhelmed with the need for a simple squeeze of her fingers to communicate that she knew how he felt.

But Parker...Parker wouldn't allow even that small comfort.

The vision of him averting Reese's hug swam before

her eyes, and Amber's lips twisted in disappointment and concern. He hadn't always been so distant. In fact, as a kid he'd been open and easy and fairly demonstrative. But that had changed as he'd grown into an adolescent. Amber had witnessed the slow transformation under his mother's treatment, and it was disheartening to realize that it remained a permanent fixture of his personality.

Bracing herself for another Parker encounter, she opened the door and entered the chaos of the noisy sports bar. She weaved her way through the throng of people, scanning the crowd.

And then her gaze caught on the back of ruffled brown hair with streaks of gold, spying Parker at a small table. He wore well-worn jeans, a long-sleeved T-shirt and the brown leather jacket. A black-haired man in slacks, a navy peacoat and no tie shared the table.

As she approached, Parker's green eyes collided with hers. 'What are you doing here?'

The words were delivered with more surprise than annoyance, but the pause that followed was uncomfortable, filled with Parker's heated gaze, chatter and the sound of clinking glasses.

The man sitting beside him sent Parker a curious look before sticking out his hand. 'Rob Winston,' he said with a smile and an accent that sounded southern. Texan, maybe. 'Ignore my partner here.' She returned his shake as he tipped his head in Parker's direction. 'His momma didn't hug him enough as a child.'

The words sent a shock through Amber's system. There wasn't a flicker of emotion in Parker's expression, the muscles in his face rigid. By the nonchalant way Rob had delivered the words, Amber knew that Parker's partner had no idea how close to the marrow his words had drilled. It was written in the way Parker was studiously avoiding her gaze.

Because she remembered...

'Don't get your ovaries in a wad, Robin,' Parker huffed, though there was no real annoyance there, either.

'Don't be such a dirtbag, Parker,' Rob said good-naturedly.

Amber had the distinct impression that these words were uttered on a daily basis.

'So—' eyes on Amber, Rob indicated for her to take a seat, but she hesitated '—how do you know my dumbass of a partner here?'

'We grew up together,' she said.

This seemed to prick Rob's interest. He sat up higher in his seat and folded his arms on the table, leaning in with a light in his gaze that was unmistakable.

'I bet you have some good stories about my friend here,' Rob said. 'Please—' he waved at the chair beside him again in invitation '—join us and share.'

Ignoring Parker's gaze, Amber bit back the smile as she sat down. It was hard not to respond to the open friendliness in Rob's face, the amusing curiosity in his eyes. Which made it easier to bear Parker's disconcerting attention.

'You're right, Rob.' Her eyes slid to meet Parker's, who was staring at her with a heat that burned her to the core, making her words just a little too husky. 'I do have some doozies to tell.'

The responding flash in Parker's gaze sent a thrill tripping through her limbs.

'Was he always an obstinate SOB?' Rob said.

Amber smiled at the memories. 'Definitely.'

'He's relentless,' Rob said with an acknowledging nod

of his head. 'He once chased a suspect ten blocks before tackling him in the alleyway of a pawnshop. And that was *after* the guy had dumped a pail of rose-colored paint over Parker's head.'

Amber laughed at the image of Parker in pink sprinting up the street.

'He spent one whole summer teaching me how to hold a crab,' she said. Remembering her yells and Parker's patient laughs, she twisted her lips wryly. 'I kept shrieking and drawing my hands away. But he kept insisting I try again, no matter how loud I screamed.'

He'd paddled like a madman to rescue her from drowning.

He hadn't given up then, either.

Tilting his head, Rob went on. 'You should see him in the interrogation room,' he said. 'Of course, my hell-on-wheels partner here is the reason we have the highest closure rate in the department.'

That Parker was the best at his job didn't come as a surprise.

Chuckling, Rob glanced around. 'We should have the waitress bring you a drink,' he said to Amber. 'So we can swap war stories. Was he a shameless flirt back then, too?'

'The summer he was seventeen he dated three girls—' eyes fixed on Rob, she leaned in conspiratorially, ignoring Parker's frown '—at the *same time.*'

'I don't remember that,' Parker said.

Gazing at Rob as if Parker hadn't spoken, Amber went on. 'Leslie Campbell, Sharon Howell and Susie Frances.' She hoped no one would comment on why she remembered the girls' names when Parker didn't. 'Once I even caught him—'

'Hey.' Clearly unhappy with the turn in the conversation, Parker waved a hand in the air between his tablemates' gazes. 'I'm sitting right here, people.' He tossed a loaded look at his partner. 'Why don't you make yourself useful and go find the waitress.'

Rob chuckled again. 'But I'm—' his curious gaze slid to his partner, where he must have seen something interesting, because Rob cleared his throat and stood '—just going to find the waitress.' He sent Amber a quick nod. 'Nice to meet you.'

After an answering smile, Amber watched the man walk away to join a boisterous bunch at the end of the bar. Her gaze lingered more from a nervousness about looking at Parker again then from any real interest in his good-looking partner.

'Why are you here, Amber?' Parker asked, his voice wary.

Feeling the need for a sense of power, she shifted higher in her seat. And from his laid-back position, legs stretched in front of him, they were almost eye to eye. Her foot brushed his, and a flash of awareness lit his gaze, an awareness that reminded her that she had been well and thoroughly kissed by Parker.

'You know why I'm here,' she said.

'We're not finishing what we started.'

Was he talking about their make-out session or the conversation where she insisted he be in the wedding?

And why was the former more disappointing than the latter?

Amber lost track of the thought when he shrugged out of his jacket to loop it behind his chair, the muscles in his chest flexing from the move. The long-sleeved T-shirt stretched across his gorgeous form nicely, the pectorals and biceps filling it in a way that made coherent thought briefly impossible.

'You need to come get measured for your tux,' Amber said.

Parker let out a grunt. 'I'm not going to be in the wedding.'

'You have to.'

His gaze pierced her. 'I don't have to do anything.'

'Please, Parker,' Amber said, all teasing long gone. 'I know it means nothing to you. But it's really important to Reese.'

At the mention of his sister, Parker's gaze slid off into the distance and Amber could see the conflict on his face. He wanted to, but he didn't. And suddenly, it seemed imperative that Parker accept this little bit of his family's affections. Or, more accurately, his *sister's* affections. Somehow Amber just knew that if he didn't follow through with this he would remain distant, not only to his family, but to, well...*life*.

'I'm busy, Amber,' he said. 'I'm here with my friends.'

'And as soon as you agree to the simple deed that will make your sister happy,' she said easily, leaning back to get comfortable, 'I'll get out of your hair.'

The twist of his lips betrayed his displeasure. But this was too important. And much bigger than just one wedding.

When he didn't relent, Amber crossed her arms and pulled the same stunt she'd pulled after he'd saved her from drowning. 'If you don't agree to be in Reese's wedding,' she went on with an expression so innocent she knew Parker could see through it, 'I'll agree to that drink with Rob.'

Parker's gaze barreled back into hers. 'You wouldn't.'

'I would.' She sent him a small smile. They both knew she had enough stories to embarrass him from now until forever. 'I bet Rob would *love* to know you listened to 'N Sync.'

'When I was twelve,' he barked, eyebrows scrunched in horrified protest.

'You were seventeen when you let Susie Frances paint your toenails.'

'That was *joke*.' He glanced around nervously, as if suddenly realizing the potential risk to his reputation. 'And besides—' the sexy smirk edged up his face '—she made the humiliation totally worth my while.'

And Amber *really* didn't want to hear how.

'Okay,' she said. Time to go big or go home. She leaned closer, and this time her smile was brilliant. 'I'll tell Rob about the time I walked in on you in the bathroom and caught you—'

'Stop.' His hand landed on the table with a *thump,* and he eyed her as if half tempted to muzzle her mouth. His voice gruff, he muttered, 'Holy mother of—'

The curse—a creative one, no doubt—died as he plowed a hand through his gold-tipped hair, leaving it more tousled than usual.

'I'll do it, okay?' he said.

The boyishly ruffled hair, his obvious embarrassment and his agreement sent a twist of affection to her heart, and she leaned in close enough to smell the leather of his jacket.

'Thank you,' she said sincerely as she reached out, overwhelmed with the need to touch his hand in simple appreciation.

He must have misread her intentions, because his gaze grew dark as he drew back out of reach. 'You've had your kiss,' he said dryly. 'And that's all you get. As a matter of fact,' he went on, lifting his brow as if in challenge. 'Hands to yourself from here on out.'

Amber was surprised the surge of heat didn't leave her in a puddle in her chair. Her nerves pulled into a knot, partly from the mention of their kiss and partly in annoyance at the reminder she wasn't his 'type.' Which apparently included everyone *but* her. She inhaled a soothing breath. Parker Robinson seemed to avoid anything he didn't want to talk about—emotions, thoughts, feelings, his *past*—by burying it in sexual innuendo.

She remember Parker arching against her body, the catch of his breath against her mouth...and the pulse of pure, unadulterated pleasure knowing that she had caused both.

Clearly, he'd enjoyed kissing her. No one could fake that kind of response. And he was still attracted, she could sense it in his gaze, in his very posture. Except he kept insisting he'd never touch her again. Any other guy and she wouldn't care.

For some reason, Parker's attitude was starting to tick her off.

'I'm measuring you for your tuxedo,' she said, amazed she managed to sound so calm. 'Touching kind of goes along with the activity.'

She forced her eyes to remain steady on his as an impressive whirlwind of emotion swept across his face. Annoyance. Resentment. And a whole lot of lust.

Lust.

Chest slowly squeezing the air from her lungs, she desperately reminded herself that she didn't do casual hookups, no matter how attracted she was. More important, she'd never, ever, seduce a guy. And she wouldn't *dream* of chasing a fellow who was throwing up caution signs all over the place. Especially like the man seated across from her, a man who was less like a stop sign and more like a road-totally-closed-ahead kind of guy.

But...but she'd wanted Parker her whole life and the desire was so strong she was seriously considering making him an exception.

'Fine,' he said gruffly. 'But I work long hours, so it will be late before I can stop by your shop.'

Visions of him in her store swam before her eyes. At night. The two of them alone. All she could hear in her head was Reese's 'You should be more proactive.'

And if anyone was worth taking the initiative to seduce, it was Parker Robinson.

Decision made, anticipation coursed through her veins, and Amber swallowed so hard it hurt.

She cleared her throat. 'I make special, after-hours appointments fairly regularly,' she said. 'Just tell me when you can be there.'

Parker heaved out a breath and grabbed his beer bottle. 'Nine-thirty tomorrow night,' he said, taking a sip as he shot her a loaded look. 'Just a quick couple of measurements and then I'm gone.'

The set of those beautiful lips and the tone of his voice made it abundantly clear he was done. But Amber...

Well, as far as she was concerned, she was just getting started.

FOUR

_____

At nine-thirty the next night Parker pulled the door open to Amber's Bridals. The bell tinkled way too merrily for a frustrating day that had started with a dead end on the Miller case, expanding the black, vast void in his chest. Which meant he'd spent the rest of today numbly going through the motions. Or maybe the numbness had been a problem for months.

Perhaps _years_.

Rolling his shoulders uneasily, he glanced around. He had to hand it to the kid, she had one helluva store. Classy to the core, the shop contained sleek hardwood floors and an abundance of white dresses lining the walls, veils, fake bouquets and pictures of models in wedding getup. And bowls of...what were those? Rose petals?

Parker couldn't help himself. He let out a shudder.

'Don't worry.' Amber's voice came from behind. 'No one has to know you were here.'

He let out a barking laugh. 'I'm losing every masculine mark I ever earned just by passing through these doors—'

Turning, he was hit with a vision of Amber that knocked him on his virtual ass. How had the geeky preteen grown into such a vision? Red hair flowed past her shoulders. She was dressed in dressy jeans and a sheer top that clung to her breasts, the long-sleeve blouse flaring at the waist and sleeves. She managed to look young and sweet and incredibly sexy.

And with the current case he was working on, he felt old and hardened and done with humanity.

Amber crossed to lock the door and then turned to face him, remaining silent. The staring contest grew uncomfortable as Parker realized he was alone in a shop with a beautiful woman who had, at the age of twelve, looked at him as if he hung the moon, the stars and the bloody sun to boot. Unfortunately, the appreciation in her face now held the weight of experience. Not to mention the lady was a walking, talking advertisement for Happily Ever After and Parker was quite convinced that Content for Now was beyond his capabilities. Toss in the fact that they were surrounded by swarms of puffy white dresses—and, holy mother, were those fake *tiaras?*— and the situation was less amusing than downright *concerning*.

She hiked a brow that didn't ease the tension. 'You ready?'

What was that supposed to mean?

'Of course,' he said.

He wasn't an amateur. He refused to be intimated by the little slip of a thing that he'd taught how to capture crabs on the beach.

As he followed her down the hall, he made a point of ignoring the gentle, seductive sway of her slight hips and the fluid walk. Fortunately, the view was easier to ignore when she stepped into a large room containing two couches, an armchair and a coffee table mimicking an elegant living room, the furniture facing a small space surrounded on three sides by floor-length mirrors. And while he was sure broad daylight and the addition of people encouraged the appropriate air for viewing a dress, somehow the whole setup hinted at something...almost erotic. Especially with just the two of them. Alone.

Damn, what had he agreed to?

'Take off your jacket and shoes,' Amber said, waving in the direction of the furniture.

Parker shrugged out of his leather jacket and tossed it on a couch, toeing off his shoes.

'Uh—' her eyes dropped to his shoulder holster containing his weapon and handcuffs '—the gun, too.'

For some reason he hesitated.

'What?' she said, hand on her hip. 'You don't mind taking off the jacket and shoes, but you draw a line at the weapon?'

'Maybe it brings me a sense of security,' he said with a small grin. When she waited for him to go on, the oft-repeated joke tripped off of his tongue. 'Most people respect the badge,' he said. 'But everyone respects Smith & Wesson.'

'Is that why you do what you do?' she said, gesturing for him to step forward to the space in front of the mirror. 'For respect?'

Black void expanding exponentially in his chest, he frowned. Shoot. He'd been teasing and she'd jumped straight to the serious talk.

'How long is this going to take?' he said as he crossed to the designated spot.

She pulled out a small, flexible tape measure and moved closer, pulling his gut a touch tighter. 'I need to measure you for a shirt, jacket and pants,' she said.

Which was really no answer at all.

And suddenly she was right in front of him, bringing her scent and the clear skin of her beautiful face close to his. He leaned back and looked down at her dubiously, his frown drawing his brows down until they tried to merge with his eyes.

'Relax,' she said. But something in her tone made the suggestion impossible. 'This isn't going to hurt.'

He elected to ignore the twitch of her luscious lips and hoped to hell she was talking about being measured for the tux. Innocent expression clashing with the knowing light in her eyes, she looped the tape measure—and consequently, *her arms*—around his neck, setting his heart tapping harder in his chest.

The slight smile on her face made him nervous. 'There's something I've been meaning to discuss with you,' she said as she took the measurement, her fingers whispering against him just beneath his Adam's apple.

The simple brush of skin on skin sent a line of goose bumps streaking up his back. And how was that possible when she was only touching his stupid neck?

'Are you going to your mother's dinner party in two weeks?' she went on.

Fortunately it was a question he could answer without thought, because thinking was difficult with her so close. 'No.'

The word came out a little harsher than he'd intended, but the feel of her fingers was sending an uncomfortable thrum through his body. And how long did it take to get an accurate measurement? She wasn't launching a nuclear warhead here. An approximation would do just fine, thank you.

'Why not?' she said as she dropped her hands and stepped over to the laptop on the coffee table.

Free of her disturbing touch, Parker let out a breath of relief.

'Because I don't have anything to say to my mother,' he said. 'And if I show up I'll have to talk to her.'

A small frown tugged on her lips as she entered the measurement into her laptop. 'When was the last time you two had a conversation?'

The gaping pit around his heart seemed to expand twofold, and Parker worked hard at *not* frowning at the memory.

'She called my cell the day my father died,' he said, remembering the feeling of desolation, the sense of aloneness. 'I didn't answer.'

She turned and stepped closer again, studying him silently for a moment. The assessing gaze, the topic of conversation and her skin that looked as if it tasted of cream made the situation wholly uncomfortable.

Without a word, she came to his side, and he stared at her profile in the mirror.

'You should talk to her,' she said.

'I've got nothing to say.'

The pause was slight, but he sensed she had more to share. The words that followed were not what he'd been expecting.

'I'm going to measure your sleeve length,' she said.

With more care than he thought necessary, she measured from the spine at his neck, to his shoulder, and then drew the tape down his arm to his wrist. His T-shirt offered no protection from the slow slide of her fingers against his bare arm, and he ignored the shimmer of awareness that came with the move.

The simple brush of skin on skin on his arm shouldn't be so arousing, either.

'You did that on purpose,' he said.

Despite the unfortunate husky tone of his voice, she said, 'I have no idea what you're talking about.' She sent him a sedate look. 'Now raise your arms.'

He shifted on his feet, uneasy. 'Why?'

She rolled her eyes. 'No need to be so suspicious,' she said. 'I just need to measure your chest.'

Something in the set of her posture and the light in her eyes told him he needed to proceed with caution. To be on guard—and not because of the conversation about his family. The mood was electric. Heck, the air was so heavily charged he was surprised they both didn't glow. And he could see in her eyes that she knew it, too.

'Arms,' she said as she stepped in front of him again.

Sending a sharp look down at her too-close-for-comfort face, Parker complied, raising his hands as if surrendering. Which he wasn't, blast it all.

Amber looped her arms around his back, and, for a moment, the world came to a grinding halt....

He couldn't think.

Couldn't breathe.

If he leaned just a fraction of an inch closer, he would be able to feel the soft press of her breasts against the harder planes of his chest. She was looking up at him with those wide, beautiful eyes, and her face almost glowed. As though she was lit from within. A light that just might be able to absorb the blackness that churned inside.

Where had that thought come from?

Looking dazed, Amber stared up at him with her arms around his torso, and the words that came from her mouth were a surprise. 'You took off your jacket.'

Her tone of voice suggested there was more to that less-than-brilliant bit of observation.

Parker's brows pulled together, the rest of him frozen. 'You told me to.'

She looked as stunned as he felt.

'No. Not that...' she said, her voice stumbling a bit. 'I mean—you still smell like leather.'

A succession of emotions filed across her face, moving on from the shock and eventually ending with something that looked like anticipation. And...damn, there was no ignoring the vibe any longer because—

'But maybe that's just your signature scent,' she mused.

—it was written all over her face.

'Are you trying to seduce me, Amber?' he asked softly.

Sometimes it was best just to punch the elephant in the room in the face.

She blinked, as if clearing her vision, and then brought her hands back around to finish measuring his chest. 'Yes.'

Apparently she had no qualms about laying her cards on the table.

Tipping his head, he paused, feeling stronger now that they'd addressed the issue. He could handle this. He'd handled her starstruck adoration as a kid and he could handle her desire now. Feeling better, he watched her cross to enter the latest numbers and then return to stand in front of him again.

Everything would be fine, if he just didn't look at her face, or her mouth, or her chest....

Bracing himself, he held his breath as she measured around his waist, her fingers skimming just below the level of his belly button, too close to more...*sensitive* parts of his body. And his abdominal muscles clenched as if punched, despite the T-shirt between them.

'You should at least come to your mother's party to see Reese,' she said as she bit the corner of her mouth in concentration.

Leaving Parker with the intense need to lick the damp spot from her lip. His head was spinning, and his shaft was thickening, and coherent thought took him a moment.

'Why?' he croaked.

See, he could form words. Sort of.

'Because she's family,' she said. 'And we all need family.'

Despite his discomfort, he let out a small huff of laughter. She thought she was going to seduce him *and* get him to talk to his family? Man, she really was a believer.

And then she knelt before him, and... *Oh, God.*

In the mirror, the vision of her on her knees in front of him sent his pulse bounding out a rhythm that threatened to burst from his body. She was joy and hope and light and the intense need to bury himself inside her, to take a little of that faith for himself, to sink into her *belief* was almost his undoing.

His mouth worked, struggling to function. 'Nothing about this scenario is going to work on me, Ace,' he said hoarsely, proud he could still form words.

'I'm just taking your measurements.'

A sarcastic scoff escaped his throat.

And then she measured from his waist to his heel, and Parker blew out a breath, relieved the act was fairly tolerable. Even being so stupid as to congratulate himself on his self-control as she entered the measurement into her computer.

'Next, your inseam.' She returned to kneel in front of him, and he braced himself. 'Spread your legs a bit.'

Sweat broke out along his lip at the erotic image her words produced. Parker was busy battling the flash of heat when Amber, with one end of the measuring tape, reached up between his thighs. His chest seized around his heart, preventing it from doing its job. And when her fingers brushed just to the left of his groin, pleasure pooled in his stomach.

Paralyzed, he used his gaze in a vain attempt to burn reason into her, his voice almost a growl. 'Does measuring my inseam include touching my junk?'

Eyes wide, she looked up at him. But beneath it all, he was sure he detected a note of false innocence. And a hint of nerves.

'Sorry,' she said as she drew the other end of the tape down to his heel.

With a wary scowl, he said, 'You don't look sorry.'

She swallowed and cleared her throat. 'Assume your normal posture, please.'

'I am.'

'You look like you're slumped over,' she said with a doubtful look.

That was because he was so hard now his body was protectively hunching around the sensitive area.

'And now I need to get the last measurement,' she said.

He should have known he was in trouble by the fine tremor in her voice. By the way she nervously licked her lips. But he was too mesmerized by the slide of pink tongue across her mouth to register what she was doing.

One hand holding the tape at his waist in back, she reached between his legs and pulled the measuring tape down his backside.

'You're measuring my ass?' he rasped.

'I need your crotch length,' she said.

Crotch length?

There was a joke in there somewhere, but, for the life of him, he couldn't formulate the wisecrack. Especially when her hand slowly pulled the tape up between his thighs.

And Parker knew he was well and truly screwed.

Breathing a distant memory, a tiny speck in his review mirror, he couldn't move as her fingers flirted with touching his erection. She skirted too close for comfort as she continued up his crotch toward the front of his waist. Wringing his insides. Dragging his nerves through razor wire. And, just when it was almost over, she lightly brushed the tip of his shaft.

Desire burst like a supernova, jump-starting his flagging brain.

'Jesus, Amber,' he ground out, grabbing her wrist. Body throbbing, he narrowed his gaze. 'Is this measurement even necessary?'

She gazed up at him, looking stunned. 'You can never have too much information,' she murmured.

'Hell yeah, you can.' His grip grew firmer around her wrist.

Case in point: her skin was warm, her pulse bounded beneath his fingers and her expression was nothing but honest—pure, unadulterated want innocently on display. Along with something else. He should have pushed her wrist as far from him as possible, but he was transfixed by the light in her eyes. As if he deserved much more than just sex.

And the crushing need to capture a little of that hope for himself, to briefly fill the black hole that had been surrounding his heart for years, was too much.

'You win,' he muttered, and he hauled her up by her wrist, gaze intent on her mouth.

* * *

Amber didn't utter a word of protest as Parker pulled her body flush with his. Her wrist still clutched in his fingers, he tucked their arms behind his back until she was giving him a partial hug. But it wasn't a real embrace, because his other hand hung loosely at his side.

Green eyes holding hers, his voice gruff, he said, 'You know this is all you get, right?'

They were pressed together from chest to groin, and she was momentarily rendered speechless by his too-blunt words and the feel of his erection. The longing to be wrapped in his arms for real was intense. But he maintained his current posture, patiently waiting for a response, and he wasn't going to continue until he was sure he'd made his point.

She'd never chased a man before, had never actively pursued what she wanted. And she *wanted* this.

With an intensity that was too great to be denied.

'I understand,' she said.

The tension radiating from him since she'd taken his measurement suddenly dissipated, and he lifted his free hand to her face, lowering his mouth to hers.

God, it wasn't fair.

He was strong and sure and oozed a confident sensuality as his lips slid over hers, as if trying to absorb something more than a simple kiss. Meanwhile she was quaking, literally *quaking* at the knees. She was a grown woman with plenty of experience under her belt. She'd been around several blocks along the way but, for some reason, this time the trip felt different.

Amber supposed it was only natural, as she'd waited for this moment since she was a preteen. Before she really even knew what, exactly, her body longed for....

She remembered the heat from innocent brushes of skin on skin as she'd accepted the crab he'd gently placed in her hand. She remembered her heart pounding from dreams too vague to recall, only that they'd contained *Parker.*

And she remembered the mesmerizing mouth that had always triggered an anxious flutter in her stomach. Parker's lips were now slicking across hers, wet and warm and working her mouth so deliciously she had to clutch his T-shirt, dizzy.

With a small movement, his tongue tested her bottom lip, and a needy catch escaped her throat as she opened her mouth wide. He finally relented and gave her what she wanted, his tongue against hers. The taste, the soft strokes that went on and on, sent her senses soaring. Twisting his T-shirt tighter, she fought to have her other arm freed from his grip.

'Slow down, Ace,' he murmured against her mouth.

Pleasure flared higher. As a kid, the nickname had always made her feel special in Parker's eyes. She hadn't been, she knew. But it was the way he said it, as if she were the only one on the planet that was important. And right now he was licking, kissing and nipping his way down her neck, leaving her feeling the same way.

Against the bounding pulse at her neck, he said, 'There's no hurry.'

Oh, but holy heaven, *there was.*

Summers of innocent longing. *Years* of fantasies.

The mother lode of mental foreplay.

'Please,' she said, pulling against the fingers wrapped around her wrist.

He released her.

Instantly her fingers gripped the edge of his T-shirt

and shoved, unceremoniously, up his torso. When he didn't lift his arms fast enough, she abandoned her plan to take it off and dropped her mouth to his naked chest. He tasted of salt and smelled of leather, as if the essence of his jacket had fused with his skin. She pressed open-mouthed kisses across his muscles, with the ridiculous thought that she could inhale this moment and keep it forever. Parker mumbled something she couldn't understand, something about taking their time, but Amber ignored him. She nosed a nipple and then licked the nub until it was raised enough to scrape her teeth across.

He sucked in a breath. 'Okay, okay.'

All thought came to a halt when his hands dropped to the T-shirt bunched just beneath his arms. Stunned, she watched the shifting of pectorals and bone and sinew as he shrugged out of the garment and tossed it aside. The strength in his shoulders, the easy play of muscle a beautiful, breathtaking sight.

Without hesitation, she spread her hands across the gorgeous display and pushed him back against the mirrored wall.

'Jesus, Amber,' he hissed.

Ignoring him, she stared at the light dusting of hair on his flat abdomen as she fumbled with his belt and the fastening of his jeans, finally pushing everything to the floor. The vision of lean hips, well-muscled thighs and a full erection left her breathless. Unable to continue.

And Parker finally seemed to grasp the urgency of their situation.

Hands and lips and teeth seemingly everywhere at once, he divested her of her clothing efficiently. When gone, she pressed her body to his, refusing to blush at the groan that ripped from her chest at the glorious feeling of, *finally,* skin on skin.

Parker swept a hand up her back and buried his fingers in her hair, his kiss raw. Mouth realigning this way and that as if to consume her from every angle. She lost track of time until the fingers in his other hand found their way between her thighs.

The visceral hit to her system left her pulling back from the kiss, gasping for air.

Lips parted, he breathed through his mouth—open hunger on his face as the fingers between her legs turned bolder. Until the desire grew so great tears pricked the backs of her lids.

Closing her eyes, she whispered, 'Parker.'

Which came out more like a strangled sound of pleasure than an actual word.

As if inspired, Parker's lips crashed back to hers. He pressed his hard shaft against the skin of her belly, as if seeking friction. The overpowering sensations were full of need. And want. And *need.* Amber could barely coordinate herself to return his kiss properly. Parker didn't seem to care, rocking his hips and nipping and pulling at her mouth for all it was worth. When he withdrew his hands, her body clenched in disappointment. Until he bent to pull a condom from the wallet in his jeans, sheathing himself.

Amber's mouth lost all moisture as she watched, transfixed, half terrified this was a dream and she'd wake up too soon.

Bracing his back against the mirror, Parker reached for Amber and lifted her up. Surprised, limbs clumsy, she didn't follow the logic until he spoke.

'Wrap your legs around my waist,' he said.

Oh, *God*, yes.

Praying her muscles would cooperate, she complied, yet all she could manage was to hold on as he buried himself inside. Eyes wide, she froze, adjusting to the pleasurable pressure that threatened to send her flying apart. A threat that escalated when he gripped her hips and began to move in earnest, each time taking her a little deeper.

Heat swamped her senses, until she was no longer frozen. She wrapped her arms more firmly around his neck. Tightened her legs around his hips.

And threw herself into a carnal kiss, scraping her teeth lightly across his tongue.

The swearword that shot from Parker's mouth into hers was explicit. He clutched her close, buried himself to the base of his shaft and then paused.

It felt *incredible*.

Chests pressed together, heart thundering against his, Amber whimpered greedily and rolled her hips, seeking more friction.

'Amber,' he groaned as he slowly slid down the mirror until she was seated in his lap, his back against the wall.

Hands on her shoulders, blunt fingernails clutching her skin, he began to rock up into her. Friction, wonderful, glorious friction again. His movements slow and sure and hard.

'I need…' he mumbled, eyes closed.

His head drifted to hers.

Each hot press of his mouth was interspersed with a flick of his tongue against her lips, all in rhythm with his hips. As if he needed every part of her, everything, all at once. The pace didn't increase, but the intensity did. Until starved, naked, needy noises began to spill from his mouth.

Nothing had ever been this ridiculously, spine-tingling delicious. The feeling of wholehearted—and, heaven help her—*reciprocated* want.

Digging her nails into his sweat-damp shoulders earned her a garbled reply.

'I can't—' he slurred.

Greedy, Amber arched her back, fitting their hips closer together, taking more.

Wringing an incoherent response from Parker. 'Ah, 'mgonna.'

With the garbled word of warning his movements grew too needy for finesse, hips bucking as if seeking fusion with every thrust. Too far gone for a coordinated kiss, their mouths pressed close, damp and hot as they breathed each other in. The feel of him slicking between her thighs, beneath her, *in* her, tightened the cord of pleasure, pulling harder. Until she was so taut she feared being stranded on the edge of this precipice forever.

Afraid she'd never take that beautiful fall.

But then he gripped her shoulders, arched and thrust hard, groaning as he shattered.

And the sound of her name on his lips as he came pushed her off the ledge. A fiery electric pleasure shot through her veins, and her orgasm burst, painting colorful fireworks behind closed lids.

With a mumbled 'Parker,' she collapsed against him, and let herself be swept away by the aftershocks.

The smell of leather and sex filled Amber's nose as her breathing finally slowed enough for her to think straight. Bit by bit she became aware of the hard chest under her cheek, Parker's pounding heart gradually recovering beneath. They'd managed to shuffle their way to the thick rug in front of the wrought-iron coffee table. Now, sweat-slick bodies cooling in the aftermath, she was draped across Parker, her palms resting on his shoulders.

His hands, however, were resting by his sides.

Parker gripped her arms, gently shifting her off, and her chest cinched tight at the movement. 'I should find my clothes,' he said, his voice rough from exertion.

She briefly pressed her lids tight, knowing he was doing more than pulling away physically. He was pulling away mentally, too, and the memory of his words punched the breath from her throat.

You know this is all you get, right?

Pushing up on her elbows, she stared at Parker. The sex had been fantastic, and now his soft hair was spiked in all directions, delectably mussed by her fingers. His cheeks were flushed from the energy he'd expended. And he'd exerted a good deal of energy.

After they'd finished the first round, while Amber was still limp and essentially incapable of thought or movement, he had rolled them over onto the rug, pinning Amber beneath him. And started in on her again.

No one had ever made her feel so sensual.

No one had ever pulled so much pleasure from her body.

But he didn't want more.

She watched him rub a hand down his face with a faint frown on his mouth, and a memory rose, unbidden, in her mind.

That last fateful summer she'd caught Susie and Parker making out, and while it was clear he knew exactly what he was doing, there was no emotion behind the act. As if he could have replaced Susie with either of the other two girls he was dating and been just as happy. And while, yes, horny teens were pretty much a given, from what Reese had said Parker hadn't changed his ways much.

Random women, random relationships and nothing that lasted longer than a few months.

Amber's gaze landed on his holster draped across the arm of the couch, an idea forming in her head. He wouldn't like it. Heck, he might even wind up *hating* her for it. But getting the stubborn man to let someone in, even if it was his sister and not Amber, suddenly overwhelmed everything else—even her intense need to flee the presence of the man she'd so shamelessly seduced.

The one who seemed incapable of wanting more.

Chest tight, nerves taut, she reached for his holster, and when he reached for his pants...

She snapped the handcuffs around his wrist.

FIVE

———

The click of the cuff around his wrist snagged Parker's immediate attention.

Rolling onto his back again, he stared up at Amber. Her hair was mussed, her lips bruisingly red from his kisses, and guilt pierced his chest. So, yeah, things had gotten a little rough there toward the end. But he was only so strong, and Amber's frantic words and feverish hands had hacked away at his control until he really shouldn't be held responsible for what came after.

The guilt stabbed harder, anyway.

'Okay,' he said, his voice like gravel as he dangled the handcuffs in the air, his body twitching with interest. 'I'm assuming you want another round.'

The edgy smile, the blush that crept up her face and the way she shifted her eyes to the left had him chuckling.

'For the record, Ace—' he stretched out his leg, resting on his elbows '—any woman who goes for the handcuffs has no business being nervous.'

She stared at him a moment more and it was as if she was looking everywhere but at his groin. Which wasn't the *only* part of his body that wholeheartedly approved of the addition of restraints, but it was the only part that could communicate its consent.

And then Amber reached for his boxers.

Frowning, Parker simply watched as she hooked the underwear on his feet, sliding them up his calves.

He lifted a brow. 'FYI,' he said, 'the addition of handcuffs usually means you're taking the clothes off, not putting them back on.'

Ignoring him, she slid the boxers higher.

Now he was *really* curious.

'Okay, I'll bite,' he rumbled. She met his gaze as he lifted his hips to allow her to pull his underwear into place, and he sent her a smile. 'You got a clothes-on fetish, right?' The thought sent a thrill working its way down his back, wrapping around his growing erection. 'I can work with that.'

Now that he was covered, she scooted until she was resting against the coffee table.

'No fetish that I know of,' she said. 'I just can't concentrate when you're so naked.'

She reached for the loose end of the handcuffs, looping it through the ornate leg of the wrought-iron coffee table before clipping it around his other wrist.

Totally intrigued now, he grinned at his helpless position—which was really kinda *hot*.

'That's one of the advantages of being naked,' he said. 'The inability to focus on anything else.'

Gaze admiring all the creamy skin before him, he took in the curve of her breasts and hips.

He shouldn't encourage her. He shouldn't be so weak. He shouldn't crave absorbing that mesmerizing light radiating from her expression. From her eyes. Seemingly from her very skin.

But he needed just a little bit more.

Desire licked at his limbs and his voice reflected his thoughts.

'You just need additional practice,' he said. 'And I'm—'

She reached for her blouse and slid it back over her head, and Parker stared, stunned. And while she had been rendered mute by the sight of him naked, he had a similar problem with the vision of her putting her clothes *on*.

When she picked up her underwear and pulled them into place, he finally found his words.

'What the hell are you doing?' he asked.

She studied him for a moment, and Parker was briefly grateful that the long expanse of her legs was available for admiring.

Amber said, 'You clearly aren't a man who likes to cuddle.'

The statement slammed into him. 'Cuddle?'

So what if the word spit from his mouth with a vengeance. He didn't like the turn in the conversation.

'And if there is anything that Parker Robinson needs,' she went on, eyeing him steadily, 'it's a good cuddle.'

Heart thumping in agitation, he was sure he made a ridiculous sight, what with being handcuffed to a table leg and his mouth opening and closing like a fish.

When he finally found his voice again, it was rough. 'Amber—'

'We're going to talk, Parker.'

The swearword that echoed through his mind wasn't fit to be uttered out loud.

Scooting over to sit by his side, Amber's eyes settled

on his. 'Why didn't you answer the phone when your mother called the day your father died?'

The one-two punch to his chest had his jaw falling open wider, and then he slapped his lips shut, his mouth growing grim.

'Damn it, Amber,' he said, struggling to prop up on one elbow, despite the restraints. 'We're not high school sweethearts.' Frustrated he couldn't even plow a hand through his hair, he went on. 'Let me up.' Anxiety pressed in on his chest, leaving it difficult to draw in a breath. 'I don't want—'

She gently cupped his cheek, her thumb landing at the corner of his mouth, and he froze, unable to do anything but blink like an idiot.

Looking up at her, he wanted to curse and rant and rail against the understanding in her eyes and the bloody confinement of the cuffs. He finally managed to pull off a sparse rattling of the chain between his wrists.

Which, unfortunately, earned him a gentle swipe of her fingertip along his lower lip. It was just a simple stroke, barely noticeable, but the tenderness curled like a knot in his belly.

'Why?' she asked again.

He lobbed a hard look in her direction and didn't spare the truth. Sweet little Amber wanted to know, so sweet little Amber was going to hear.

'You were following me that day,' he said. 'You heard what she said.'

Amber didn't pretend she had no idea what he was talking about.

Her gaze warm on his, she said, 'I heard some of what your mother said, yes.'

Unsure of which parts she'd missed, he gave her the

full version. 'Marrying my father was a mistake.' His next words came out louder than he'd intended. '*I* was a mistake.'

Letting the words echo in the room, he forgot to breathe for a moment.

'I was just a symbol of everything my mother had done wrong,' he said. 'Of everything she regretted.'

None of it mattered.

The mantra had served him well in the past. He'd learned as a kid it was best to exist on the surface and ignore or bury or compartmentalize the rest. Because it was the rest that bit you in the ass.

Be polite to your mother, but don't try to get her to show you she cared. Hugs weren't necessary, but an occasional expression of some sort of affection would have been nice. He'd given up looking around the age of ten.

None of it mattered.

Or at least, that's what he'd told himself.

Until the summer he was seventeen and he'd tried again. But the years of being the rowdy boy who only got noticed when he got into trouble had taken a toll. Maybe by then his mother couldn't have cared, even if she'd wanted to.

'She hated my father's job,' he said. 'Looked down on what he did for a living.'

And Parker had *despised* her for being such a snob.

'Which was exactly why you followed in his footsteps,' Amber said as, still cradling his cheek, she stroked his lip again.

His mouth twisted beneath her finger. Man, she always was such an observant little thing. Even as a too-sweet, freaky stalker of a kid.

'Maybe in the beginning,' he said, though he knew she

was absolutely right. Growing weary of his awkward posture, he laid down on his side. 'But now...'

Well, not *right* now. Cuz right now everything was dull and flat and he got little enjoyment out of much of anything. But there was a time when helping victims' families find justice had been incredibly satisfying.

'You've always been good at taking care of people,' she said.

Barking out a laugh of disbelief, he tilted his head as he stared up at her, amazed she was still cradling his face. Strangely, he was starting to like the comforting feel of her palm.

'Who did I take care of?' he said.

'Reese,' she said. 'When we were kids, anyway.'

She gazed down at him, like she had as a kid. That same light in her eyes. He just didn't get it. What did she see in him then? What did she see in him now?

And then she went on. 'And you took care of me....'

He couldn't talk about how he'd felt that summer he left his mother's home and never went back. As a seventeen-year-old he'd been too cool to admit he'd missed Reese's and Amber's company. As an adult it seemed too late to confess the truth.

With a huff of humor, he said, 'You're just saying that because I saved you from drowning.'

Finally dropping her hand from his face, she sent him a small smile. And he didn't miss her touch. Not at all. Damn it.

'Your father loved you,' she said, and he swallowed back the groan.

Apparently, nothing in his history was sacred.

His dad hadn't been the type to hug or tell you he cared with his words. But he'd shown him in other ways.

'But then he died,' Parker said, and he hated the way the words came out so harsh. So bitter. He tried to ease the mood with a small smile, failing by a mile. 'Cuz life is mostly just a nasty little bitch who's looking to collect.'

Amber's expression shifted into one of sadness and he hated that he put that look on her face. The urge to take it back, to put a smile on her mouth, was overwhelming. And then suddenly she was crawling over him and sliding onto her side to lie next to him. Shocked, he didn't move as she wiggled her way up between his cuffed arms, settling against him as she embraced his chest.

Staggered by the comforting contact, the press of bodies from torso to toes, he took a moment to respond.

'You know,' he said dryly, 'I don't do the morning-after thing.'

'I'm not asking you to.'

'And hugs don't count if they're not freely given.'

'I know,' she said as she gave him a gentle squeeze. 'That's why I'm freely giving this one to you.'

Paralyzed, he didn't know what to do with himself. Silence stretched between them as they lazed on the floor, wrapped in each other's arms. His by force. Hers by choice

And it was really intimate in a way that sex usually wasn't, and wasn't that just the kicker?

Something in Parker shifted. Just a little, but enough to voice the thought he'd been having for weeks. 'Plenty of people have it worse than me,' he said quietly.

He didn't know why he needed to say the words. Other than the fact that they were the brutal truth. And if there was anything he was comfortable with, it was the brutal truth. Maybe it was the comfort of her arms that seduced the words from his mouth.

'Who?' she asked. 'Who has it worse?'

He didn't want to look into her eyes, so he stared up at the chandelier on the ceiling. 'I'm working on this case,' he said. The dark cloud encasing his heart grew thicker, denser. Something he hadn't thought possible since the day his dad had died.

An acid rain just waiting to break.

'Our current suspect is just a stupid seventeen-year-old,' he said. 'And his parents...'

He didn't want to repeat the words they'd said about their son.

'You know,' he said instead, his voice hoarse. 'Family should stick by you, no matter what.'

Man, now the woman had both hands on his cheeks.

Turning his head to face hers, her gaze clear, she said, 'Yes, they should.'

Staring into her amber eyes, he clenched his jaw.

The case had been eating at him for a while, draining what little color remained in his already-mucked-up life. He refused to lean into the warmth of Amber's palms, but the urge was there. He remembered the stricken look on her face when she'd overheard his mom that day, and the comforting hand Amber lay on his shoulder later.

Not that he'd wanted her sympathy. No, he'd hated the caring in her touch, the gesture of concern from a twelve-year-old when he couldn't even get that kind of emotion from his own mother.

Something in him had died that day, something vital that he'd lost. And damned if he knew how to get it back. He was pretty sure he didn't even *want* it back.

Blocking Amber's beautiful gaze, Parker closed his eyes and concentrated on keeping his breathing even. She held his face, and her sweet scent surrounded him, the silky legs entwined with his. But it was the warmth of her body that captivated him the most. Surprisingly, he wasn't really thinking of her skin in a sexual sense, but more of the gentle give-and-take of shared heat. It was refreshingly simple. And kind of nice.

Like a handful of summer sun on a dark winter's day.

But the unfamiliar feeling of comfort, of contentment—of...*happiness?*—scared the bejesus out of him.

Parker didn't know how much time passed as he grappled with the dueling urges to push her away or pull her closer. Maybe he should do something more productive, like bang his head against the nearest wall.

'You're right, family should stick by you,' she said, and he lifted his lids. 'No matter what.' Amber raised her chin to look up into his face, her eyes warming him in ways he'd never imagined. 'Which is why you should come to your mother's dinner party,' she went on, and Parker didn't bother suppressing the groan.

Christamighty, not this again.

'To support Reese,' she went on.

Without warning, she slid down from between his arms, and he instantly missed the feeling of warmth.

That tiny bit of...security, for lack of a better word.

'You should go to the party, Parker,' she said again.

After sitting up, she slipped on her jeans. Her shoes came next, and he absolutely did not panic that she was dressing to leave. Because that would be a stupid thing to do.

'Why?' he asked.

'Because your sister loves you,' Amber said as she stood to look down on him.

Something inside him rejected the notion, and not just because Reese had never said so in as many words.

'And if you can't do it for Reese,' she went on. Her voice

dropped an octave, creating an ominous pressure in his lungs. 'Then do it for me.'

This time the word came out harsher. 'Why?'

Reese stared down at Parker, her heart pumping wildly in her chest.

'Do it for the kid who saw you as worthy of adoration all those years ago,' she said.

The rest was on the tip of her tongue as she hesitated. But her insecurities suddenly seemed so insignificant compared to all that Parker had been through. He deserved the truth. He needed to *hear* the truth.

So she went on. 'And do it for the woman who's falling for you now.'

Denial, exasperation and a massive dose of confusion flared in his eyes just before he slammed his lids shut, muttering, 'Damn.'

She hadn't started out intending to share so much. But suddenly her choice to tell Parker the words that were so simple and complex, the words she was pretty sure he'd never heard in his life, was important—not just for Parker, but for herself. An extension of her decision to finally *fight* for what she wanted. And she wanted this man in her life.

Not the boy she'd obsessed about in the past, but the *man* of today.

Ironic, given it might be too late for Parker to ever truly let himself love anybody.

When he finally opened his eyes, a blank look on his face, she simply picked up the holster containing his keys and gently dropped it by his foot. Going on, she looked at him and spoke the words she knew he needed to hear.

'I'm falling in love with you,' she said. 'And you deserve to be loved, Parker Robinson.'

SIX

_____

Whywhy*why?*

Two weeks later Amber was dealing with her last customers of the day and preparing to leave for the Michaels' dinner party, still unsure she'd made the right decision to abandon Parker with his keys to free himself. Which he had, of course. She'd checked, just to be certain. Part of her thought she'd been making a statement by walking out, taking the first step in seizing control of her romantic life by seducing the man she'd dreamed of for ages, sharing the truth of how she felt about him and then exiting with her head high. The other part knew the truth.

Cowardcoward*coward*.

Because she didn't have the strength to stick around and *really* deal with the repercussions of her confession.

Fabulous, Amber.

Staring at the couple deciding on the style of the tuxedo for their wedding, she smiled, a tiny bit envious. When the groom-to-be leaned over and kissed the top of his fiancée's head, Amber's lips twisted. Such a simple gesture, shared and accepted so freely. As if the act was a given.

For some people displays of affection came easily.

Amber's cell phone rang and, grateful for the distraction, she turned her back on the couple and answered.

'Amber,' Reese said. 'You'll be there tonight, right?'

'Of course.' Without thinking, she went on. 'Have you heard from Parker?'

My. God.

Would she always sound like that twelve-year-old little girl who loved Parker Robinson?

'No,' her friend said with a sigh. 'But at least he agreed to be in the wedding, so thanks for that.'

Amber murmured a 'No problem.' And how did she tell Parker's sister that the only reason he'd agreed to be in the wedding was because her friend threatened to tell embarrassing stories to his partner? Maybe Parker really was that shallow. Deep in her heart she knew he wasn't.

But if *Parker* believed it, then the truth didn't really matter.

Clutching her phone, Amber forced herself to focus. 'Your dress is due to arrive next week,' she said to Reese. 'I'll set up a time for the first fitting.'

Reese's enthusiastic 'Good' was heartwarming. She knew Parker had his doubts about his sister's marriage, but Amber envied Reese and Dylan because their relationship always looked so comfortable and easy. Just as Amber always thought love should be. Of course, Parker's very DNA made acknowledging the possibility of forever near impossible.

Behind her, the tinkle of the bell over the door signaled another customer. Signing off the phone, she slipped it in her pocket as she turned...and spied Parker just inside the entranceway.

Her head spun, her gut tensed and her heart hurt too

much to function. Unfortunately the overly dramatic angst of her teen years didn't compare to the real, grown-up pain of a woman. Falling for him again was turning out to be easy. Doing something about it would be hard.

Now that she'd adjusted to his presence, her eyes roved lovingly over him. He wore jeans and his leather jacket, as usual. The only difference was the button-down shirt that he wore.

No matter, Amber was sure it smelled of leather. She'd spent enough time in his arms, kissing every inch of his skin to know his scent inside and out.

When the couple called out their goodbyes, Amber waved, working hard not to feel a sliver of jealousy as they held hands on the way out. Uneasy, she glanced at Parker, who was watching them leave. The slow barrel roll her belly was attempting wasn't helping her nerves, and she swiped a damp palm down her dress pants.

'Tuxedo rental,' she managed to say lamely, nodding at the retreating couple.

His brow furrowed in humor. 'Did you measure his crotch, too?'

'It wasn't necessary.' Despite everything, she had to bite back the smile. 'Only for you.'

His mouth quirked. 'I figured as much.'

Five heartbeats pounded in her chest before the awkward silence was broken.

'So...' Parker leaned a shoulder against the wall, crossing his arms with that earthy easiness that was so seductive. And how could such a simple movement be so sexy? 'What kind of woman leads a guy on by handcuffing him to a table and then up and leaves?'

'I put the holster with the key in reach of your foot,'

she said. 'I knew with a little bit of time and effort you'd eventually escape.'

Parker let out a cocky *hunh*. 'I was free and out the door in two minutes.'

Clearly he was proud of his skills.

Hiking an eyebrow at the expression on his face, she said, 'Ten.' She tipped her head. 'It was *ten* minutes.' And when he shot her a sharp look, she gave a small shrug. 'I was watching your car from the window.'

The pleased look on his face was comical. 'You worried I wasn't going to get free, Ace?'

And here he was, choosing the shallow route again. As if the amount of time it took him to retrieve his key from the holster and unlock the cuffs around his wrists—not an easy task, she was sure—was the most important thing they needed to discuss.

'I think we already established that I *do* care,' she said.

Parker closed his eyes, and the easy look on his face died, his voice low. 'Damn, Amber.' He rubbed his neck and met her gaze again. 'I got good news today, so I'm in a first-rate mood. And you were the one who convinced me to go to my mom's tonight.'

Her heart soared at the words, and she realized that also explained his button-down shirt.

Frowning, Parker went on. 'But I don't think I'm ready for...'

He dropped his arm to his side and looked at her. Shifting against the wall, his movements were now stiff. He looked as if he was braced for battle.

A million questions crashed through her mind like a ten-car pileup, but she decided to start out simple.

'What's the good news?' she asked.

'That teen I was telling you about? The suspect in my

latest case?' he said. 'Turns out he's innocent. He's been cleared.' The small shrug was simple yet meaningful. 'I don't know if that will help him with his parents or not, but at least he's got a second chance.' The relief on his face was obvious.

And *this* was why she was falling for Parker all over again. He liked to pretend he was above those pesky things called emotions. To pretend he felt no fondness or affection or hope. To pretend he didn't care. But it wasn't that he had no heart. The problem was his heart was so big, had been through so much, the need to protect himself was automatic.

Today was an encouraging step, but there was a real risk this instinct might never be undone completely.

'I'm glad you're going,' she said. 'I know Reese will appreciate it.'

Thick dark lashes slowly blinked across a mesmerizing green gaze as he stared at her for several moments. 'I'm not going just for Reese.'

Her breathing stalled, and she barely managed to murmur, 'No?'

Two pounding heartbeats passed as she longed for him to clarify.

'No,' he said. 'I'm also going for me.'

And while she breathed out a sigh of relief that he'd finally decided that he wanted family in his life, a small part of her was crushed he wasn't going for *her*. She'd known all along the most she could hope for was to help him reconnect with Reese, and this was as good a start as any. In truth, it was a miracle he was going tonight. And while Amber was glad Reese's wish would come true, the truth was, having him here—having him near *her*—was hard.

Because a part of her would always long to be loved by Parker.

'Well,' she said, shifting closer to the exit. Distance. She needed *distance*. Time to regroup. 'Your sister will be happy to see you.'

'Yeah, but I can't say I'm thrilled with the idea of making polite conversation with my mom and stepdad,' he said, his feet firmly planted in place. 'Cuz I know things won't have changed.' His expression grim, he went on. 'William Michael of the Park Avenue Michaels hates any reminder that he wasn't my mother's first husband. My mother is weak, petrified he'll leave her. And, way back when, Reese was too young to notice,' he said with a tiny shrug. 'I've accepted all that.'

By the look on his face she knew it was true. He cleared his throat, suddenly looking uncomfortable.

'I was hoping we could go together,' he said. 'Having you around might make things a little...smoother.'

A confusing mix of tenderness and disappointment flushed through her chest, and she picked up her purse, heading for the exit. 'Then let's go.'

Amber could feel him following.

'But the other reason I came was because I wanted to see you first,' he said.

Her feet stuck to the floor.

'About—about what you said,' he said from behind.

Clutching her purse harder, she turned to face him.

'You know...' He shrugged awkwardly. 'Before.'

I'm falling in love with you.

The lag time from one heartbeat to the next seemed to lengthen to uncomfortable levels. So much so Amber was amazed she didn't pass out.

'As a kid—' he puffed out a breath grimly '—it sucked

not getting what I needed from my mom. And it's...' With a small scowl he plowed a hand through his hair before gesturing at Amber. 'You're...' He dropped his hand, frustration etched in his every word. 'You know everything I don't want *anyone* to know.'

The raw, naked look on his face lasted several seconds before he let out a scoff.

'Which makes you the last person on earth I should want to see,' he said.

My God, this wasn't getting any easier.

'After that night,' he went on. 'I spent the first few days thinking you had some sort of...*misguided* sense of hero worship because of the whole drowning incident.'

She could hear the hesitation in his voice.

'And then I spent the rest of the time hoping it was more than that,' he finished in a low voice.

Her voice resolute, she said, 'It is.'

Now the lag time between heartbeats was ridiculously short as she watched the emotions parade across his face. Relief. Followed by something that looked like contentment before landing on that cocky smile she loved so much.

Parker stepped forward, all awkwardness gone. The easy stroll was back, carrying him right up into her personal space, and her stomach swooped at the sight. The gorgeous green eyes. The ruffled hair. And that mouth, that beautiful, beautiful mouth that had first captured her attention oh so long ago. Little had she known then how good it would feel pressed against hers in a *real* kiss.

'But the rescue was an incredibly awesome move on my part,' he said with a grin.

She rolled her eyes, delighting at his responding bark

of amusement. When he reached out to brush the hair from her cheek, her stomach swerved.

He paused, his voice uncharacteristically riddled with self-doubt. 'Even the thought of trying for something that lasts past a few months scares the crap out of me.'

Inhaling slowly, Amber steadily held his gaze. She'd spent years pining after something that could never be hers. Parker, specifically. And as lame as the idea was, especially given she'd been just a ridiculous *preteen,* it was time to admit the years of unrequited feelings had had a profound influence on her choices in life. And the thought of putting herself in a vulnerable position again was almost incapacitating. But Parker had spent years hoping his mother would change, and was willing to venture back into her circle again with little likelihood that the relationship would improve.

'That's the thing about letting someone in,' she said softly. And if he was willing to put his heart on the line for his sister, for *himself*...well, then maybe she should take a risk, too. 'It's both a beautiful and a dangerous thing.'

His eyes searched hers. 'So why me?'

Drawing in a deep breath, she tried to put her thoughts into words.

'I think over time,' she said slowly, 'the closer you get to a person, and the closer you let them *get to you,* the more the light and the shadows inside become more vivid. Clearer. More sharply defined.'

Love wasn't easy. And sometimes, especially with a man like Parker Robinson, it would be especially difficult. But she loved the parts of him that were dark just as much, if not more, than she loved the lighter bits. Because they defined him the best.

And for a moment, she almost felt sorry for Reese and Dylan. A comfortable relationship would definitely take less work, but Amber wouldn't trade the conflict or passion she shared with Parker for all the ease in the world.

She reached up to cup his face, and nothing, *nothing* would ever be as wonderful as the slight tip of his head into her palm. The contact wasn't much. But enough.

Encouraging her to go on. 'And knowing all those bits about a person makes it both more difficult, and—just as important, I think—more imperative that you take that chance.'

The tiny, nervous lick of his lips was almost heartbreaking.

'So...' he said. 'You want to give this thing a whirl?'

'Do you think it will work?'

'Almost definitely maybe.' His mouth curled at the edges. 'We have several things in our favor.'

'Such as?'

'First, I'm adorable and you worship the ground I walk on.' She lifted her eyes heavenward with a 'whatever' look, and he let out a chuckle. Amber wasn't sure if his shallow reply was a coping mechanism or if he just liked to see her reaction. She suspected t was a bit of both. 'Second,' he went on. 'I *want* it to work. And third...'

Amber didn't miss how quickly he'd rushed through the second, almost as if embarrassed. She'd let it slide. For now.

'And third?' she asked.

The quirk in his lips was adorable. 'I'm just stubborn enough not to give up.'

Eyes stinging, she swallowed back the mushy words and sent him a smile.

'I'm not going to have to handcuff you for every hug I want, am I?' she said.

He reached out and took her hand. The gesture was hesitant, the fingers that squeezed hers gentle. But the light in his eyes?

Sizzling.

'Oh, you'll need the handcuffs, all right,' he said, his voice husky.

And then Parker Robinson drew the sexy smirk like a gun from a holster. 'Just not for a hug.'

* * * * *

REQUEST YOUR FREE BOOKS!
2 FREE NOVELS PLUS 2 FREE GIFTS!

HARLEQUIN® KISS™

YES! Please send me 2 FREE Harlequin® Kiss novels and my 2 FREE gifts (gifts worth about $10). After receiving them, if I don't wish to receive any more books, I can return the shipping statement marked "cancel." If I don't cancel, I will receive 4 brand-new novels every month and be billed just $4.30 per book in the U.S. or $4.99 per book in Canada. That's a savings of at least 13% off the cover price! It's quite a bargain! Shipping and handling is just 50¢ per book in the U.S. and 75¢ per book in Canada.* I understand that accepting the 2 free books and gifts places me under no obligation to buy anything. I can always return a shipment and cancel at any time. Even if I never buy another book, the two free books and gifts are mine to keep forever.

145/345 HDN FVXQ

Name _____ (PLEASE PRINT) _____

Address _____ Apt. # _____

City _____ State/Prov. _____ Zip/Postal Code _____

Signature (if under 18, a parent or guardian must sign) _____

Mail to the **Harlequin® Reader Service:**
IN U.S.A.: P.O. Box 1867, Buffalo, NY 14240-1867
IN CANADA: P.O. Box 609, Fort Erie, Ontario L2A 5X3

Want to try two free books from another line?
Call 1-800-873-8635 or visit www.ReaderService.com.

* Terms and prices subject to change without notice. Prices do not include applicable taxes. Sales tax applicable in N.Y. Canadian residents will be charged applicable taxes. Offer not valid in Quebec. This offer is limited to one order per household. Not valid for current subscribers to Harlequin Kiss books. All orders subject to credit approval. Credit or debit balances in a customer's account(s) may be offset by any other outstanding balance owed by or to the customer. Please allow 4 to 6 weeks for delivery. Offer available while quantities last.

Your Privacy—The Harlequin® Reader Service is committed to protecting your privacy. Our Privacy Policy is available online at www.ReaderService.com or upon request from the Harlequin Reader Service.

We make a portion of our mailing list available to reputable third parties that offer products we believe may interest you. If you prefer that we not exchange your name with third parties, or if you wish to clarify or modify your communication preferences, please visit us at www.ReaderService.com/consumerschoice or write to us at Harlequin Reader Service Preference Service, P.O. Box 9062, Buffalo, NY 14269. Include your complete name and address.

HKI3

KISS™

She hadn't seen him in ten years and he chose
her wedding day to show up...

THE UNEXPECTED
WEDDING GUEST

"Surprised to see me, Park Avenue?" The familiar, sexy rumble
and the nickname added to the surreal nature of being trans-
ported back ten years in time when she had laughingly told
Mason her college roommates' nickname for her, Park Avenue
Princess. And then he'd made the name his own, dropping
the *princess* part. Which for some strange reason had pleased
her no end.

But she was not pleased to see Mason.

Days away from her *wedding*.

Reese gritted her teeth, struggling to retain her cool as the
anger finally built high enough to surpass every other emotion—
shock, doubt and dread, just to name a few. Why was he coming
to see her again? After ten years, why *now*? Right when all of
her dreams were finally about to come true.

She forced her voice to remain smooth. "And the last time
I saw you, you were dodging the dog tags I hurled at you."

"Your aim was good."

"I should have used your baseball bat."

"It still made a nice punctuation mark for your demand for
a divorce." The corners of his eyes crinkled. "Claimed irrecon-
cilable differences, if I remember right."

She tipped her chin higher. "Temporary insanity was more like it."

"A *lust*-induced state of insanity." Heat flushed through her like a flash fire, though he steadily held her gaze. His expression more reflective than affected, he murmured, "A drug, that."

Her chest pinched, making breathing more difficult. Bad enough he had to still look good, now the unwanted memories invaded. Memories of Mason making love to her. The incredibly intense state of happiness they'd achieved, right before it had all been blown to hell. Correction, right before *Mason* had blown it all to hell.

Remember, Reese. Never again.

Never *again.*

"The sex wasn't a drug," she said, though at the time, she'd thought the same thing. But God knows she'd learned her lesson the hard way. She was no longer susceptible to the whims of her hormones. "It was quicksand."

And just as deadly to her peace of mind. Her sanity.

He hiked a brow and studied her a moment more. "Maybe," he said softly, his lips curling at the edges. "But what a way to go."

**Pick up THE UNEXPECTED WEDDING GUEST
by Aimee Carson, on sale June 18,
wherever Harlequin books are sold.**

Four friends. Three weddings.
Two explosive secrets.
One unforgettable
summer!

THE WEDDING SEASON

Reese, Cassie, Gina and Marnie were best friends.
Until *that* night.

They haven't seen each other in years, but now Reese is
getting married and she wants everyone there.

It will be a reunion to remember—and the wedding of
the year! But what these feisty women hadn't planned
on are the sizzling, scandalous and *very* surprising
consequences....

**Look for this fabulous quartet from these talented
Harlequin KISS authors—Aimee Carson,
Amy Andrews, Heidi Rice and Kimberly Lang.**

Starting June 18 with
THE UNEXPECTED WEDDING GUEST
by Aimee Carson

HARLEQUIN® KISS™

www.Harlequin.com

If you loved WAKING UP MARRIED, you will love

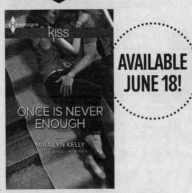

ONCE IS NEVER ENOUGH

by *USA Today* bestselling author Mira Lyn Kelly

His reputation preceded him!

Nichole Daniels has had her share of heartbreak. Two broken engagements and a single bed are proof of that. But when a blue-eyed stranger offers her a taste of every nighttime fantasy of three long years, she's considering putting an end to her prolonged dry spell!

Garrett Carter's reputation as a ladies' man? Absolutely right. A danger to her health? Definitely. The man for her? Not on your life.

Nichole has no intention of getting involved with the man known to whisper almost any woman into bed! But she soon discovers that his reputation isn't for nothing. When it comes to Garrett, one night will never be enough....

HK20721